UNYIELDING HEART

A.T. BUTLER

UNYIELDING HEART

Historical Women's Fiction Saga

COURAGE ON THE OREGON TRAIL
BOOK 4

A.T. BUTLER

CHAPTER ONE

The door to the cozy, faded gray farmhouse slammed shut, practically rattling off its hinges with the force. Beth McKinnon jolted where she stood next to the stove, surprised by the sound. She had only just sent Boyd and Ross out to feed the pigs and had come into the kitchen to check the pot of chicken broth that had been simmering most of the day. These bright, winter afternoons when she could send the children out of the house were generally peaceful for her, but she couldn't take a single moment for granted. There was always plenty to keep her busy, children underfoot or not.

Without turning around to look, she scolded the small boy who had just run in. "Alexander McKinnon!" Beth called to her son. "You know better. How many times do I have to tell you?"

"Sorry, Mama!" he yelled as he ran past her. His dog Prince, a yellow labrador, followed closely on his heels, not wanting to miss a moment of his master's adventure.

She shook her head indulgently. Only six years old, and already that boy knew how to get around her. He must be a quick study, watching how his older siblings teased and cajoled. From Boyd, he would learn how to exaggerate and alarm her with his drama. From Lizzie, maybe, Alexander would learn to ask for a series of small privileges that added up over time. So much of her life was centered around her children, Beth couldn't help but give in to their whims as much as possible.

All she had ever wanted in life was a happy, healthy, large family and all that came with it.

In this case, however, her small son leaving the door banging open to the frigid January snow was one of the small drawbacks that came with such a large family. With a sigh, Beth replaced the lid to the pot of broth and made her way to the back door that still swung open on its hinges. But before she could make it back to the stove again, Alexander was tearing down the stairs, Prince just behind him, and through the kitchen again.

"Close the door!" Beth called after the child as he dashed off into the cold.

The pair tore through the door, out into the snow again.

The door bounced back, flung into the door-frame without latching.

"Goodness," she said under her breath as she crossed to the door to close it tightly. From the doorway, Beth looked out over the wintery farmland, at Alexander's small form running toward the barn. As he ran, he pulled his hat back down over his dark hair.

Their plot was just outside Lancaster, Pennsylvania, in a community Beth had loved her whole life. Tall, bare oak and maple trees peppered the property around the house before their acres stretched out beyond. The land itself had been in her husband's family for generations, going all the way back to the mid-eighteenth century. Every time she looked out over their property, Beth could feel the pull of those roots, that history, anchoring her to this home.

Humming to herself, Beth returned to the warm kitchen, which was the heart of her home in the winter. The cozy, bread-scented room drew her hungry children and her chilled husband, all looking for comfort and love. She loved her home, crowded though it may be. They had a history here, not only her own immediate family, but her husband's family going back two generations. More than a dozen McKinnons had been born in this house, and she was proud to be the current stewardess of it.

"Mama!"

Baby Tara, only two years old but the perfect age for getting into places where she shouldn't, called out to Beth from the sitting room. She had quietly played with the wooden blocks handed down from her older siblings for nearly thirty minutes before losing interest. Beth smiled to herself as she closed the door and turned toward her youngest.

"Baby girl," she cooed. "My little Tara, darling loveliest girl."

Her older children sometimes teased Beth for all the loving praise she heaped on them every day, but she wouldn't have it any other way. She squatted on the floor next to her youngest child, who sat beaming up into her face. How could she call this perfect angel anything but darling and beautiful? How could she be expected to speak to a toddling infant the way she did her oldest children?

"Look, Mama!"

"What have you got there?" she asked Tara, who had something gripped in her chubby fist.

Tara blinked at her and held out the candle snuffer. Beth laughed and took it carefully from the baby's hand, carefully holding the sharp end away from her. It looked like a pair of scissors with a small bowl placed on top, but fortunately, the pointed end was well dulled.

"Where did you find this?"

She had been looking for the snuffer all over the house for the last several days. It had been a wedding gift years ago, and while always useful, in such a busy house, it was also the kind of item that was regularly misplaced and easy to do without. Ross, in particular, took great pleasure in blowing out candles, never thinking about trimming the wick.

"There," Tara pointed, in answer to her mother's question.

The corner of the room that Tara pointed to was home to the family's rocking chair, Beth's sewing basket, a basket of various items of clothing waiting to be mended, and a bucket of wood shavings from her husband's occasional attempts at carving. No wonder she hadn't seen the snuffer when she had scanned her eyes over that area.

"Well, thank you for finding it, beloved." She kissed the top of the baby's head and stood again to return the heavy metal snuffer to the drawer of the side table under the window where it would likely not stay any longer than the next morning.

Sighing contentedly, Beth again returned to the kitchen, to the stovetop, and tried to remember the next thing she had intended to make that afternoon. More and more, she was finding that the exertion of keeping her household running, especially as the children grew older and had more of their own specific interests to cater to, took all of her attention. And then, when such was compounded with interruptions from said children, it was a wonder Beth got them all fed and clothed every day.

She grinned to herself as she lifted the lid of the chicken broth to check its progress, forgetting that she had only just done so. Truth be told, she didn't always get all six of them fed and clothed. More than once, she had had to patch the seat of a little boy's pants early before school or serve only one side dish with supper because she had run out of time to shell the peas or shuck the corn.

That thought reminded her of what she still needed to do before supper that evening. With a final glance into the sitting room, Beth wiped her hands on her apron and set to work. Supper for eight people was always an elaborate affair. Though she knew her oldest daughter Claire would be coming breathlessly into the kitchen at any minute, apologizing for being late, Beth still had plenty to keep her own hands busy.

Several hours later, she had managed—with the help of her daughter—to complete everything she had intended to complete, and the rest of her family had filed into the dining room for supper. Every day around this time, Beth reached the end of her relatively quiet afternoon, and the noise and chaos of all of her children descended on the house.

She and her husband had been married nearly twenty years and had six children to show for it. Claire was fifteen, the oldest, and the rest went down like steps of the stair: Boyd, his father's right hand already, Ross, Lizzie, Alexander, and baby Tara, who was quickly growing out of her baby phase. They all crowded around the table, elbowing each other, settling into their usual chairs, snitching a taste of the canned peaches before their father had said grace. Exactly as they had behaved every evening at supper as long as Beth could remember, as long as her family had been growing.

"Okay, now, settle down," she said over the din, as though any of the children were paying attention to her. The sooner they all sat, the sooner they could eat, but Beth knew that reminding them would do nothing. She would just have to be patient.

Her husband Robert caught her eye across the table and chuckled lightly. He had sat in his usual place at the head and was waiting along with her.

How blessed she was to go through life side by side with this patient, easy man.

"Mama, did you see what Boyd did?" Lizzie cried, pointing to her older brother across the table.

"What?" Boyd wore what his mother recognized as his trying-to-look-innocent expression while clearly already had his mouth full of food.

"Swallow whatever is in your mouth, Boyd, and sit."

Claire had just entered carrying the last platter of pork chops and moved to take her seat.

"All right, you lot. Everyone have what they need?" Beth looked at each of her children in turn. "Pa is going to say grace now. Bow your heads."

Beth looked around her as each of the children closed their eyes, bowed their heads, and took the hand of their brother or sister sitting next to them. She sighed contentedly. If every day was like this, she could die a happy woman. She closed her own eyes and listened as her husband thanked the lord for the bounty before them and the sweet security of their home.

CHAPTER TWO

Her oldest son wore his best trousers and a starched collar, but as he tried to slip past her, Beth didn't even need to look twice before making her verdict.

"Boyd McKinnon, go back upstairs and wash behind your ears. You know perfectly well that was supposed to already be done. Hurry now. You're going to make us late for church."

Beth pretended not to hear her son sigh in frustration as he spun on his heel to return to his bedroom and the washbasin therein. She was still too busy getting the two youngest children ready to leave the house to spend too much time managing the older ones, who really should know better.

"Honey," she said, turning to her husband, "could you—"

But he was already on his way out the door, heading to hitch up their wagon and saving the family those few moments when it came time to leave. As ever, Robert was ready when she needed him, supporting whatever the rest of the family asked of him.

In this instance, she just hoped the rest of the family didn't ask too much. Sundays were the only day that every single member of the family had to be dressed, clean, and ready to leave at the same time. And invariably, Sundays were the only day that Beth truly lost patience with the children. The target of her frustration would change from week to week, but rarely a Sunday went by when she didn't need to seek out a quiet, isolated spot to calm herself. This week it was Boyd, who had somehow talked his mother out of a bath the night before, and now thought he would get away without performing the basic steps of cleanliness before church.

Beth occasionally despaired for the boy's future wife, but that always resolved her to do more now to train him up properly.

"Ross!" Beth called up the stairs. Her third child was the most serious of the bunch, and she never had to remind him to wash what he was supposed to wash. Accordingly, moments later, she heard his footsteps descending the staircase. He soon appeared in front of her, clutching his Bible to his small chest. "If you're ready, will you go wait in the wagon, please?"

"Yes, Ma," he responded before darting out the door.

Looking around, Beth took a deep breath. Lizzie was already outside—she wanted to kick stones while she waited, and Beth didn't have the energy to forbid it in the girl's Sunday shoes. Better to dirty her shoes than her hands, at least.

That only left...

Where had Alexander gotten to?

But before she had to go looking, both he and Boyd came thundering down the stairs, with Claire walking swiftly behind them. Beth glanced at the clock and decided to simply trust that Boyd had done as she instructed. They were running too late for her to put up with another fight.

"Claire, carry the baby, would you please?"

"Come on, little one," the girl murmured as she reached for her youngest sister.

Beth took one last look around the kitchen before grabbing the small wooden crate waiting near the door and followed the rest of her family out to the wagon. Once she got the children, and the crate of jars, situated in the back, she heaved a sigh and climbed up on the wagon seat next to her husband.

"Well, we'll likely be late, again, but I don't know what else to do."

He nodded and clicked his tongue to the horses, starting them down the long road to their church.

"I brought the preserves for your brother," Beth continued. She and Robert often had one-sided conversations like this. He was not one to waste words and never spoke unless he had something to say.

"Ma, are we going to Uncle Stuart's after church still?" Claire asked from where she sat just behind her mother.

Beth glanced at her husband before responding.

"As far as I know. Seems he wouldn't let your father tell him no, the way I heard it."

She had expected Robert to chuckle at that, but he simply watched the road ahead. His older brother's overbearing nature had long been a source of amusement in the McKinnon household. More than once, Beth had said a quick, grateful prayer that she had married the quieter of the brothers. But now, Robert seemed to be finally irritated by his brother's antics.

The rest of the journey passed in silence, but Beth persisted in wondering what was going on in her husband's mind.

When they reached the church, the bells signaling the start of the service had already started. Beth and Robert hurried their children into the building, admonishing them to be quiet, and took their seats in one of the rear pews without a moment to spare. In the calm, steady rhythm of the sermon, Beth took a moment to be grateful for the quiet and for her family. God himself knew this might be one of the few quiet moments she got that day.

After the church service, Beth said hello to many of her friends and neighbors as she ran into on her way out of the building. There was no lingering, however. They were expected at Robert's brother's home soon.

Robert said nothing more as he drove their wagon the short distance to the other McKinnons' farm. Not that he ever said much. Beth had learned long ago to just trust that he was listening to her, even if he rarely responded himself. Perhaps the afternoon with his brother would open him up more.

They arrived at the McKinnons' farm, and Robert drove the wagon as close to the house as he could to let off the rest of the family. Beth was climbing down from her perch when she noticed a new, larger building next to where the old barn sat.

"Did you know they had built a new barn?" she asked her husband quietly.

He nodded. "Stuart's always got some project or other. I'm sorry, I thought I had mentioned it."

She looked again at the grand structure as Robert drove the team of horses to the paddock where they would wait for the McKinnons through that cold afternoon. The expense of an outbuilding of that size told her a lot of things; mostly, it pointed to the fact that Stuart must be expecting an exceptionally prosperous year. She could think of no other reason he would be willing to spend that on his animals over his own family.

The children had run on ahead of her, so Beth made her way to her in-laws' front door on her own. When she stepped through the door, she handed over the box of jars of preserves to Stuart's wife, Ann.

"Here you are," Beth said, trying to keep her voice light through her irritation. It was difficult to relinquish so much of her hard work graciously.

What had started as a kindness to the other

McKinnons each year had somehow turned into a tradition of a tributary. Just because Stuart, as the oldest, technically held the deed to Robert's farm—the longtime McKinnon family estate—he acted as though they owed him everything, including, apparently, what he jokingly called a tithe of a portion of their harvests. Beth had vociferously sounded her objections to her husband time and time again, but Robert had always just found it easier to give in to his brother.

And so, she made extra preserves each fall, knowing that her self-important brother-in-law would be the beneficiary.

This winter, however, Beth had gone as long as she could get away with without handing over such a large portion of her labor. She had been done with her canning months earlier and conscientiously stored them all in the cellar for her own family. Stuart began to ask about what she would be bringing him the very next time he saw her, and the hints and subtle digging had never stopped.

"Is that what I think it is?" Stuart asked as he came into the room to greet them. Robert had caught up with her, and the brothers shook hands. Stuart leaned down to kiss Beth's cheek. "I've been looking forward to these for a while now."

"Yes, well," Beth started awkwardly. "I do make delicious preserves. As does your wife, of course."

"Of course. But then Ann does quite a bit around here, and your little gift each year is always appreciated to give her a break."

Beth flushed with anger and looked at Robert,

but the man merely smiled at his brother and changed the subject.

"I see you finished the new barn."

"It's quite the investment," Beth added. "I wonder at choosing to build a whole new barn instead of something a little more... Oh, I don't know, practical?"

"I think you'll find that anything I do to improve this land is practical." Stuart smiled down at her condescendingly. He seemed to think such business was beyond her pretty little feminine head, but he would humor her. "When the day comes to sell or mortgage the property, you can rest assured I'll be getting my money back and then some."

"And you're certain of that?" Beth asked, trying to keep the incredulity out of her tone. "Why, Robert doesn't spend even half what you do, and I'm sure our farm is still worth a lot."

"Well, you're right about that," Stuart interjected with a laugh. "Robert has never put a dime into that farm, and yet I can tell you without hesitation it's bound to sell for more than you think."

Beth opened her mouth to defend her husband, but Stuart had already turned away. When she caught Robert's eye, he shook his head slightly. Something was going on between these two, and she wanted to know what it was.

"Supper will be ready in an hour or so," Ann said, serenely glossing over the awkward moment between brothers.

"I'll help," Beth offered, following her sister-in-law into the kitchen.

Her husband didn't need her to mediate. Whatever was eating at Robert, he could handle himself. She had always been able to trust him before and would do so again now.

"What can I do?" she asked Ann as she tied on an apron and got to work.

CHAPTER THREE

Beth blinked in surprise as she looked into the dark interior of the cookie tin that sat on the top of the cabinet in the dining room. It had long ago ceased to hold cookies and was now where her husband deposited the cash that she needed for the household supplies. Today she had time to do some shopping, but as she reached in, her fingers brushed against the bottom of the tin instead of against the banknotes she had been looking for. She had thought there was more money in there. It had been more than a week since she had had to visit the general store in town, but the funds in the tin were barely enough to purchase a few pounds of coffee.

Frowning, she returned the tin to its place and reminded herself to ask Robert about it. There was certain to be a reasonable explanation. And she had plenty to do without that shopping either way. She pushed the worry from her mind.

Beth stepped into the sitting room where her

oldest daughter was curled up by the window read-ing. She hated to interrupt the girl. As she got older, Claire rarely got a quiet moment to herself; Beth often relied on her for help around the house and with her siblings. But this invitation would be worth it.

"Did you still want to come with me, Claire?"

The girl's eyes lit up. "Are you going to see Poppy Lynch's trousseau?"

In that instant of delight on Claire's face, Beth could imagine the years ahead, her daughter meeting a man, planning her wedding, living her life with her own family and all. She just hoped Claire wouldn't move too far away from them when the time came. What would she do without her?

"Yes," Beth continued. "Her mother invited me over sometime today if we have time. I was going to also stop by the dry goods store, but..." She trailed off, thinking again about how strange it was that Robert had left her without enough. "Never mind that. We'll call on the Lynches and have a lovely afternoon."

Claire set the book on the arm of the chair and sat up straight. "When are we leaving?"

Thirty minutes later, the two women, with Tara carried by her mother, arrived at their neighbors' home. The brisk walk in the January cold was biting, but the opportunity to mingle with their neighbors in Lancaster was not to be missed. The Lynches lived at the end of a short drive, the small farmhouse nestled between a pair of bare ash trees. In spite of the cold of the day, not all of the visitors had made their way inside. The front porch was already starting to fill with women who had come to call on a similar errand.

"Mrs. McKinnon!" They were greeted at the door by Poppy Lynch's older sister, Agnes, a tall, angular woman who, even after she grew out of her teens, seemed to be all awkward limbs and corners.

"Why, we didn't expect to see you here yet," Beth exclaimed. "How long have you been in town?" They followed Agnes inside as she led them through the crowd, talking over her shoulder.

"Me either. Of course, I had planned to come for the wedding, but my husband just insisted I come early. You know how much work this all can be. So I'll be visiting for a few weeks yet, and Fred will come later and travel back to Maryland with me."

Beth marveled at how young people seemed to have no qualms or hesitation in picking up stakes and move all over God's green earth. When Agnes Lynch married Fred Laton three years earlier, they didn't bother trying to find a home right here in Lancaster but instead settled south, across the river.

"But I know you didn't come to hear me jawing. Let's go find Poppy."

She led them up the stairs, passing a trio of other neighbors in the sitting room, happily sipping tea and gossiping with Mrs. Lynch. The older woman looked up at the McKinnons as they passed, offering them a cheerful little wave.

"Is everything set for the wedding?" Beth asked Agnes. "Your mother seems surprisingly relaxed."

"Mostly," she replied over her shoulder as they

continued up the stairs. "Of course, she was a disaster when I got married three years ago, but this time, I don't know if it's that Poppy is just more organized than I am or if Mother has realized that something will go wrong whether she frets about it or not." Agnes chuckled. "But it *is* nice to see her not working herself into a tizzy. I can tell you Poppy is a lot happier for it, too."

They reached the doorway to Poppy's bedroom, where she had laid out her new dresses and finery for her visitors to admire. The bride herself stood on the opposite side of the room, nearest the window, as she talked to the young woman Beth knew to be her bosom friend, Jane. The smile on Poppy's face was as bright, and she subconsciously played with the delicate ring she wore.

"Poppy?" Agnes called as they entered.

The young woman's smile broadened even further when she saw that she had more guests to show off to. Beth's mind went back to her own betrothal. She'd had nothing like this spread that Poppy boasted of, but the joy and pride were there all the same.

"Mrs. McKinnon, Claire, thank you so much for coming." Poppy kissed Tara on the top of her head when she came to greet them. "I know this is all just an excuse to brag to friends, but it is so nice to have a reason to invite you all here."

"No, don't look at it like that," Beth scolded kindly. "This is a way for your loved ones to share in your happiness. I'm sure every lady downstairs is as proud of you and happy for you as they would be for their own children."

"Are you?" she asked teasingly.

"Of course." Beth glanced at her fifteen-year-old. "More, maybe. Claire finds any excuse she can think of to not have to sew or hem for her own hope chest."

"That's true," the girl said, laughing.

"Well," Poppy said, laughing with them. "In that case, come be proud of me. The dresses were fit by Emily Norbert, but the linens and things I made myself."

She gestured to the frippery, ruffles, and sleek fabric spread out over the coverlet; the collection more than took over her entire bed.

In addition to the three new, gorgeous gowns, Poppy would also be taking into her marriage the fruits of her own labor for the last several years. Linen handkerchiefs, new bedding, half a dozen towels, and a silk nightgown were among the treasures she had stored up in anticipation of this happy time.

Beth watched Claire as the girl reverently fingered the delicate lace and machine-stitched hems of Poppy's new dresses. She had always been the first to notice a friend's new gown or point out changes in the latest fashion. Beth had taken to letting her daughter choose her own dresses for the last few years and strove to give her the best she could. Though she never complained, it was apparent that Claire wished for something finer than the attire her mother could afford to dress her in.

Though Claire's own marriage was likely several years off yet, Beth didn't see how she would be able to offer her daughter a trousseau anything like this.

"Will you be married here in the parlor?" Beth asked. "Or did Joe want to get married in the church?"

"The parlor. Just family and a couple friends, you understand. With a wedding supper afterward here. We're still deciding on the menu, but my grandmother will be contributing her famous birds-nest pudding for certain."

Beth half-listened as Claire peppered Poppy with questions about the wedding and their plans afterward. She was too busy imagining her own daughter's wedding and worrying over what she would be able to offer the girl. And then after her would be Lizzie and Tara, with the boys sprinkled in between.

The responsibility of setting her children off in the world as prepared and cared for as possible weighed heavily on her shoulders. She and Robert did their best to give their children everything they could, but that was not the same thing as everything the children wanted or deserved. Where Agnes and her husband had moved to a neighboring state with the funds they had saved up or been gifted, Beth wondered if she should start preparing for one or more of her children to live with their parents into their adulthood.

When Robert and Beth got married, his older brother had allowed them to take over the McKinnon family farm. Stuart had charged them only a nominal amount of rent for the use of the buildings and land that rightly belonged to him, but somehow, they hadn't managed to ever get very far ahead. With six children and all the illnesses and essentials that went along with them, Beth found herself grateful every day that her home at least was owned by the family, if it couldn't be in her husband's hands. They were safe, and they were blessed to be putting down roots in the same place their family had for so long.

As for where all the money from the tin had gone, Beth would have to ask Robert. There was certain to be a reasonable explanation, and it was not as though she hadn't had to make do in the past. Everything would be just fine.

CHAPTER FOUR

Once they returned home from the Lynches', Beth didn't have time to ask Robert about the missing money before she had to get right to cooking supper. The girls' visit had lasted longer than Beth had expected; Claire kept coming up with questions. She wanted to know every single detail about Poppy's courtship, not to mention the wedding, and Beth didn't have the heart to interrupt. So, as a compromise, supper that evening was a bit of a thrown-together catch-all, consisting of cold chicken leftover from the day before, biscuits, and more than one canned vegetable opened to serve.

As she whirled around her kitchen, trying to pull everything together, Beth kept telling herself that one of these days, she would get ahead of her chores. One of these days, she'd find the extra time in the day to finally get everything under control. In spite of this conviction, every day, it seemed as though something unexpected came up, and she fell further and further behind. Today it was Poppy Lynch, but tomorrow would be something new.

"Come to supper!"

Beth stood in the doorway to her kitchen, with the toddler Tara on her hip, and called out into the yard. It hadn't snowed in over a week, and the thawing, dirty slush helped disguise the children playing in the twilight. She could only see the top of the head of one of her children but knew the rest were out there somewhere. Sure enough, in just a couple of minutes, the kitchen was a whirlwind as half a dozen small bodies ran in, yelling, laughing, bumping into things, and elbowing each other over the basin.

"Wash your hands," Beth called over the din. Of course, she reminded herself, she had trained them well enough to know that was precisely what they were doing.

Without being asked, Claire caught up the basket of biscuits in one hand and the jug of water in the other and brought both to the table. Boyd helped Ross and Lizzie get their own hands washed, only getting a small part of the front of the girl's dress wet in the process. Alexander filled Prince's bowl and carried it carefully out to the porch where the dog could have his own supper. As a family, they all worked very well together.

"Where's your father?" she asked the room at large. None answered her, but it was no matter. Robert should be along shortly. She had plenty to keep her busy getting the rest of supper on the table in the meantime. "Come along, everyone."

Somehow, in the chaos, Beth missed Robert

entering the kitchen from outdoors and washing his hands before sinking into his usual seat at the head of the table. She blinked in surprise when she sat across from him and saw the apologetic expression on his face as he looked at her more intently than she could remember him doing.

"Are you—" she began, before changing her mind. Now was not the time. Not in front of the children. "If everyone is ready, Pa will say grace."

A chorus of 'yes, ma' sounded around the table, and all the children bowed their heads and took each other's hands. Beth stole one last look at her husband before closing her own eyes. Something was worrying him. It had been for days, and she couldn't think of how to solve it. But, just as with the supper, she didn't have time to pore over the problem thoroughly. She was dishing out food and correcting table manners before she could give the problem any more thought.

As supper neared its end, the children grew quieter, more tired, and there was a lull in their usual chatter. In that small moment, Beth leaned back in her chair and savored the quiet and peace. She let out a long, slow breath of contentedness.

Robert cleared his throat. "Elizabeth," he said.

She looked up sharply. Though Robert never said much, she had learned to interpret much from his tone or the sparsity of words he chose. In the nearly twenty years they had been married, they had developed a shorthand. When he spoke only her first name—her *full* first name—he required her dedicated attention.

"Claire, can you take the young ones upstairs and help them get ready for bed?"

Clara looked at her mother. It was still a bit early for the older children to go to bed. She didn't protest, however. She could read her mother's expression the same as Beth read her husband's. She nodded and stood.

"Come on, boys. And Lizzie. I have a new story to tell you as we go to bed."

Claire herded the chattering children up the stairs, leaving her parents alone.

Beth's hands shook as she tried to prepare herself for whatever Robert was about to say. Her mind went to so many different possibilities. She tried looking at him but couldn't bear the anguish of trying to guess or interpret his expression, of trying to prepare herself in just a few short moments for innumerable disasters that he might be announcing. Instead, she focused on her hands. To keep them from shaking, she clenched both together, wrapped in her apron in her lap.

Her life was about to change; she could sense it coming like a runaway horse. And there was nothing she could do about it.

"I'm sorry," Robert said softly.

Not a single other thing would have induced Beth to look at her husband at that moment, but an apology was so unexpected, so out of place, that she had to. The man had always taken such good care of her and their family that there had rarely been any reason for an apology. Which made these two faintly uttered words all the more alarming.

"Sorry? About the money that is gone from the tin?" she prompted, hoping it was nothing more serious that was making her husband look like that. "I meant to ask you. It was not a problem today, but I'll need—"

"No," he said, interrupting her for the first time in her recollection. "We— I lost the..." He swallowed hard and looked down at his hands. Beth's mind whirred. "We gotta find a new place."

"A new place? A new place for what?"

"A new home, Elizabeth."

"I don't understand."

"We can't live here anymore."

"But... *this* is our home. This has been our home since the day you brought me here as a bride. Robert. Look at me, please."

"Come now," he said miserably. "You know it was never truly ours. We've just been renting. You insisted we marry anyway."

Beth's mouth fell open. "Nearly twenty years ago, that was, Robert McKinnon. Do you mean to tell me in all those years we still have not made any progress in buying this place from your brother? Have you asked him about it?"

"Well, there was the drought, of course, and the doctor's bills when Boyd broke his leg. And we needed to replace the smokehouse..."

He trailed off, but Beth had stopped listening. What on earth could he mean, tearing her from her home? She was furious. She didn't deserve this. Her blessed children didn't deserve to lose their home. After everything she had done to keep this family together, to keep every person fed and clothed. After all she had sacrificed, all she had poured into their home here. She was expected to just walk away from all of it?

"Well, what are we supposed to do now?" she whispered.

Robert cleared his throat and shifted awkwardly in his chair.

"How can we leave our home?" she said a bit louder. "How could you do this to me? Have you *talked* to Stuart about it? Why would he just throw us out in the cold? What is wrong with the two of you?"

Her husband remained silent, offering no more apologies or even suggestions.

"Robert?"

Beth was furious with him, but at the same time, had already begun thinking through the various solutions she could come up with for this problem. She could go to Stuart himself and beg for another chance. She could sell all the furniture and stock on the place, maybe even rent out a room somehow to raise the money to buy it. If they absolutely had to leave this home, maybe her parents could take in the family for a few months while they found another farm. Beth started wondering what extra work she could take on to help raise enough money to purchase land of their own. She had never been that strong of a seamstress, but maybe with more practice—

"He offered to help us some, Elizabeth."

Her thoughts were interrupted by this mysterious addition of her husband's.

"What? Who did? What kind of help?"

"Stuart. He felt bad about turning us out like this—"

"Then he shouldn't do it—"

"But the money he's making from selling it is too good to pass up," Robert continued smoothly.

So, this is what that man was laughing about the other day, she realized grimly.

"We're family! This is your family home. Where is that man's heart or sense of decency?"

Robert shook his head, and Beth knew she would not win this. She could already see the end result as clearly as she could see the agony on her husband's face. There were a good many things that Robert would do for his wife and children, but going against his own brother was not one of them.

The two sat in silence for a long moment. Beth wondered how Claire was entertaining the children. But, bless that girl, she seemed to sense that her parents needed space and was staying out of their way.

There was no possible way out of this horrendous situation that Beth could devise. Somehow someone was going to have their heart broken.

It would likely be her.

Stuart wasn't completely heartless, but if the money for selling this land, even if it was his long-time family estate, was enough, he certainly would not hesitate to turn a deaf ear to her pleas.

"What kind of help is he offering?" she asked dejectedly.

"Well..."

"Remember, of course, that no amount of money can replace what we will lose by leaving this home. The best we can hope for is to somehow be able to stem the outpouring of pain caused by this upheaval."

"He's offering us enough for a wagon."

"A wagon? We have a wagon, what are—"

"A wagon and supplies to get us to Oregon. We can take the children, and start a new life there, build a home of our own. Free land. It's our best chance."

Beth burst into tears.

CHAPTER FIVE

Beth did not speak to her husband for two days.

After he broke the news to her that they would have to give up everything they knew in Pennsylvania and move their family to the Oregon Territory, she needed time to cool down and figure out what she would do next. Leaving the town where she had lived her whole life and raised her family seemed impossible. There had to be another way. She spent those two days considering every other possible option, but without the financial support from Stuart, they really didn't have anything.

The oldest McKinnon brother had made it very clear that his offer was greatly favored as a way to help them settle out west. With Robert his usual reticent self and Beth not speaking to him anyway, Stuart and Ann each spent hours trying to help Beth come around to the idea of resettling in the territories. Her brother-in-law even went around the county enquiring about other farms for sale, so she had all the information. Options were already limited in January, but farms extensive enough to support their large family were impossible at the price they were looking for.

How she wished she had asked Robert about their financial situation years ago. Or that they had been given more notice. Or that some other miracle had occurred that could have shielded her from this disaster.

Nevertheless, she wasn't willing to give up. Poring all through their house, Beth found a couple of pieces of older, though sturdy, furniture that might fetch some kind of price. The pastor's wife spread the word, and soon the McKinnons had cash in hand for the sixty-year-old armoire and the pair of armchairs that Claire favored for reading.

It still wasn't enough.

As the time passed, the deadline for them to move out was approaching, and Beth grew more and more frantic. Her husband kept trying. He wanted to make her happy and solve this problem for them. But when his brother came over to discuss it, Beth watched Stuart shaking his head at Robert's tentative questions out of her earshot.

Soon, she realized that her disaster planning was leaning more and more toward what they would need to cross the continent instead of focusing on what they would need to stay in Lancaster. She was involuntarily giving in, despite her heartbreak. Looking forward to the next solvable problem was her very disposition.

There wasn't any other belonging that Beth

could stand to part with, and there wasn't any other reasonable option for her family. It was an utter shock and a heartbreaking disappointment, but Beth McKinnon would soon be forced out of the home where she had lived since she was first a bride.

"Elizabeth," Robert said softly.

For a brief moment, Beth had forgotten where she was. She was standing in the middle of the second floor of their farmhouse, at the top of the stairs. Glancing at each bedroom door in turn, Beth had been racking her brain to try to come up with some other way they could make the money they needed. She remained confident that there must be something that would allow them to stay in this town she had lived her whole life.

"Elizabeth," Robert said again as he climbed the stairs toward her. "The children."

He didn't say any more, but he didn't have to. Beth knew. The children were getting restless and hungry. The winter sunlight had almost disappeared altogether; none of the lamps upstairs had been lit, and she had been standing in the near-dark. She had put off starting supper until she had solved this problem, but now it seemed as though she wouldn't be able to.

"I know." She sighed. "I know. I'm coming. I can pull something together quickly, so we don't all starve."

Beth started down the steps, but when she got to where Robert stood in the middle of the stairway, he blocked her path. There was no more fight left in her, no more will to even ask him to step aside. She sighed.

"Robert," she whispered, her shoulders sagging. She was on the step above him, but with his height, she was still only barely high enough to look her husband in the eye. What she saw in his expression when she looked up at him broke her heart. They had always been a good team, and she knew he had been trying in his own way just as much as she had.

He opened his mouth to say something. She waited. He looked down, shaking his head, and put his arms around her waist. Robert pulled her close to him, his face resting on her shoulder in a familiar, intimate way that he hadn't held her in years. In turn, she wrapped her arms around his broad shoulders and hugged him close. His body sagged under her embrace and nearly twenty years of things unsaid rested between them.

She knew he had done his best. He only ever had done his best for the family. It had irritated Beth to no end to hear other women complain about their husbands—how they didn't listen or they never gave the children attention. Take that home and deal with it there, she had always thought, while at the same time being grateful she had nothing even similar to complain about herself. Yes, there were undoubtedly times that Robert tried her patience, especially with his near-constant silence, but he was always doing his best.

"All right," she said, pulling away. "All right. I know."

Beth looked directly into her husband's eyes,

placing a hand on each shoulder. Leaning her forehead against his, she whispered, "I know. I'm sorry. We can do this."

"We can do this," he echoed.

Beth waited a single moment longer, with Robert's arms around her, with his face close to hers and the confidence of their love and strong family buoying her.

"Right," she said finally, with steel in her tone. "Supper. Those children are going to tear each other apart if we don't get down there soon."

She pecked her husband on the cheek and continued her way down the stairs with his chuckling behind her.

It took Beth several more days to come around to the idea that Oregon was the best option for her children, but once she did, she dove into the necessary plans to emigrate with full force. She found herself crying over the selling of their livestock and over the folding of the little ones' clothes to pack, but she did it all. No one ever protected their family the way she did, and even with all her fear and uncertainty, Beth managed to get through all of it.

With the decision now made, she forced herself to turn her attention to the future and to whatever new opportunities they would have in the new territory. For one, they would be able to own their own farm, a difference that would provide for their children for generations. The government was literally giving acres away, an opportunity they would not get anywhere else. And Claire likely wouldn't be expected to have an elaborate trousseau; their neighbors would be living just as humbly as the McKin-nons. The boys would have opportunities to grow and learn in ways that staying in Lancaster would never afford them. This didn't have to be all bad, she kept reminding herself.

For the most part, Beth thought she was practical and efficient in her packing. She talked the boys out of bringing their collection of birds' eggs. The oldest and most worn of their clothing were given to the Albrecht family, who had several young boys of their own. Even Claire was convinced to pare her books down to only her four most beloved volumes. As much weight and superfluity they could do away with before leaving Lancaster, the better.

There was much that the McKinnons shed, trying to fit everything into one wagon. Even so, Beth went back and forth on her decision whether or not to bring their candle snuffer with them to Oregon. She knew, really, that it wasn't a necessity. It wasn't light, and it performed a function that wasn't truly essential. But, since she was losing the home she had come to as a bride, Beth found herself more and more attached to the items that had come into her life at the same time. The wooden chest gifted by Robert's parents, though heavy, could hold blankets and dishes for the journey. Her bright blue mixing bowl that had been a family heirloom since her great-grandparents had come over from England would be useful anywhere. But the candle snuffer she could not make excuses for.

But still, in it went, wrapped in a dishtowel so the sharp end wouldn't scratch the interior of the trunk where it had been tucked away. When Robert found it later that day, he looked at her questioningly.

"I know," she said in response to his silent query. "But I just can't let *everything* go. A person can't survive on just potatoes and quilts."

"You can keep the candle snuffer," he said, "but maybe you could also keep the fears to yourself. Or just tell me, please? I overheard Lizzie yesterday telling Alexander that they would have to learn how to 'talk Indian,' in case they get kidnapped." He implored her with his eyes.

"No, you're right," she said. "Goodness, that poor child. What a burden for her to take on. I'm sorry. I... I promise I will do better. I'm sure everything will be fine. We just have to be careful. I will do my very best to stay positive for you. For all of us. I'm sorry."

"Thank you." He reached out and squeezed her hand.

Once she had made the decision, Beth wanted to be gone from Lancaster and everything they had to leave behind as soon as possible. Everything they needed was packed into their wagon; everything else was sold. Where one day she was hearing all about Poppy Lynch's wedding plans, only weeks later Beth was saying her good-byes to those same neighbors.

Before they left, Beth read the Oregon Trail travel guide Robert had brought home from cover to cover. Having a better idea of what to expect on their journey made a small difference in her willingness to leave her home. The larger effect it had, however, was planting in her mind the seeds of fear that would grow over the following weeks as they traveled toward Missouri. She had never given it much thought, but the things that could go wrong on such a long journey seemed innumerable.

She had to believe this opportunity was the best thing for her family, but at the same time, she prayed that they would all reach said opportunity safely.

Finally, the day of departure was upon them. Beth and the older children would have to walk most of the way, as their sole wagon was full to bursting with food, clothes, tools, and every other household item she couldn't bear to part with. With a heavy heart, Beth turned her face toward the west, away from her home, away from her family, away from everything she had ever known.

CHAPTER SIX

The McKinnons arrived in Independence, Missouri, on a rainy day in late March 1850. The children had been restless and quarrelsome for weeks. By the time the family finally reached the gateway to the west, all Beth wanted was to separate them. They would have to stay in one room for a few weeks while they stocked up on the supplies needed for the six months of travel. How they would ever make it until October living out of a wagon she didn't want to think about.

Claire, at fifteen years old, did her best to lighten her mother's load, but even she was no match for the pure mischievousness of her brothers. Robert did his part as well, enlisting both Boyd, thirteen years old, and Ross, ten, into chores and labor that would keep them busy and make them tired each night. Somehow, in spite of all this, Boyd found ample opportunity to prank his younger siblings and wreak havoc.

The next youngest, Lizzie, tried hard to help her mother and older sisters, but as she was only seven years old, she got in the way more often than not. To this end, Beth had put little Lizzie in charge of keeping Alexander, who was six, and Tara, who was only two years old, entertained as their wagon rolled over the stones and ruts on the road from Pennsylvania to Missouri.

But once they reached Independence, the family still had so much to do to be ready to continue the journey west. The first step was to commission the building of a second wagon. They would need to purchase and train another team of draft animals, purchase all the supplies they would need for the next six months of travel to Oregon, connect with a company of other emigrants they could travel with, and sometime in there educate, entertain and keep safe all six of the McKinnon children. All of this was somehow to be handled while living in a cramped hotel room in the middle of the busy frontier town in just a few weeks that spring.

Beth was managing; she had a running list of tasks in her head and thus far had not missed an important one. But she wasn't going to pretend it wasn't difficult.

"Isn't there anywhere quieter?" Beth had asked in despair.

The day they arrived in Independence, Robert had ridden ahead to secure the family and their animals a place to stay. Boyd had been left in charge of the team, driving them the rest of the way into town, but after only an hour, he had required his mother's help. She all but bit her tongue to keep from snapping at the boy as she tried to keep an eye on the younger children and help her oldest boy drive a team of oxen.

And now, after all that, Robert had found them again. He took over the team and led his family to the Delaware Hotel, where all eight of the McKinnons would be sleeping in a single room for the next month.

This was all exactly as they had expected and frankly better than they hoped for. And yet, Beth was surprised by the depth of her own disappointment.

"I know we're lucky to get a private room at all," she insisted to her husband as the children played on the boardwalk that stretched along the street to either side of them. "And, I know..." She swallowed hard. "I know that it won't be any better in the wagons for the next several months, but couldn't we just... Is there really nowhere else?"

It was nearing supper time, and they stood in front of the hotel, which was situated at the corners of Main Street and Kansas Avenue. Though Beth reminded herself that this was surely not the case, it seemed as though every man, woman, and child in the town had to pass along the streets on either side of this hotel. There was a constant flux of bodies, traveling in both directions and unconcerned about the smallest McKinnons who might land in their way.

Robert offered no defense, no comfort to his wife, but that was fine because Beth knew all the reasons anyway. Nothing he said could change things. At least the Delaware Hotel was a full block away from the town square. At least they were all able to fit in one room and didn't have to be separated. At least it would only be a month, and they would be out and about most of the time anyway. She knew it could be worse.

Beth had this silent negotiation with herself before sighing in acceptance, after reminding herself that she had vowed to stay encouraging and hopeful for the children's sake. Her own complaining would only fan the flames of theirs.

"Gotcha!" Lizzie yelled as she lunged forward to tag her brother.

Beth turned just in time to see her youngest son, Alexander, trip in his haste to avoid his sister and tumble right into his mother's skirts.

"Goodness!" she exclaimed as she caught him. "Be careful, please."

"We could camp outside town if you prefer," Robert said softly. "Spread out a little more?"

Beth looked at her husband, marveling at how he made his choice about when to speak and when not to. But that thought was pushed aside as she briefly considered, then dismissed his suggestion. This would be her last chance at a proper bed for months, cramped though it may be. The safety these four brick walls afforded were worth the noise and the expense.

She smiled bravely at her husband and then down at her son, still struggling with his sister.

"Come along," she said, righting Alexander to his

feet. "Your father has found us a lovely place to stay. Let's take our clothes and things inside and then we'll explore the town. How does that sound?"

"Prince too?"

Robert shook his head, and Beth added, "Hotels are not for dogs, dearest. He can wait out here for you. It won't be long at all."

Over her son's complaining and the other children's laughter, wonder, and questions, Beth managed to herd her family into the crowded lobby and up the stairs after Robert. At the top of the stairs, he unlocked the closest door and held it open for them. Tentatively, Beth stepped past his outstretched arm into her new temporary home.

The room held only two large beds, and when she sniffed, Beth wondered if the chamber pot had been emptied at all recently. Tears stung her eyes when another wave of disappointment hit her. But, she reminded herself for the hundredth time, it wouldn't be for that long. And she had plenty of blankets in the wagon brought from Pennsylvania. The boys could sleep on the floor, and all would be safe and warm.

Because that was what really mattered after all— that her family was together, safe and secure. Their physical needs were taken care of, and Beth kept reminding herself that all would be better once they got to Oregon. It had to be. If a crowded, loud, not-quite-clean hotel room was the worst she had to deal with, she was a blessed woman indeed. That was what was most important.

That's what she kept telling herself, though the

strain of all the new problems to deal with was wearing on her. But perhaps if she repeated it often enough she might begin to believe it.

The McKinnons settled into their routines in Independence quickly, though Beth wished there was a way they could all stay a little closer to their temporary home. As it was, her husband and children seemed as though they scattered to the winds every morning. Baby Tara was left with Beth, but Claire had taken charge of the rest of them. Each evening they returned to the tight room to regale their parents with stories of their adventures of the day, this time visiting the blacksmith to deliver the order for nails they need.

"And then he let me hammer the metal when it was hot," Ross said with a grin as wide as the Mississippi itself.

"And what did you say, brilliant son-of-mine?" Beth admonished with an indulgent smile. How she wished she could have been there to see her son handle such tools for the first time. How much that must have thrilled him. "I imagine the blacksmith must have been very busy."

"I said thank you," Ross insisted, sternly, as though insulted that his manners had been questioned. "Twice!"

"Have you ever done smith work, Mother?" Boyd asked her.

That child was at the right age to learn what fun it could be to tease his mother. He hadn't yet crossed the line into impertinence, and Beth rather enjoyed his sense of humor most of the time.

"Why, didn't you know? Your mother made all the horseshoes in Lancaster County in her youth."

Boyd's face fell, his eyes wide in wonder. "Wait, really?"

Beth laughed. "No, you goose. I'm teasing you. What a silly question."

"We also met someone who said you should come find her," Claire added. "A Miss Atkins. I told her what wagon company we would be joining, and she said she will be there too. And—you'll never guess—she's a teacher!"

"A teacher? Going to Oregon? Is she by herself?"

"I think she's traveling with a family. Not her family. I don't know all the details, but she did say she hoped to hold at least some classes over the summer as we travel west. And she's promised to lend me her books too." Claire's eyes sparkled with excitement.

"That sounds wonderful," Beth said.

And she meant it. Her own days had been full of a million small worries; she hadn't had time to think about such luxuries as schoolwork. She wanted better for her children. If a teacher was willing to take on some of their training over the following six months, so much the better.

"What did you do today, Mama?" Alexander asked as he settled himself in her lap.

Beth wrapped her arms around her small son, taking a moment to breathe in the scent of the top of his head before answering.

"Well, I made a friend too. A nice woman named Mrs. Hudson and I were both in the dry goods store at the same time and got to chatting as we waited for the clerk to help us. She'll be in the same wagon company too. And I finalized our order for the cots we need for the wagon. It will be a tight fit, but we'll manage."

"How long till we leave?" Alexander asked.

Beth looked at her husband.

"Only two more weeks," he said.

"Two more weeks," Beth repeated. "Two weeks left to sleep under a roof. Two weeks to sleep on a real mattress."

"Two more weeks until you have to be in charge of a team of oxen," Claire said pointedly to her brother. "Are you sure you're ready?"

Boyd looked affronted. "Of course I'm ready."

Ross piped in then with his own question for his brother, and Beth sat back and listened. Only two more weeks. She wasn't sure she would ever feel ready for an adventure such as this.

CHAPTER SEVEN

Beth wasn't sure she would ever get over the heartache of having to leave her home in Pennsylvania. However, every day she was in Missouri was one more day when the worries and tasks of her current life blocked out the memories of her past. And, goodness, were there a lot of worries when they were setting out to emigrate across the continent. Her family needed her, and Beth McKinnon had always been willing to do what needed to be done.

The morning the wagon company was set to leave Independence, Beth was up before dawn, far earlier than any of her children and much earlier than she really needed to be. The week leading up to this moment, she had found herself waking earlier and earlier, seeking out the quietest moments of the day, before the rest of the town was up to their bustling, before the animals stirred awake, before the sun even. The quiet, velvety darkness before the day properly started was when Beth felt most that she had everything under control. In the weeks to follow, when any time to herself would be scarce, she wanted to have the calm memory of these mornings to look back on.

That last morning in Independence passed in a blur, however. Soon Robert was up, dragging Boyd and Ross with him to the wagonmaker's yard to hitch up their new team. The girls and Alexander stayed behind to collect the last of their belongings that had been strewn throughout the small room over the previous weeks. Together, they were to bring the family's horses and Prince to where they would meet the loaded wagons. Each member of the family had their job. By the end of the morning, the McKinnons' two wagons had been packed full, the teams were hitched, and all were rolling behind other wagons down the main street out of town and toward their next camp.

Beth wanted to be in several different places at once, keeping an eye on everything that could possibly go wrong. Robert, as ever, counseled patience.

"You need to trust them, Elizabeth," Robert said gently. "Trust that you've taught them what they need to know. They'll be grown in no time and need to be able to do all these things without their mother holding their hands."

"I know. It's just so much. You're sure Boyd will be all right?" Beth asked him. "Those oxen are so strong."

"I was twelve when my father had me driving our harvest into town every week. Remember how much work that was?"

"But you were far more serious than he is, weren't you? I just worry he won't take his responsibility seriously, driving a whole team by himself every day. It's so much."

They were walking along the dirt road in a small caravan of families who were all leaving Independence that day to head west to Missouri. They would make camp that evening and connect with the other members of their new wagon company. In the preceding weeks in Independence, Robert had asked around and managed to secure the McKinnons' inclusion with a large wagon company. The Sullivan-Mills company boasted both a doctor and a schoolteacher among its members. For Beth, there was not much else that she could ask for during their next six months of traveling. The group of men and women they traveled west with could be the difference between life and death.

"This first day, when we still are near enough to town to make repairs or get replacements, if necessary, is the best time for us to learn how Boyd will handle it," Robert said calmly.

"All right," she said with a sigh and one final look behind them to where Boyd was. "I'm sure you're right."

Robert said nothing, but he reached for her hand and gave it a squeeze.

The stretch of trail between Independence and

the first camp seemed to go by quickly for Beth. She walked along the trail, step after step, but wasn't thinking about her feet. With all of the overseeing she had to do to make sure all of her children were safe and accounted for, not to mention ensuring that Boyd was as focused and serious about his role in leading the team and wagon as he needed to be, it was no wonder that they arrived at their destination without her realizing it. She was surprised when her husband guided the family to a camping spot just as the sunset at the end of the day.

Taking off her bonnet as the boys arranged the wagons in place, Beth took a look around at where they had stopped for the night. This was not only where the McKinnons would be meeting up with their wagon company, but it was where most of the companies gathered outside of Independence. As such, the field of white canvas wagon tops seemed to stretch for miles. Hundreds of wagons were gathered in camps around this single water source. The sheer number overwhelmed her. Each of these families was looking for their own new start in the west, just as the McKinnons were.

Beth was exhausted. She was hot. She was cranky. Her dress itched around her collar, and she had sweat through her bonnet under the April sun. But she had work to do. As Robert showed the oldest boys what needed to be done with their animals, wagons, and making camp every night, Beth steeled herself for more hours of work. She picked up two of the family's wooden buckets and followed the general crowd of women and girls to the small stand of trees just at the foot of the hill that signi-fied the camp's water source.

All around her, as she followed the trail, Beth heard the cheerful chatter of introductions and the sympathetic murmuring of women. Though they were likely all just as tired as Beth herself, she didn't hear one harsh word among the crowd. Many of these women would be her friends and neighbors, not only over the summer as they traveled west, but also perhaps once they reached Oregon. Though Beth and Robert hadn't discussed in any detail where they would settle out there on the coast, she had to assume with the number of families in this company, at least some of them would live near the McKinnons.

Beth jostled her way to the water's edge, eager to get her supply and get back to camp.

"Excuse me," she said, trying to squeeze between a pair of young women and a tall shrub that reached out with thorns for her skirt.

"Oh!" the older one said. She noticed Beth trying to get by and turned back to the younger. "Amy, move. Get out of the way."

The younger girl, maybe Claire's age, seemed surprised to be pulled out of the way. She had been too focused on watching the activities of a spider weaving its web between two branches to notice anything else.

"It's fine," Beth assured them with a smile as she snuck around them. "Not to worry. We'll likely all find ourselves in the middle of somebody's path between here and Oregon. Are you two with the Sullivan-Mills camp by any chance?"

"We are!" the younger girl said, looking away from the web. "We heard there was a doctor with that company. Do you know about that? Do you think he does dissections?"

Beth sputtered awkwardly. "I'm sorry?"

She looked between the two young women, wondering if there was something more that she should be wary of.

"Never mind her. *I'm* sorry. Nora Cole," the older girl said, gesturing to herself. "And this is Amy, my sister."

"My name is Mrs. McKinnon." She paused before continuing cautiously. "And to answer your question, I think if the doctor ever did dissections, it's unlikely that he will do any of that on the trail."

"Oh." Amy seemed disappointed. "That's probably true. Amputations, though, maybe, right?"

"Amy," Nora hissed.

"Um. Yes, maybe. You know, I have a daughter about your age," Beth said to Amy, trying to smooth over her sister's embarrassment. "Her name is Claire. She helps me a lot with my younger children and with chores and such, but maybe the two of you, or three of you, might like to play together some time."

"We'd love that," Nora said brightly before Amy could answer. "But of course, we have chores of our own to get to."

"Of course."

"It was lovely to meet you." Nora smiled at Beth,

handed one of their buckets to her sister, and nudged her back up the trail away from the water.

Beth chuckled to herself, watching the sisters go. She had known plenty of girls like Amy Cole when she was growing up, so completely unconcerned with what other people thought of her to the point of social awkwardness. She didn't envy Nora her role in guiding her younger sister, but maybe both could be good for her own child.

For that short time, Beth had forgotten how tired she was. She resolved that pushing her children toward making strong friendships would be a goal of hers over the next few months.

When she got back to her own campsite, Beth found that someone had started the campfire going already. But when she reached the opening in the canvas of their second, supply wagon, she was surprised to find all of her children already meddling about in the crates and barrels, making a mess of things.

At the moment that she watched, Ross backed into a tall stack of crates, knocking the top one to the floor, where half a dozen tin cups clattered.

"What are you doing?" Beth said, startling the children from their focus.

"I wanted to get started," Claire began, "but then..."

She gestured to the younger ones as she trailed off. Beth could fill in the blanks just fine.

"Did your sister ask for your help?" she directed to the others.

"No, but—" Lizzie started.

"But we're so hungry," Boyd cut in.

"And she was taking so long," Alexander added.

"We thought maybe dinner could be sooner," Ross concluded for them. "Five heads are better than one, right?"

"And five pairs of hands make a bigger mess than one," Beth said. "Out. Everyone out. You too, Claire. Thank you for trying, but…"

She shook her head. Amidst some grumbling and protests, the children were soon out of the wagon and out of her way.

Beth stood in the dim interior of the supply wagon and took stock of what they had with them. They had left Independence in such a hurry; none of her dishes or tools were organized the way she wanted them to be. And now, with the children moving things around, it would be even more difficult to find what she was looking for. One thousand pounds of flour sure took up a lot of space. Six hundred pounds of bacon sounded like a lot, but with these children, she wasn't sure. One hundred pounds of coffee should be more than enough. Tea, sugar, lard, beans, oats, dried apples, and so much more, all of it needing to stretch out as long as she could manage.

They had all these essentials to carry with them across the continent. It seemed like an immense amount of food, but split between eight people—including three growing boys—it would barely last the six months they had planned to be on the Oregon Trail. If there were any accidents or spoilages, Beth didn't know what she would do.

There was so much that could go wrong and so many things that could keep her up at night with worry.

Keeping the children safe and fed was all she needed to worry about for the next six months. She could do this. With a deep breath, Beth pushed up her sleeves and got to work.

CHAPTER EIGHT

The next morning, the smell of freshly brewed coffee was on the air, floating throughout their campsite, and the sounds of children playing surrounded Beth.

"Mama! Mama, watch!"

Alexander called to his mother for what felt like the ninetieth time, and Beth was running out of energy to give him. She only had the day and was supposed to be reorganizing her supply wagon. Good, focused work today would set them up for a far easier journey, but she kept getting distracted. Everyone seemed to want something from her.

The Sullivan-Mills wagon company was spending a full day at the camp. This allowed some straggling members to catch up with the group and allowed the members already there to ease into their journey. Earlier that morning, one of the other companies of emigrants had pulled out of camp, arranging themselves in a long train of white-topped wagons rolling westward. Beth had watched with longing—she wanted her family to be on their way—but she trusted that the company leaders to which Robert had hitched their future were the best, and safest, choice for their family.

As such, they had a full day to wait, but also—as Beth cheerfully told her children—a full day to make friends, to rest before the hard part, and to organize their wagons exactly as they wanted them to be. They couldn't be certain when they would get such time again. It could be time well spent. Claire had heard all about the Cole sisters from her mother, and the company seemed to be full of other little ones. Beth had her eyes out for more children who might befriend her own family.

But now, Alexander had evidently run out of other ways to entertain himself. He had spent the last twenty minutes repeatedly trying to jump over the narrow gap where the two wagon lips overlapped while Prince followed joyfully behind. It was far too high for the boy to leap over, and he had likely bruised his chest and ribs more than once in the attempt. Nevertheless, Alexander repeatedly called for his mother to watch him attempt the feat.

"My darling boy," she called to him when she finally acquiesced to his calling. "You are so good at that. I see you. I'm so proud, but I have to finish this repacking before the sun goes down."

"But you didn't even see—"

"I did."

"Nuh-uh. No, I did it differently this time. You didn't see!"

Beth smiled, tired but still enamored with her child. There must be a tiny shred of patience left in her. With a deep breath, she stood up straight and gave him her full attention.

"All right, then. One more time. Just once, and then I really need to finish this."

"Okay, okay, okay!" he blurted excitedly as he returned to his starting position. "Okay! Just watch. Here we go."

This time—and to be fair to the child, it was different than she had seen previously—Alexander stepped up on the spoke of one of the wheels and used that to launch himself over the lip. Wind-milling his arms, the boy barely kept his balance. His landing was awkward, however, and Beth winced to see the knees of his trousers slide in the dirt.

"Did you see?" Though bruised and dirty, Alexander seemed quite pleased with himself.

Beth applauded. "I did see. That's wonderful, dear. You did so well. But why don't you see if the Jones family or the Abbotts or anyone has any other little boys your age? Maybe you can make a friend today that will be good company for you?"

"I don't know..."

"And then you could show him your special jump," she concluded.

He shrugged. "I guess."

"Or you can sit here and play with Tara?" She gestured to where the youngest McKinnon was sitting on a quilt in the grass next to the family's wagon. All the older children had a horror of being lumped in with the "baby," no matter their age. That nudge was exactly what Alexander needed to spur him away from the family's camp. He sprinted off with Prince close on his heels.

And that left Beth alone—finally—to focus on what she would need over the following months. The items that would be used more needed to be moved nearer to the end. The items that they may not need until Oregon would be packed farther back. She would need to plan and ration and make sure to keep a good balance of all the food for each meal, remembering how much each of her children would need on these long days of walking along the trail.

Such planning and looking ahead filled her day. The pastor, Mr. Montgomery, came by their wagon to introduce himself, as did Mrs. Fields from the wagon next to theirs. Several other families, couples, and women passed by their camp and smiled their greeting without stopping. Robert reported meeting several of the other men from their wagon company at a brief meeting the captains called. He pointed out the Buchanans, the Sullivans, the Franklins, and others to Beth, though she hadn't had a chance to introduce herself yet. It was a lot to take in all at once. Beth had to remind herself that she wasn't missing anything. She had six months on the trail, plenty of time.

After that full day in camp, everything had been set. The company hit the trail the following morning. Beth was relieved to be on their way, finally. The journey to Oregon that had been the focus of all of her attention for the previous several months was actually beginning. Somehow the moment the wagon wheels began rolling, the moment they crossed out of the tall grass onto the crooked dirt track, felt like the start of everything.

When Beth had finally acknowledged that they needed to leave Pennsylvania, she had quickly turned her focus westward toward the future and all that she would need to do. Now that the moment had arrived, she felt both relieved and overwhelmed.

The Sullivan-Mills wagon company was finally on the way to Oregon.

There was no more preparation she could do.

She was as ready as she would ever be.

The caravan didn't stop for a midday meal that first day, as they had started late that morning, but not long into the hot afternoon, the wagons ahead of them slowed to a stop. Beth had been walking alongside her oldest son. He'd needed her help driving the wagon that final day before they reached Independence, and she couldn't be certain how much better he would do now. So far, she was pleased with how he was handling the team. Still, when her husband's wagon ahead of them stopped, she immediately began worrying again.

"What do you think it is?" Boyd asked, trying to peer over the vehicles. "Why did we stop?"

She shook her head but didn't put words to her fear. It could be anything. The list of dangers and obstacles between them and Oregon was endless.

They waited in near silence for the wagons to move again or for someone to come give them different instructions, as Beth grew more anxious with every moment. When they finally started again, the caravan was led off of the trail, in the grass and around some impediment.

As they drew closer, following behind Robert's wagon, Beth began to feel a knot of fear in the pit of her stomach. Whatever had happened that had driven them off the trail was not likely to be pleasant. The caravan curved around, and she caught the first glimpse of the obstacle in flashes between the wagons. There was a mess of wood and limbs and blood, and nothing seemed to be in the right place.

"Oh no," she said. "Oh—" A rising sob cut off her words. She couldn't bear to look at it, but she also couldn't look away.

One of the wagons ahead of them had somehow overturned, and in the chaos or confusion, a man had been crushed underneath it. Even now, she could see a pair of men valiantly trying to lift the felled wagon off of the victim, but it seemed futile. A woman and small children stood off to the side, watching helplessly.

"What is it?" Boyd asked, craning his neck to see over the animals.

"Nothing," Beth answered sharply. "It's nothing. Keep moving. Keep your eyes ahead on your father's wagon."

As they drew level with the overturned wagon, it was clear that the accident had only just happened. Beth couldn't be sure how far ahead of the McKinnons the Buchanans had been in the line of wagons, but so little time had passed that it seemed as though there were still frantic efforts being made to save the man. Maybe it wasn't too late. The doctor—what was his name? —should be there any moment. Surely someone had sent word to him.

A part of Beth wanted to rush to Mrs. Buchanan's side, to help her guide her children, to aide her through whatever the next step was, be it caring for an invalid or burying a partner. She wanted to do *something*. But out here, in the virtual wilderness of the plains, Beth had to remind herself that her children were her first responsibility. Six little ones depended on her.

As the caravan of wagons rolled slowly around the downed vehicle, Boyd stumbled, tripping over something and falling to his knees in the grass next to the trail.

Beth screamed in terror. She clutched for the reins that her son had inadvertently dropped and all but leaped over his prone form to put her body between him and the oxen.

"Ma, it's okay," he mumbled, hurrying to his feet. Boyd brushed the dirt off his trousers, his face red with the embarrassment of his fall and her reaction. "Ma, give me the reins. It's okay. I'm all right."

Though she had successfully suppressed a sob only minutes earlier when she saw what the Buchanans had suffered, now that her son had scared her so, Beth could not hold back.

"Boyd!" she choked out. "Don't ever do that again!"

She wanted to clutch him to her. She wanted to send him far away from the big, strong animals. She wanted to take them all back to Pennsylvania, where

Boyd wouldn't need to drive a team of oxen two thousand miles. Every fear and panic that she had put aside since they left their home all came back in a rush.

"Ma," he protested.

Her hands were still shaking when she handed him back the reins. He was just a child; what was Robert thinking putting him in charge of such creatures, putting him in the way of such danger?

But it was too late now. They had committed to both wagons, and the only alternative was if Beth herself were to drive the team. Maybe they could hire an older teenage boy to help out, but she didn't see how they would be able to spare the money.

She glanced back at the Buchanan family. Mrs. Buchanan had gathered the children to her, ten feet or so away from the wagon, and her husband crushed beneath it. Even from this distance, Beth could see the grief hanging heavy over the woman. She had known accidents like this could happen any time on the Oregon Trail, but she didn't think it would occur quite so soon.

Clasping her son's free hand in her own, Beth faced forward again, walking alongside Boyd as he led the team of oxen to follow his father's wagon.

Death and injuries were an accepted fact of the emigrants' journey. It would be up to her to keep her family safe from all dangers.

CHAPTER NINE

After the shock of Jeb Buchanan's death, the Sullivan-Mills wagon company seemed to be holding their collective breath. Though every member of the company had told themselves to expect some tragedy, none thought it would occur so soon into the journey. They had barely had a chance to realize they were on the Oregon Trail before it claimed one of them.

Word went around the camp that Mrs. Buchanan had elected to continue on her own way west to Oregon. Her children were too small to be of much help, but she hired a couple of the older boys from other families to help her drive the repaired wagon across the continent. Selling the few supplies she could do without helped pay for that, but none of this was what the poor woman had planned when she first set out from home. It would be far more difficult than the original harrowing journey the woman had thought she was on, but she seemed determined to keep on.

Beth thought she might attempt to make friends with the strong, brave woman. It must be so trying to suffer such a loss, especially so early in the journey. She had so hoped that the community of this wagon company would help make up for what she had left behind in Lancaster. Unfortunately, she could never find a moment. For the time being, she was too exhausted keeping track of her own children and acclimating to life living on the trail. The first bloom of excitement was off the rose, and the harsh realities of their new life weighed on her.

When the McKinnons had traveled from Pennsylvania, they were able to take whatever time required or travel at whatever rate they chose. Robert was in charge of all of it, with Beth by his side for whatever he needed. Now, however, they were in a wagon company of nearly fifty families, with even more wagons than that. Dozens of children, along with more than a hundred head of livestock, had to be accounted for each day. The company leaders had to balance the needs of their weakest members against the very real and pressing deadline of reaching the Blue Mountains before the snow fell that autumn. No matter what Beth wanted to do for her own small family, she had to go along with the will of the company.

The thought of another wagon accident or even one of the children getting caught under the hooves of an ox haunted her. The presence of a doctor in the company only eased her anxiety so much.

Running out of food before they could resupply worried her. The easy preparedness she had worked so hard for seemed to be draining away. As the days passed, Beth felt a growing sense of panic at having so little control, but she tried to cope.

Keeping her children close was the first step.

"Yes, Lizzie, you can go play," she said sternly to the little girl after breakfast one morning when they had been on the trail a few days. "You know the rule. You must be taller than the grass where you play, and you must be within hearing of my voice. And don't let Alexander get too far either."

"Yes, Mama," she sang back before darting away.

"You know they will run off again as soon as they think you're not paying attention?" Claire said with a laugh as she scrubbed hurriedly at the dishes.

"Yes, I do. Just like I know you're rushing through that chore so you can go see what the Cole girls are doing."

Claire blushed. "I don't have to if you need me."

"Nonsense," her mother said. "I'm pleased you've made friends. But just you make sure you get those dishes done right. I don't want any grease still making them slick when you put them away."

"Yes, Ma," she said.

"Lizzie!" called a new voice.

She turned to see a small girl, roughly her daughter's age, skipping through the grass. It was Marigold Abbott, whose family wagon was camped nearby. She called out again. As Beth watched, Lizzie turned toward her new friend, jumped up in delight, and the two little girls embraced as though they had gone years without seeing each other instead of merely less than a day.

Beth chuckled.

Not far behind her, walking far more slowly, was the woman Beth knew to be the little girl's grandmother. Beth waved at Mrs. Fields as she approached.

"Good morning, Mrs. Fields! Would you like some coffee?"

"No, no coffee, thank you. I just came to return your rolling pin."

The family who followed directly behind the McKinnons' second wagon—their sleeping wagon driven by Boyd—was Curtis and Emma Fields. Beth had introduced herself to the older couple on their first day out on the trail; they would be neighbors throughout the entire journey, after all. She soon learned all about the Fieldses' plans for Oregon, as well as about their family. Their daughter and her family traveled in the wagon just behind them, and they had left a couple sons behind in the eastern states. Emma Fields was friendly, talkative, and easy-going in a way that Beth herself had never been. The few chances she had had to speak with the older woman had been lovely, including offering to let her borrow the rolling pin Beth had stashed away just in case.

"Oh, thank you. How was the pie?"

Emma laughed. "I intended to save you a piece as a thank you, but there's not a scrap to be had. I suppose you might say it was a success."

"I must confess to being disappointed," Beth

teased. "From the way you described it, your recipe sounded delicious. I never would have thought to put cranberries in an apple pie."

"No?"

Beth shrugged. "I'm not one to deviate from what I already know to work, I suppose. Better to stick with what's safe. It just seems easier that way. Less to worry about. Goodness knows these rascals"—she gestured to Lizzie and Ross playing in the grass beyond the wagon—"give me plenty to think about otherwise."

"Oh, I understand that. I'm the same way about my dresses." Emma sat carefully, leaning against the back lip of the McKinnons' wagon. "My daughter-in-law, back in West Virginia, makes the most cunning little dresses and shirts for her little ones. Just whips them up off the top of her head, whereas I stick to the same patterns I've always used."

"It's easier that way," Beth agreed.

"But I suppose after raising four children, feeding them all with the same recipes over and over would have worn on me. It's just a fun little adventure to try at times."

Just then, the girls' playing erupted into shrieks and peals of laughter. Beth looked up to see that Marigold had taken off at a run, with Lizzie following behind her. Whatever game of chase or tag they were playing seemed to be delightful.

"Goodness, is that Marigold?" Emma asked.

Beth looked at her in surprise. "You didn't know? She got here just before you. I had assumed you had walked over together."

"No, I had no idea." She chuckled. "I'll wager no one else does either."

"Does she need to go home?" Beth asked. "Does her mother know where she is? I don't want her to worry."

"Oh, don't you fret, child. I'll tell Jenny. She doesn't worry much about the little ones anyway. They can only get so far."

"I..." Beth's mouth fell open in confusion. "I don't understand. The child is what, seven? Eight? Her mother's not worried?"

"She's just turned eight, yes. Which, I'll allow, might be a little young. But Marigold has always been headstrong. In fact, the first week she first started going to school a couple years ago, there was one day she just decided she was done with school. She didn't say a word to the schoolmaster, but walked home on her own. Six years old and just strolling all by herself through town as confident as you pleased."

"Oh my." Beth rested a hand on her chest. "Was her mother angry when she got home?"

Emma laughed even harder. "Marigold didn't even come home. Jenny knew nothing about it until supper that night. The girl had somehow realized that she was supposed to be somewhere else, so she hid in the hayloft until the afternoon when she could pretend to be coming home from school."

Beth gasped. "So no one knew where the child was for hours? She could have been badly hurt!"

"Of course, you're right. But she wasn't. That's just Marigold. At supper that night, her older brother ratted her out. She was punished quite strictly if I recall, but that hasn't seemed to detain her. Never you fear. I'll mention this to Jenny when I get back. But the child seems fine, doesn't she? I'm sure there's nothing to worry about."

Beth was silent and turned back to watch the little girls playing.

She couldn't understand how the girl's mother could be anything but panicked, not knowing where her child was. Beth couldn't think how to word all of her mountain of worries. Though Emma Fields had been a mother—and now a grandmother—far longer than Beth, she didn't seem to have the same caution or vigilance. Not being anxious about every move her children made seemed foreign to Beth.

"Were you the same way when your own children were young? Just letting them..." Beth gestured help-lessly. "I don't know..."

"Letting them be children?" Emma smiled kindly. "I'll admit there were more broken bones and hurt feelings than there might have been if I had been more vigilant. But, then, all my children have grown up to be happy, healthy adults, with a solid sense of their own limitations."

"Hmm."

"Mind you, Thomas learned the hard way that he couldn't fly from the roof of the smokehouse, but he did learn it. Children are smarter than we probably give them credit for." Emma stood up again. "I should be getting back. Sounds like the wagons will be starting up again soon. Thank you again for the use of your rolling pin, my dear." She placed an old, wrinkled hand on Beth's arm and beamed into her face, patting her hand a few times.

"Please, feel free to borrow it any time. It's no trouble."

Once the older woman had left, Beth turned her attention back to putting away the dishes from breakfast. She tried to ignore the laughter and shouts from the children only thirty feet away; she told herself she could give them space to learn the way that Emma had. But the practice of doing so was far harder than the theory. She tried to put thoughts of turned ankles or snake bites from her mind.

In the end, Beth resumed her watchfulness over the little McKinnons. They seemed unharmed by her attention. All in all, the McKinnons seemed to be settling into their new life pretty well. Soon they would be reaching the wide Kansas River, marking the first of the landmarks on the Oregon Trail that they had been looking forward to.

CHAPTER TEN

The emigrant families traveled ever westward across the flat plains of the Missouri Territory. Each morning the spring chill roused them out of sleep, and each day they walked or rode as many miles as they could muster under the hot sun. Captains Mills and Sullivan tried to keep the caravan to a strict schedule. They had thousands of miles to go, still, and setting a precedent for the rest of the journey was paramount. There was a calm and a rhythm to each day that Beth clung to. Routine comforted her, and that comfort helped keep her from worrying about the unknown in front of her.

When the Sullivan-Mills wagon company approached the wide Kansas River ahead of crossing it, Beth had already spent the previous several days instructing her six children on everything that was expected of them to stay safe, secure, and, hopefully, dry. She still worried, but at least she could console herself in her belief that she had done all she could. After supper the evening before, before she tucked them all into bed, she tried again to make sure they knew what to do.

"And, what will happen when it's our turn to cross?" she asked Boyd, who at that moment was trying to get their horse to eat a small twig. "Boyd!"

"Huh?" He looked up at her.

"I asked you a question."

Ross giggled.

"I know, Mama!" Alexander piped up.

Beth smiled at her small son. He wanted so badly to be included with the bigger boys; he didn't realize that his very enthusiasm was part of what made his brothers dismiss him.

"Boyd?" she prodded.

He shrugged.

"Mama," pleaded Alexander.

"All right, yes. Tell me what happens when it's our turn."

Alexander wriggled like an eager puppy and stood up straighter. "When it's our turn, the men helping will put both of the wagons on the platform. And the animals," he added as an afterthought.

"And where will you be?" his mother prompted.

"Not on the wagons," Lizzie said.

"I *know*!" her younger brother insisted with a frown, put out at the interruption.

"Lizzie, let your brother tell me."

She and Ross both giggled this time.

"Go ahead, Alexander."

He nodded seriously. "We will be holding on to

the rail, next to you, Mama. And stay out of the men's way. And away from the oxen. And hang on tight."

"Unless...?"

"Unless... Um..." He screwed up his face, trying to remember all the details his mother had warned him about.

She looked to her other children. Beth wasn't worried about Claire, old enough that her judgment could be trusted. Lizzie and Tara would stick close by their sister. The boys, however, were another story. She could never be quite sure how well they listened or how much stock they placed in her caution. The boys seemed to disregard all of her warnings as an overreaction and never quite believed that anything so bad could happen to them that their loving parents couldn't fix it.

"Ross?" she prompted. He had taken to pushing Boyd playfully, getting between him and their horse. "Boyd?"

"Boyd!" Alexander yelled.

His stunned older brother frowned but finally gave his mother his attention. "Yes?"

"Under what circumstances are you to *not* hold tight to the rail of the platform as we cross the river?" Beth prompted.

"Um... If it tips, right? If the thing... if something goes wrong and the wagons start rolling, and it seems like we're going to, you know, um, go over, we should jump into the water, right? And swim across."

"And upstream."

"And upstream," he repeated, grinning proudly

that he had remembered. "Right. That's what I was going to say. So we don't get pulled in or run over if the platform does go over."

"And you will watch out for your siblings, won't you?" she continued.

"But, Ma, they all can swim. At least a little."

"Boyd," she said patiently. "The water will be cold. Everyone will be scared and tired. I need to know that if the worst happens, you will look out for each other."

"Yes, Ma. I know," he said as Ross tugged him away to go play.

"Won't you be in the water too, Mama?" Alexander asked.

"Of course I will, my love," she assured him. "And this probably won't happen anyway. Mr. Mills and your father and all the other men have everything quite under control, and not one of the wagons has gone into the water yet. I just want to make sure you're safe and prepared, just in case. If we all have to go into the water, I'll be there too. I promise."

He nodded seriously at her vow, but only briefly, before grinning and running off to see if his brothers would let him play with them.

Beth sighed, watching him run. The line between protecting and guiding her children was so fine. The best she could hope was that she was preparing them for everything that the world could possibly throw their way.

Fortunately, all her worrying was for naught. Though she was tense the entire time, when the

McKinnons' wagons were loaded onto the platform, everything went as smoothly as possible. Several of the younger men from the wagon company were on hand to help, and nothing more was asked of Beth than to keep her children out of the way of the heavy vehicles and stressed animals. They were over the water and leading their wagons to the campsite on the other side by early afternoon.

And with that adventure safely behind them, Beth settled in for the rest of the day. She had been planning to use the time to bake extra johnnycakes that the children could eat cold when they were hungry. Planning ahead for all possible eventualities, as usual. After withdrawing promises from the children that they would not leave the range of her voice, Beth focused on getting as much done as she could in the little time she had.

Finally, near sunset, she had prepared supper and tried to gather the family to eat.

"Boyd! Ross!" Beth called. The bigger boys were filthy from their playing under the nearby trees, but at least they were within shouting distance as she had asked. "Come to supper!"

Once she saw that they were heading toward her, Beth looked around for her smallest son.

"Alexander!"

"I haven't seen him," Claire said as she added some dried grass to the campfire. "Maybe he's playing with the Jones boys?"

"Maybe," Beth murmured as she stirred the pot of beans just starting to steam. "I told him not to go far, though. I'll find him."

After offering Claire a few quick instructions, Beth wiped her hands on her apron and headed toward where the Jones family wagon had settled for the night.

"Alexander?" she called again.

There was no stirring, no apologetic child running to her from the campsite. She got within thirty feet of their wagon before she turned. Where had the boy gone? Beth racked her brain for a memory of him mentioning any other child's name. Were there any other clues that had been planted over the previous weeks of where he could be now?

Weaving her way between campsites, she reached the outer edge of the company's campsite. Surely the boy could not have ventured this far away. He had been told again and again that he needed to stay where he could hear her, where she could see him. After this long day of waiting to cross the river, Alexander must have been aching for a little bit of freedom—she just wished he could have done it nearer to camp.

"Alexander!" Beth called again. "Alexander McKinnon, it's supper time! Where are you?"

Still, she heard nothing beyond the chirping of the crickets and the conversations from the campsites behind her. Ahead of her, the fading sun illuminated the landscape, reflecting hard beams off the water's surface and turning the plains of grass beyond a fiery yellow. For a brief moment, Beth caught her breath. The strength and power of such a landscape overwhelmed her. She felt tiny in the wide, never-ending empty continent. Where her home in Lancaster had been cozy, well-worn, and comfortable, here living in the veritable wilderness, she was struck by how wild every step felt.

Such thoughts were dashed from her mind when her eyes lit on a small dark figure in the water. From this distance, it was impossible to see what it was; all she knew was that in the river, about six feet from the shore, something substantial floated on the surface, breaking up the otherwise even reflection of the sun.

Before she gave it another thought, Beth was striding into the water. She had to see what it was. She had to prove to herself that her gut feeling was wrong. Soon she was in the river. To her ankles. Up over her boots. She was knee-deep in the shallows as the river coursed around her. Her petticoat and skirt billowed up to the surface, and the water seeped even higher, up through her shirtwaist. With every step, Beth's dress took on more and more water, acting as a kind of anchor holding her back, keeping her safely in ignorance of what the floating thing was.

Dread seemed to choke her as every step brought her closer to the truth.

"No," she murmured to herself as she drew closer. A pale flash of white surfaced from under the dark.

A child's hand.

"No," she sobbed out desperately.

But she couldn't deny the evidence of her senses. What she had hoped in vain was a log or even an empty barrel, tumbled out of someone's wagon while crossing, was revealed to be a young child, bobbing face down in the shallows.

Finally, fighting against the current and against the weight of her own clothing, she reached the child. Tentatively extending a hand, she forced herself to take hold of the small shoulder and turn the body over.

Her worst nightmare had come true.

A heartbroken wail tore itself out of her as Beth pulled her son from the water. His small white face was already turning blue. His fine black hair was plastered to his forehead and cheeks, framing his cherubic lips, lips that even now she knew would never again open in the bubbling laugh she so loved.

"No..." she sobbed, repeating over and over her denial of the loss, her rejection that this was her child.

How could she have let him out of her sight? How could it have come to this, after all her vigilance and care?

Holding her youngest boy in her arms, Beth ponderously made her way through the water to the shore, wet skirt dragging her down with every step. Her tears blurred her vision. She wanted to give in and sink down into the dark water herself, but she would not let her precious Alexander remain in the river any longer than necessary.

As she took the first steps onto dry land, she felt the comforting presence of her neighbors surrounding her. One woman wrapped a blanket around her while another helped her to sit on the shore. Some kind soul took the child from her, mercifully, as she had lost all strength in her body. Beth all but collapsed, but was propped up, supported, and comforted as best the crowd of Good Samaritans could manage while Beth sobbed her broken heart to empty.

CHAPTER ELEVEN

Someone thought to find Robert McKinnon and bring him to where his wife huddled wet and grieving on the shore of the Kansas River. Beth couldn't say how long she had been sitting in the grass next to the water, next to where her beloved son had lost his life. Her skirts were still damp, but by the time her husband sat silently next to her, they had dried somewhat. Some time must have passed, though it was all a blur to her.

She didn't look at him; she was afraid she would start sobbing all over again, and she didn't know how much more she had in her. Instead, Beth sat hunched over, leaning forward and resting her forehead on her arms.

Alexander was gone.

She hadn't watched him closely enough, and he had slipped from her grasp.

Her youngest son, her angel, her precious, joyful child, was dead.

Robert put an arm around her and leaned his own head against her shoulder.

They sat in silence together for several long minutes.

Beth willed her husband to say something, comfort her somehow, or promise her this wouldn't happen again. Though he had always been the strong, protective man she knew him to be, there were times like this one when she needed more from him. She needed words from him. She needed to hear from his own lips that he was in as much pain as she was.

It felt as though she was mourning Alexander completely on her own, but she didn't see how she could possibly manage to do any of this by herself.

"Say something," she whispered, without lifting her head.

He cleared his throat. "I'm sorry."

That set her to crying all over again.

"I'm sorry," he said again. "I'm so sorry, Elizabeth."

"Sorry? All you ever are is sorry. You're sorry we had to leave Pennsylvania. You're sorry you couldn't keep our home. Sorry we might run out of food before we get to Oregon or get stuck in the snow. Now you're sorry that our son has died. It's not enough, Robert."

Even as she lashed out at him, she dimly realized she was being unfair, but she couldn't help herself.

"Sorry is nice," she continued. "But sorry won't bring our son back." Her voice cracked at that last, and she swallowed the rest of her sentence. Robert's arm tightened around her, but he didn't say anything.

Part of her wanted to get up now and hug all the rest of her children and never let them go. But part of her was still drowning with Alexander; all her limbs felt weak, and any exertion seemed too much.

There seemed to be only one option that she truly wanted to take.

"Let's go back home. To Lancaster. We could go back," she pleaded. "It's not too late. We could just turn around and be in Pennsylvania by the end of the summer. Our family is all there, and our friends. Our children would be safe. *Safe* in a home that they are familiar with, instead of out here in the wilderness where anything could happen. Robert, please." She turned her body to look at him fully. "There will be more rivers they have to cross, and maybe Indians and the chance of a wagon overturning. Every day, Boyd has to work with those enormous animals, and he could make a mistake and suffer the same fate as Jeb Buchanan."

"Elizabeth," he said gently. "We can't go back. We have nothing left there. We will have less in Pennsylvania than we did before."

"But the children," she pleaded with him. "I can't do this again. I can't risk it. Please, just think about it. We could be ferried across again tomorrow morning and be on our way. I'll make sure the others stay safe, but I don't know if I can do that as we get farther and farther west, farther into the unknown."

He shook his head but didn't say another word. Instead, Robert climbed to his feet and offered a hand to Beth as well. She wanted to rail at him, demanding that he take their family back to Pennsylvania, but she had lost all energy. Every scrap of her will had drained away with Alexander's life. She couldn't do this on her own. Hanging her head, Beth allowed Robert to lead her back to their campsite, where the other children sat quietly.

Supper had long ago burned in the bottom of the pan with no one to pay attention to it. Someone must have told the children something—they were unnaturally subdued—but Beth couldn't be bothered to learn what. This family was no longer whole, and she could not pretend otherwise.

Robert deposited Beth next to the campfire and wrapped a light blanket around her shoulders. "Warm up," he said. "Your skirt is still damp."

She could have changed, she supposed, but that seemed like too much work. Instead, she bent her head, again to rest on her arms, while the children shuffled and sat silently around her. Robert disappeared off somewhere. Beth didn't notice where but now she was left in charge of her remaining five children.

As she sat there in the growing dark, with the comfort of her family all around her, Beth thought about all the mistakes she had made and everything that had gone wrong that day. There was no doubt that this was her fault, and she would never forgive herself. She should have made it more clear to Alexander where he needed to stay. She should have gone looking for him sooner. She should have taught him to swim better or forced one of his brothers to keep an eye on him.

She should never have brought them west.

She should have never let him go.

Now, at least, one thing was certain: she wouldn't make the same mistake with the children she had left. Not a single one of them would be permitted to go off alone at any time.

Beth sat up and looked around her.

"Where's Ross?" she asked in a panic.

Boyd pointed behind his shoulder. "He went to the big tree—"

"Get him," Beth demanded sharply. "Go, just... I need him here. He needs— *Get him*, please, Boyd. Please."

"Okay," the boy mumbled as he stood.

"Wait, no, take your sister. Claire, please go with him. Don't get separated. Stay with each other and bring Ross back here to me. Please. Be careful. Please," she pleaded.

"We'll find him, Ma," Claire said quietly as she went off into the dark with her brother.

When they returned a few minutes later, they were accompanied by their father and a woman Beth recognized but had not yet had a conversation with —Mrs. Mills, the wife of the company leader.

"Why—" Beth croaked, hastily getting to her feet. She was furious with her husband for bringing a guest into their midst. Didn't he know she was in no fit state to—

"Please," Mrs. Mills said kindly. "Stay seated. I don't want to worry you or put you out in any way."

Beth almost protested, but she didn't have the energy. Gratefully she sank back down and pulled the blanket more tightly around her. Gazing at Mrs. Mills, she realized she didn't much care why the woman was here. She couldn't muster even the politeness to ask. What was a neighborly visit when her son was dead? Surely this woman couldn't expect anything of her, not today of all days.

As such, Beth didn't bother to try to make her guest feel welcome. Mrs. Mills could do whatever she pleased. If Robert had brought her here, Robert could worry about it. She rested her head on her arms again, sinking back into herself.

Through the haze of her grief, she felt a presence sit next to her, close enough to feel their warmth, though they didn't touch Beth. Raising her head, she saw that Mrs. Mills had taken a seat nearby, but she kept her eyes on the campfire and staying quiet.

"Children," Robert murmured as Claire returned with the younger ones. He guided them toward the sleeping wagon, offering the two women some modicum of privacy.

Mrs. Mills stayed quiet, and Beth found herself resenting the woman's infringing on their family grief. What had Robert been thinking?

"I'm very sorry, Mrs. McKinnon," Mrs. Mills said, finally. Her eyes stayed locked on the campfire as though her mind was somewhere else entirely. "I know how hard tonight must be for you. I wanted to make sure you and your husband know that if there's anything we can do—my family or the company alto-gether—please allow us to."

"Thank you," Beth mumbled coldly.

"And Pastor Montgomery is prepared to hold a service first thing in the morning," she continued gently. "I've asked a couple of the young men to dig the grave over under the trees, but if you object to any of that, we can do whatever you choose. I'm so sorry."

Beth paused before responding, torn between her utter exhaustion and her anger. "That's what everyone keeps saying. That they're sorry. But nobody knows—nobody can possibly imagine how painful this is."

There was a small beat of silence, as though Mrs. Mills was debating how to answer, before she said, "A number of women here have lost a child, Mrs. McKinnon. You may find more sympathy among this community than you expect."

Beth was stunned with that realization only briefly before she continued. "None of that sympathy will bring my boy back. For all the talk of community, not a single person noticed my son was..." Her voice broke, and she swallowed to regain her composure. "Not a single person was paying attention when he was... When he was in trouble."

"Mrs. McKinnon—"

"I don't know why we're even here," Beth said. "We were far better off in Pennsylvania. Back home. And I've told Robert so. I intend to head back to Lancaster as soon as I can get him to agree."

"Yes," Mrs. Mills said. "That's why your husband came to me, in fact. He told me you wanted to turn around and asked for my help. I believe he wants to stay with the company."

"I'll talk to him. I'll make him see."

"Maybe," she allowed. "Or maybe it would be better to find the good parts of the journey west to Oregon and of this wagon company. I would hate to see you pining for something you can't have, especially on top of your son's death."

"All this entire trial has been is a series of pining over things I can't have," Beth said, not caring how rude she was being. "You have no idea what I've given up."

"I'm sure you're right," Mrs. Mills said evenly. She stood, smoothing down her skirt as she did so. "Even so, I hope that you will find a way to be content here. And as I said, my family is available if you need anything. We're happy to take on whatever you need. My deepest sympathies to you, Mrs. McKinnon."

Beth looked away, shunning the woman with all her good intentions. She didn't know what it was like; she couldn't understand how much Beth was hurting. No one could.

Without a proper good-bye, Mrs. Mills left Beth to her pain and her mourning. She had been sitting alone for only a few minutes when Robert appeared.

"The children are in bed," he said. "They wanted me to tell you they love you."

Beth nodded, tears smarting her eyes.

He sat next to her and sighed deeply.

"Please," she said in a desperate whisper.

"Robert, this isn't the place for us. Please let's go back to Pennsylvania."

"No," he said with a deep sigh. "Elizabeth, we have already decided. This is done. There is no going back. We will just do the best we can do, but we will do it while traveling west to Oregon."

She allowed another storm of sobbing to overtake her. As her husband held her close, Beth sobbed out her heartache and regret.

CHAPTER TWELVE

The following morning, Beth found herself standing with Robert's arm tightly around her from one side, all but holding her up, and Lizzie's hand holding hers on the other under the canopy of the wide oak tree near the camp. Keeping her eyes locked on the small, wrapped form of her smallest son sitting gently in the dirt, Beth was blind to the crowd around her. Her only thought was to sear into her memory the precious smile that she had so often seen on her son's face. She had no concept of how many of their neighbors had come to see little Alexander McKinnon into the afterlife, so focused was she on his memory.

She imagined Pastor Montgomery's funeral service for the boy was heartfelt and somber, but Beth didn't hear a word of it. She couldn't focus on anything in the present, as she was too busy anxiously worrying about the future.

Once the service was over, going through the

motions of getting ready to leave was as much as she could manage. Everyone had packed up their campsites, and the company was on the trail again before Beth realized all over again that they had left behind her baby boy, and she burst into tears while walking along the dirt track. Her son Boyd looked at her in surprise, but she couldn't calm herself, even for him.

That day—each step taking her farther away from Pennsylvania and farther away from Alexander —was perhaps the worst day of her life. And she had no recourse. Beth just had to keep walking west.

Fortunately, the neighbors and other emigrants in the wagon train knew that Beth and Robert needed help, even if they weren't up for asking it themselves. That very first day after Alexander was buried, Pastor Montgomery approached the family when the company stopped for a midday meal. Beth had not managed to pull together anything but a pot full of beans for her children. She stirred them listlessly, forgetting whether or not she had added salt, while her mind worried over all the dangers that were still ahead of them between here and Oregon.

"Excuse me, ma'am? Mrs. McKinnon?" the pastor began cautiously. He removed his hat respectfully as he approached. "I was wondering if I could maybe borrow your little ones for the afternoon?"

Beth looked up at him, struggling to focus on this virtual stranger standing in front of her and what he was asking of her. The children were all sitting quietly around the campsite, waiting for the food to be ready, but perked up when they had a visitor.

"Why?" she said abruptly. "You want me to let them leave my sight? Absolutely not."

"No, of course not." He reversed course. "How thoughtless of me. Of course not. Maybe I could help out here, then. Read to them or...?"

"Why?"

He looked around at the small faces listening to the conversation. She noticed his hesitation, sighed, and began dishing up the food for her children.

"Ross, Lizzie. Here. Take this." She handed over tin bowls and gestured with her head toward one of the wagons. "Take the others. Go eat in the wagon for now while the pastor and I talk."

It was a testament to their upbringing and maturity that not one of the children complained about eating in the stifling wagon. Maybe the older children had whispered instructions to the younger, or maybe they just all sensed that their mother needed grace right now. They made themselves scarce.

Once they had gone, Beth turned again to her visitor.

"What is it I can help you with, Pastor? As you can imagine, I have a lot on my plate. Please just speak your mind."

"Yes, ma'am."

"We're still grieving, you understand," she said, putting as much pain into that single word as she could. "And to have a stranger just interrupt and demand to take my children..."

"I understand," he said. "I had a thought that maybe if someone—myself, perhaps, or my wife— could relieve you and Mr. McKinnon of some of your responsibilities, maybe you would have the freedom to grieve the way you need to."

She narrowed her eyes at him. "Like what?"

"Well, at the very least, I can try my hand at keeping an eye on the little ones during part of the day. Read to the baby, or look after the older ones when they play. You would know better than I, ma'am, but if you can trust me to keep them safe, maybe you can rest your own worrying for an hour or two."

Beth's immediate reaction was to decline, to deny that she needed help at all, to even be affronted at the man's suggestion that she couldn't watch over her own children. But as the idea began to sink in a bit more, she felt only relief. Try as she might, Beth couldn't hold up the whole world. She had two eyes, two hands, and nearly half a dozen children to keep safe from the dangers of this world.

"I... That might be nice," she said finally. "I'm mighty tired."

"I'm sure you are."

He looked as though he wished he could do more but knew better than to offer. Beth sighed.

"Would you like some beans?" she offered half-heartedly.

So, for a few days, Pastor Montgomery became part of the McKinnons' every day. He would join them sometime in the late morning and stay until supper, if not later. Some of the other families learned to seek him out with the McKinnon family, and Beth watched her children blossom when they met other members of the company.

But the pastor had learned, and never again did he suggest taking the children anywhere that Beth couldn't at least see or hear them. Keeping her family close and keeping them safe was the only way she could get through every day.

"Wait," Beth called to her son Ross as he set off in a run up the caravan. "Where are you going?"

The Sullivan-Mills wagon company had just started out on the trail for the day. Her husband Robert drove the team of oxen that led the McKinnon family's supply wagon, and her oldest son Boyd followed behind, leading their sleeping wagon. Claire rode in the sleeping wagon playing with young Tara while Lizzie walked next to her mother in the grass parallel to the trail. The routine they had established was set, and the repetition at least offered some semblance of security.

Each and every family member was accounted for. Beth had reminded her children innumerable times over the previous few days since their brother's death that they were not to leave her sight. Ever. For any reason at all. Even if they needed to relieve themselves, they should tell their mother where they were going, so she didn't worry. If at all possible, they should take another person with them, just in case.

Just in case. It was all but a form of punctuation in Beth's vocabulary now. She could sense her family —Robert included—becoming frustrated with her with all her insistence, but there was no way she was going to risk losing another one of them. The more boundaries and safeguards she established, the calmer she felt.

So now, when Ross left his father's side to run on ahead, Beth yelled for him.

"Ross McKinnon, get back here!"

The boy paused, turned, visibly sighed, and trotted back to where his mother and sister were walking.

"Where are you going?" Beth repeated.

"Pa said it was okay—"

"I didn't ask about that, Ross. I asked where you are going. What if I need to find you and your father isn't around to tell me where you went? What if something were to happen? You know the rules, Ross. Where are you going?"

"Mr. Goldman said I could help drive their cattle today if I wanted."

"Drive cattle?" Beth exclaimed. "Why on earth would you want to do that?"

He shrugged, suddenly embarrassed. "I don't know. Ethan has to do it every day, so I thought maybe I could help?"

Beth clenched and unclenched her fist, trying to calm the fear in her heart. The idea of her son being so near so many enormous animals petrified her. Having Boyd lead the team of oxen was bad enough, but for her last remaining son to also be at risk was too much.

"Oh, son, no. I'm sorry. You can't—"

"But—"

"I know you want to spend time with your

friend, and I appreciate your generous heart in offering to help, but I just can't let you be away from me for that long. Especially near all those big animals. It's too dangerous."

"Mama," he protested in a whisper. "Please."

Through all of this, Lizzie remained silent. Her brother Alexander had been only one year younger than her, and the two had been as thick as thieves. His loss seemed to have stunted the little girl. Beth didn't know how to help her. She didn't know if she even was the right person to help her, grieving as she was. Even now, Beth couldn't find the words to reassure her daughter that everything would be fine—she wasn't sure she believed it herself. So, instead, the two stuck close together, quietly honoring Alexander in their own ways while the rest of the wagon company moved on.

Before Ross could protest any further, there was a deep clap of thunder. All three McKinnons looked at the sky, surprised to see that a heavy layer of dark clouds had rolled in low across the prairie.

With her face pointed up, Beth felt the first light drops of rainfall. She closed her eyes, feeling the heavy pressure of the storm and the increasingly intense precipitation. Even nature herself was mourning the death of Alexander. At that moment, Beth forgot about her two still-living children standing next to her; she forgot about how Ross had gotten pneumonia just the winter before. She forgot her responsibility to the here and now for just a couple seconds until another clap of thunder woke her from her reverie.

The rain was falling harder now, quickly soaking through her dress and bonnet. When Beth opened her eyes again, she realized the storm had descended without warning. She had to move fast.

"Go," she said to Ross and Lizzie, struggling to be heard above the rising wind. "Go to the wagon with your sisters. Stay there and dry off. Get warm. Be careful."

They nodded and ran off through the quickly forming mud, as Beth ran toward the other wagon. Robert and Boyd couldn't leave their posts by the sides of the teams, so it was up to her to do what she could to protect them. Tucked into a trunk near the front of the supply wagon was a collection of oilskin wraps that Robert had bought in Independence. Beth pulled three out, wrapping one around herself immediately, before climbing out of the wagon. Luckily, the caravan's overall speed had slowed as each man had to worry about not getting his wheels stuck in the mud. Beth brought a wrap to both Robert and Boyd. They each nodded their thanks but remained grimly focused on the task at hand.

With nothing more to do to help, Beth returned to the wagon where the rest of her children were waiting out the rain. As soon as she entered, Claire handed her mother a dry quilt.

"We had a visitor a little earlier," she said, as Beth dried herself as well as she could. "Before the rain. When you were walking with Lizzie."

"A visitor?" Beth frowned. "In the middle of the day like this? Who was it?"

"Miss Atkins, the schoolteacher? She said she was trying to talk to all of the families today."

"Why'd she want to talk to the families?"

"Miss Atkins wanted to see how many students might be interested in her putting together a little school," Claire said. "She says there are so many young ones, at all different ages and skills, that she needs to plan separate classes and things."

"And what did you tell her?"

"Well, I know Tara is too young, but Lizzie—"

"I don't know that I want any of you going over there," Beth said.

"But, it's school, Ma." Claire frowned in confusion. "Why wouldn't you want us to go to school?"

"It's not only school, Claire. You know that. It's letting you loose on the prairie without my supervision. I feel as though I have been quite clear that I don't want you out of my sight, but now you're talking about going over to some unknown person's campsite for hours at a time. And what am I supposed to do during that time, worrying myself sick?"

"She's not unknown, Ma," Claire retorted. "She's Miss Atkins. Everyone knows her."

"Everyone does not know her," Beth insisted. "I don't. No, I'm not sure I want you all to have any part of that. I don't want to hear another word about it."

Beth pretended not to see Claire and Ross exchange a look between them. Let them be angry with her if they must. They could be as angry as they liked, as long as she could keep them alive.

CHAPTER THIRTEEN

Preparing for all eventualities, risks and chances was one way Beth reconciled herself to this frightening adventure. But, if there was one thing Beth had known was unpredictable when they had first begun planning for their emigration to the Oregon Territory, it was the weather. Big, destructive storms had become legend on the Great Plains. As they were spending months crossing the grasslands, it was inevitable that such acts of God would catch up with them.

The rain continued for the better part of two days, and Beth took some satisfaction in knowing that no one would be sending their children to Miss Atkins's lessons. She could keep her children close and safe, and no one would think anything of it. Though the storm and muddy trail slowed them down, the company leaders kept the wagons pushing ever westward. They only made five or six miles each day, but it was more than nothing. They had to assume that obstacles impeding their progress could come at any time, so if they could keep moving, they should.

Beth loved the rain, feeling a perverse satisfaction in knowing that everyone else was just as miserable as she was. At times, the chill of wind made her teeth chatter, and still, she walked alongside her wagon, keeping an eye on her oldest son while the rest of the children remained safe and dry inside the wagon. It even kept Pastor Montgomery away. Though Beth missed the small feeling of relief knowing her children were safe with him, she still treasured the days of tight quarters and constant companionship.

Beth McKinnon may have been the only member of the wagon company to enjoy the rain, however. On the third day, the sun finally broke through the clouds, the same day the company was scheduled to arrive at a campsite on the banks of a narrow river. Mr. Mills sent his son around camp with the word that they would be staying put at this site for an entire day. It would allow the emigrants time to dry, repair, or rescue anything that had been damaged by the incessant rain.

As the caravan pulled into a circle, tightly chaining the axles together, Beth began to feel that now-familiar fear again. Without the rain to keep her children cooped up, they would ask to run free, visit a friend, or even go play in the water. Furthermore, staying so close to a water source brought all of Beth's fears to the surface.

She managed to keep all her panic inside until

the following morning. Claire was scrubbing the dishes after breakfast while Beth went through the family's sleeping wagon to gather up all the dirty clothes she could find. Who knew where boys put their socks? She was on her knees, searching under the cot, between the crates wedged in there, when she heard Lizzie's voice behind her.

"Mama, Marigold invited me to come play today. Can I go?"

Beth straightened up and turned to look at her daughter. Her hopeful expression was almost enough for Beth to acquiesce.

"Play in her campsite? Near her mother?"

"Um..." Lizzie looked down at her hands, and Beth noticed she had them tightly clenched together.

"Lizzie."

She looked back up at her mother and winced, even as she injected enthusiasm into her voice. "She, uh, we were going to play in the big trees over there."

"Trees?"

Beth tried to remember where she had seen trees when they made camp the night before and suddenly realized the only big trees anywhere nearby were along the banks of the stream.

"No, no, no. No, I don't think so," she said hurriedly as she straightened and turned to her daughter. "No, I want you to stay here with me. I need you to stay where I can see you. If Pastor Montgomery comes, or if Marigold wants to come here, you can play with her here at our campsite. But

I don't want you wandering off. I don't want you near that water."

Lizzie's face fell, but she didn't argue.

As her daughter walked away, presumably to tell her friend she couldn't come, Beth had a moment of panic. Her chest tightened, and the constricting feeling of knowing she would need to keep all five of her children safe *and* entertained for a full day in camp overwhelmed her. But she was resolved. What other choice did she have?

Staying as they were on the banks of a narrow river, it would have been an excellent opportunity to bathe. Beth had not been in a full tub of water since they had left Independence, and goodness knew her children could use a bath as well. But as soon as she started thinking about collecting their soap and towels to find a spot in the shallows, her fear overtook her.

So, no. It was decided. She would just have to find something else to occupy five energetic children, ages two to fifteen, for the entire day, without allowing them out of her sight. Looking around the dim wagon interior, she started plotting what chores and tasks she could assign to each of them to keep them busy.

Though it took the better part of the day, Beth hauled and heated enough water to wash her own hair and that of her children. Claire attempted to suggest that going down to the river would be more efficient, but seeing her mother begin to cry had stopped her abruptly. She couldn't even allow the boys to help her haul water; Beth kept thinking about how they would need to get their feet wet, how close they would need to get to the currents in the middle of the narrow river if they were going to fill their buckets. She couldn't stand it. So instead, Beth gathered all the water herself, trip by harrowing trip.

The first couple of excursions down to the water, she came across half a dozen different women taking the chance to bathe. After that, she diverted her path farther upstream, so she didn't have to hear the conversations. Every moment Beth spent on the banks of the river, she was thinking about Alexander. The laughter and chatter only hurt her more, all those cheerful faces who seemed to have forgotten her son completely.

She had set Claire to watching over her younger siblings as they each took a turn in the large tin tub that she generally used for laundry.

Though she had to cajole and practically beg Boyd to climb into the small laundry tub for a bath, eventually, he gave in. Beth had her hands full heating more water for him when Pastor Montgomery came by their campsite again.

"Ma!" Boyd exclaimed, turning his back to the man.

The pastor chuckled and averted his eyes. "I'll only be a moment, young man. I didn't mean to walk into anything."

"What can I help you with, Pastor?" Beth said, stepping between the pastor and the rest of her family.

"Oh, I just wanted to check on how you all are

doing and see if I could possibly take any of the children off your hands for longer. No offense intended," he began, forestalling her objections, "but as you know, my wife and I have just the two of us. If it would help for Ross or Lizzie or even Tara to come spend a couple days in our wagon, we're happy to have them."

"Really?" Beth was too shocked at first to be anything but curious. "Mrs. Montgomery is okay with this?"

"I'm sure she'll love it. Some sweet soul like Lizzie would give her some company during the day, for example."

Beth added a little fuel to the campfire as she thought. She didn't get any further than imagining going to bed that evening without her little girl in the wagon with her before she rejected the suggestion outright.

"I couldn't. No. Pastor, please don't ask this of me. Thank you, but I couldn't."

"All right, Mrs. McKinnon, all right. I'm very sorry. I just thought—"

"No," she said again, more firmly. "The children belong with their mother. With their parents. Here where I can keep an eye on them."

"I understand."

"In fact, maybe it would be best if you saw to some of your other responsibilities instead of coming here every day."

"Ma'am?"

Beth noticed Boyd looking over his shoulder at her curiously. "I can look after my own family, Mr.

Montgomery. We don't need you on hand every minute of the day."

There was a pause before the pastor bowed his head in acquiescence. "Of course, ma'am. I'm... I understand. And if you do find that you need anything from me, you know just where I am."

"Yes. Well... Thank you."

He offered a tight smile before turning back the way he came. When the pastor was out of earshot, Claire spoke up.

"He didn't mean any harm, Ma. It's been nice to know we weren't worrying you any."

"Oh, I know," Beth said tiredly. "But not knowing my own self that you all were safe was causing me more worry than not. It will be better this way. You'll see. Our family doesn't need anything but each other."

Claire didn't answer, but Beth caught her exchanging a look with Boyd.

CHAPTER FOURTEEN

When the Sullivan-Mills wagon company left the banks of that narrow river, they did so only after filling every empty barrel, pot, canteen, bucket, or any other possible containers with water. The following several days' worth of traveling followed a trail near no usable water, and they had to carry enough for each man, woman, child, and animal. Given how many horses, cows, oxen, and other creatures were being herded west, there was no room for error.

Robert insisted that the boys, at least, help their parents haul all the water they could to the wagon. Though she protested, Beth gave in and instead spent her time vigilantly watching every move Boyd and Ross made when they were within a few feet of the river. Eventually, the family had collected all they could, the boys could stay away from the stream, and Beth was able to rest the tiniest amount.

On the other side of this water-less stretch would be yet another hurdle for Beth's nerves.

Even as they traveled days using as little water as possible, each step brought the company closer and closer to more danger. From her reading of the guidebook, Beth knew that there were innumerable streams and creeks the wagons would need to cross through on the way to Oregon. Few would be as wide and as strong as the Kansas, the river that had claimed her son. But any day now, they would be reaching the Platte River. Not only would they need to cross the wide expanse of river, but the trail would actually run parallel to it for a number of days.

Every single moment of those days, Beth would have to be on guard, protecting her family.

She wasn't sure how she would manage it.

Through the several days of travel they had on the way to the Platte River, Alexander's precious face kept flashing in her memory. She had no portrait or even sketch of him; instead, she tried to spend time every day remembering her son, what he looked like, sounded like, what he enjoyed. The poor dog, Prince, still looking for his playmate, trotted alongside Beth next to the wagon and looking pleadingly up at her.

Finally, the wagon company climbed a low hill and reached the top of the ridge that looked down into the valley where the Platte River lay waiting. To Beth, it was like a snake waiting to strike, curving around, lurking immediately next to the very trail that they would need to follow for days. She had been walking next to her husband as he guided his team but stopped abruptly when she saw the water.

"That's the Platte?" she asked.

Robert slowed his oxen but continued following behind the Gladwell family wagon. "Yes," he said simply, leaving her where she stood.

"It's so wide."

"It's very shallow," he assured her. "It's perfectly safe."

As Boyd's wagon reached the ridge and followed his father's wagon, Beth uprooted her feet and hurried to catch up with Robert. The guidebook had claimed the Platte River was a mile wide and a foot deep, with not a drinkable drop. Such concerns of the children ingesting it were nothing compared to Beth's fear of what the currents could do, weak though they may be.

"I can't," she said. "How can I? How can we?"

"I know," her husband said. "But we can."

"How long?"

He cleared his throat. "The trail follows the river for three days."

"And then it crosses."

"And then it crosses."

She watched the slowly moving current a few moments longer. "We have to go into the water?" Her voice caught on that last. "You're sure there's no other way?"

He nodded, watching her carefully.

She shook her head.

"I don't know."

"It will be fine, Elizabeth."

She had her doubts, but she tried to stay calm in front of him. There would be no convincing him.

The next several days were excruciating. The trail wound along the banks of the Platte River, and each night they would stop to camp near to the water. Every moment, Beth was terrified, lashing out at Lizzie or Ross the moment they came within ten yards of the water. Not a single member of the McKinnon family forgot for an instant how they had lost Alexander. By the third day, none of her children even mentioned the river to Beth.

After a week of being so close to the river, when the trail finally forked, and they had to cross the water, Beth's nerves were stretched almost to breaking. It didn't matter how many times she read their guidebook or how strenuously Robert tried to reassure her; the fact was that Beth was terrified to cross the Platte. She wouldn't even let herself think about how many more rivers they would have to ford before Oregon.

It was about mid-day when the McKinnons' turn to cross came. Beth had once again reminded her children of what she needed them to do to stay safe over and over again. She had insisted past the point of what was reasonable, she knew, and the patience of her children had worn thin.

She did not let that stop her.

"Ma, I can do it," Boyd insisted.

"Absolutely not. You will stay in the wagon. I don't even want to see your head poking out. Your father and I will lead the teams, and when we get to the other side, then I will allow you to take over."

"It's not even that deep."

"Boyd McKinnon, you know perfectly well the Kansas River wasn't all that deep when it took your brother. That is far from the only factor. I know what I'm about, and you will be just fine in the wagon."

"It's so cramped, though," he whined. "I don't want to be in there with the babies."

"Who's a baby?" Lizzie interjected.

"Well then," Beth continued over her daughter, "you'd best stop chattering to me and let me get on with it."

"Ma, I just want to—" Boyd began climbing out of the wagon, and Lizzie's little face appeared in the opening of the canvas just behind him.

"No! You stay," she said, almost desperately. "Claire, you have to— Please, little ones, just stay put. For Mama. I know it might be scary, but I promise, if you just hold tight, your father and I will get you to the other side as quickly as we can."

Grumbling but cowed by her tone, Boyd sunk back into the small space between the cots. Beth reassured herself that there was plenty of room in the sleeping wagon. They were all in there each night, after all. They would be fine.

They would be safe.

"Don't you think Boyd can at least help you?" Robert suggested, appearing at her elbow.

"You too? No, I don't. No, no, absolutely not. He's only twelve, Robert. He's not strong enough. I can do this, and he can stay safe inside the wagon with the others. Safe and dry."

Robert gazed at her a moment longer before nodding. "All right, then. If you're sure."

With that, he returned to his own team, leaving her to lead this two-thousand-pound wagon and enormous oxen on her own. If that was what it took to protect her children, she would do it gladly.

Calling the team, Beth guided the oxen closer to the water. It was just about the McKinnons' turn as the chain of emigrants inched forward, and she tried to speak soothingly to the big animals. They would resist walking right into the water, but she knew she could do it. A firm hand, determination.

She could do this.

As she neared the edge of the river herself, though, the reality of what she was about to attempt came up to the surface. Churning butter or patching trousers was no trouble for her. But coaxing four two-thousand-pound oxen into a river when they had no desire might be beyond her skill. She had been so focused on keeping her children where she knew they would be safe that she had given little thought to what was required of herself.

Her toes stopped at the edge of the Platte River, lapping gently against the dirt. Beth dropped the reins. Her hands were shaking too badly. All she could think about was how a river of this size had taken her sweet little boy. She couldn't bring herself to cross this one as well.

But she had to. If she couldn't manage this, all of her insistence and efforts to keep Boyd and the others safe would be for naught.

Beth closed her eyes, took a deep breath, and let it out slowly.

The moment the breath was done, she opened her eyes.

Catching up the reins again, Beth took her first step into the water.

She felt as though she was going to throw up.

"Athena, girl," she said to her lead oxen, even as her voice shook. "Come on now."

Each step was excruciatingly slow, but Beth needed to be sure the wheels wouldn't get caught in the mud below. At one point in the middle of the river, the strength of the current surprised her. She stopped. She wished she could retreat, but that wasn't a choice.

Curtis Fields crossed the river behind the McKinnons and, in fact, led his team so much faster than Beth that he went around, slightly upstream, and passed her, reaching the opposite shore before she did. But she didn't care. Her wagon held precious cargo. Even if the water only reached just above her knees at this stretch, that was still plenty deep to be dangerous to Tara, or even one of the older McKinnons.

So, Beth kept moving little by little, slowly. Even the oxen seemed impatient to get across.

When Robert had led his own wagon to the other side, he put the team in some other man's hands and came back to meet her.

"I'll take that," he said, gesturing to the reins in Beth's hand.

She shook her head stubbornly, not taking her

eyes off of where she was stepping. "I need to do this."

Without another word, Robert waded through the current, back to the rear of the wagon. She heard him calling to the children and them responding in turn, though Beth wasn't paying close enough attention to know what they were saying. All she could think about was avoiding any stone that might turn her ankle or break a wheel.

Step by careful step, she felt her husband at her side as he placed his hand on the small of her back, supporting her, though letting her do it all herself.

Finally, after what seemed like an interminable length of time, Beth felt firmer ground under her feet. One more step, then another, and then her family was across the wide river, safely and wholly.

And all because of her.

She let out the long slow breath she had been tensely holding and willed her legs to stop shaking.

CHAPTER FIFTEEN

After successfully leading one of the McKinnons' wagons through the shallow Platte River, Beth stumbled up the bank depleted and anxious. She could be grateful nothing terrible had happened yet, but still expected it at any moment. Her hands shook from the stress of it all.

"You stay put," she called back to her children, who remained in the wagon interior, waiting out the traversing. It wasn't until she had guided the oxen a good thirty feet away from the water's edge that Beth let herself stop and let Robert take the reins from her.

When they felt the wheels finally stop, she heard Lizzie call out, "Can we get out now?"

"Yes, all right," Beth responded.

She hurried to the back of the wagon to help lift Tara out and otherwise check on the children's safety, but her skirts and boots were still soggy from her wading through the river. She felt like it added dozens of pounds. Her muscles, already sore from the strain of leading the wagon, began to shake. By the time she made it back there, all five children had already eagerly made their way out. Ross and Boyd shoved each other playfully, getting out energy that they'd had to keep bottled up during the river crossing.

"Be careful, please," Beth said. "Tara, why don't you come with Mama?" She held out her hand for the little girl to take it, guiding her farther away from the water's edge. "I've got to get dry, and you can come with me."

"Why don't you go lay down, Ma?" Claire suggested timidly. "You could change and rest in the wagon."

"I can't. We're not staying here. We've still got a couple miles of trail to cover before camping for the night."

"But you don't need to do anything. You can lie in your cot while Boyd drives the wagon. That river crossing was hard on you, wasn't it?"

"Oh, honey," she said, placing a hand on her daughter's shoulder. "I appreciate what you're trying to do, but I couldn't possibly just lie down in the middle of the day. You all need me too much." Tara squirmed in her arms and whined to be put down. "But I will let Boyd drive the wagon again. I don't need to do that again this moment."

Beth offered her daughter a bright, hopeful smile and pushed away all thoughts of exhaustion.

．　．　．

The next day, the terrain the wagon company had to cross changed dramatically. Far from the even, flat plains that stretched on indefinitely, here the ground seemed to burst with stones and boulders as though the very earth was disgorging them. The rolling fields of Pennsylvania were a far cry from this rocky surface they now needed to cross.

The path was so difficult that even if Beth had wanted to keep Boyd safe and far from the crunch of the wagon wheels, she knew that she would not be able to drive the team of oxen herself. The men and boys leading their respective wagons had to move excruciatingly slowly, making sharp turns and coaxing the wheels carefully over the rocks they could not find space around.

What man had thought this was a reasonable trail west, Beth wondered. It seemed that any time they saved by going straight across the stony field instead of around must certainly be lost by their necessity to go so slowly.

But what choice did they have?

"Claire, I want you to stay far away from the wagons. Take Tara and the other two, and lead them through on foot, but not close to us. But also, be sure to watch out for snakes. And take care not to turn an ankle. In fact, maybe you should just wait here for your father or me to come back and go with you." Beth looked up ahead to where Robert had already slowly started his team through the stones.

"Ma..." Ross whined. "We'll be fine. It's just walking."

Beth looked at him in surprise. That this child of

hers, this serious, cautious, mature child, had been the one to speak up made Beth pay attention.

"All right," she said. "Just be careful, please. Just yell for me if anything happens, and I'll be there immediately."

"We will," Claire assured her, lifting Tara in her arms. "We'll see you on the other side."

Boyd had watched this entire exchange while waiting to cross the stony field himself, but Beth had forbidden him from starting without her.

"Can we go now?" Boyd asked. "It's going to take long enough."

"Yes, okay." Beth didn't have the slightest idea how they would do this, but if so many emigrants before them had made it, then the McKinnons could, too. "You go ahead, and I'll just keep an eye out for anything you might miss, all right?"

"I can do this, Ma," he said.

"Of course you can," she said, though she had no intention of leaving him alone to do so.

Her twelve-year-old son clenched his jaw and set off into the broad field of stones, rocks, and danger at every turn. Beth did her best to help and guide him, but he didn't seem to be as observant as she was, or maybe he wasn't as careful as she had hoped. Together they tried to lead the wagon through the path, following directly behind Robert, but as time went on, they fell farther and farther behind.

"Be careful, Boyd," she said sharply.

The boy wasn't paying attention. She could see at least half a dozen ways this could go wrong. He seemed to be heading straight for the biggest and sharpest stones.

"Right there," she said, pointing to an indescribable patch of clear land that Boyd didn't seem to notice. "Slowly now."

As with crossing the Platte, Beth's wagon was moving so slowly, the families behind her caught up and tried to pass her. Here, finding the easiest path through the stones was far more difficult, however, and even without looking, she could sense several wagons backing up and crowding behind her.

"I can't go any faster," she mumbled to herself.

Looking ahead, she saw that Robert was nearly clear of the worst of the boulders. He should be able to return and help her any minute.

But until that happened, she needed to focus.

"Wait!" she said, and then darted ahead to push a smaller stone out of the way of the wagon. It was surprisingly heavy for its size, but better she strained herself moving it than the wagon get marooned or broken somehow.

Boyd sighed audibly. "I think it's probably—"

"Just wait," she said again, nudging the stone a few inches. "All right, now, slowly. Go ahead."

Accordingly, he called to the team again, guiding them forward, until his mother called out again for him to wait while she tried to move another stone. In this stop-start manner, they progressed a few yards. But they still had so far to go. Beth could see part of a path that would work, but making that clear to Boyd would be a problem.

"Over here, son," she said, pointing, though it

was clear from his blank expression that he didn't see the same thing she did. She brushed her filthy hands on her apron. The scrapes in her palms from her effort with the boulders would need to be seen to and possibly bandaged. But not until they had gotten through the field.

"Um... All right..." Boyd mumbled.

"Oh, just let me," she said. Whatever patience she may have had that morning had long since been used up. "It'll be fine. I'll take care of it. Step back a bit, Boyd. I don't want you to get in the way in case something goes wrong."

Sullenly, he handed over the reins to his mother. With the sharp leather cutting into her bruised hands, she strived to coax the oxen back the opposite direction from where they were headed. With a good ten yards to go before the edge of the rocky field, Beth was overwhelmed by all the things that could possibly go wrong. At least now she had control of the wagon and could manage it.

Coaxing the team slowly, she came to a mostly flat stone that could not be moved. The wheel would have to roll over it. Squaring her shoulders, prepping herself for the task, Beth led the oxen, keeping one eye on the wheel, one eye on where the animals were headed, while also trying to keep an eye on her son and where she put her own feet.

She failed on that last.

Trying to keep track of too many things at once caused her to step back awkwardly onto the slippery side of another stone. Her foot lost purchase, and

Beth lost her balance, just as the wheel of her wagon was rolling over the top of the stone.

As she scrambled to her feet, the wagon stalled without her to keep the animals moving. The balance was all off, the weight shifted, and before she could backup or push them forward, there was a loud crack.

Beth almost didn't want to look. She furrowed her brow, contemplating. Just the thought of what such a crack could mean brought tears to her eyes. It was more than she could bear.

"Ma!" Boyd exclaimed.

Reluctantly, Beth forced herself to look.

The wagon sat at an unnatural angle, tilted up where it rested on the stone.

The wheel had broken.

A sob escaped her lips.

She dropped the reins.

But Robert was by her side in a moment.

Without a word, he took the reins from her, gave an instruction to Boyd, and she was led away from the wagon. There was nothing else she could do but stay out of the way.

In no time at all, men from elsewhere in the wagon company had descended upon where they had gotten stuck. With enough muscle, they were able to lift and move the wagon off of its perch. They had to find stones and other tools to hold the wagon up while the broken wheel was removed, and there was a scrounging for wood that could be used to replace the broken spoke. Watching Sean Gilroy bending over a hot fire under the afternoon sun as he hammered the McKinnons' iron wheel rim back into place consumed Beth with guilt. This was her fault. She had failed, and now these poor men had to pay the price.

Even when she was the most careful, something still went wrong. She had kept an eye on everything she could, and she still couldn't keep everything safe. The children, who she had allowed to go on ahead, were absolutely fine, but the wagon where Beth had stayed to pay special attention had been what failed.

She thought again to her idea of turning around and going back to Pennsylvania. It was too late to do so now—she knew that—and unsafe to do so without others. But maybe it also was too late to be able to protect every single part of her family. Maybe failures like this would just be something she would have to deal with.

In her frustration, she had made a mistake. Now not only her own family but the whole wagon company was also delayed and would have to work to make up for it. Beth busied herself with making sure her children stayed far away from the precarious wagon and hot metal.

Some of Beth's guilt at delaying the entire wagon company was assuaged when she learned that the McKinnons' wagon was not the only one to need a repair that day. As the dozens of families passed slowly through the field of stones, three different vehicles found themselves caught and battered. Spokes cracked, wagons shifted, and frantic repairs were made before they lost too much light. The wagon company had so much distance to make that day, it was fortunate only three wagons needed repair. Poor Mr. Gilroy, the blacksmith, had his hands full.

Just past the worst of the field of boulders, the ground cleared somewhat, and Mr. Mills led the caravan to a narrow chasm that opened up. The company was headed to a campsite at the bottom of that ravine, but first, they had to make their way down the steep incline. It would be just as perilous and just as risky as crossing the rocky terrain, but they would be rewarded with fresh water and shady trees at the bottom.

After their harrowing experience resulting in the broken wheel, Robert insisted on handling both of the McKinnons' wagons himself.

"You carry Tara down," he prodded. "Take charge of the children. I can get one of the Davis or Kirk boys to help me with ours."

Beth opened her mouth to protest.

"I'll manage," he insisted. "They need you just as much."

She accepted the grace, kissing his cheek before she turned away with their smallest child in her arms. Truthfully, she didn't know how she would have been able to cope without such a strong and capable husband. Knowing that she could trust this to him went a long way for her to get through the day. She would help when she could, but Robert was such a bulwark.

Getting down to the bottom of the ravine was a trying experience. A narrow trail cut into the side of the gorge, but it was so steep that the men had to chain their wagon wheels to ensure nothing went careening out of control. Women and children walked down separately with the herds and other animals. Though many of the other women smiled kindly at her, Beth had her hands full keeping all five of her children with her, and didn't attempt any conversation. Boyd, in particular, seemed ready to go running down ahead of everyone, with Ross following as usual, so relieved was he to not be leading the wagon at that moment.

Beth thought she noticed Mrs. Fields start to cross the open campsite toward her, but her attention was so pulled by her worry over her sons that by the time she looked back, the older woman had disappeared. With a pang of homesickness, Beth realized she missed having the time to visit with friends. How long had it been since she had sat down with a cup of tea to hear about a neighbor's newest project or child's milestones? So much of her day was filled with merely surviving; she didn't see how any of the other women managed to maintain any kind of social life.

I'll just have to try harder, Beth thought resolutely.

The campsite at the bottom of the ravine was like an oasis. After the chalky, unusable water of the Platte and the uncompromising terrain they'd had to cross since then, finding a green, lush spot to stay for two days seemed an incomparable treat. Both animals and people needed this break to fill up on food and water after the difficult journey so far.

"All right, McKinnons," Beth called to her children. "You know what to do. I need fuel for the fire, but don't go too close to the water and don't leave my sight."

"Mama, can I go play with Jeremiah?" Lizzie asked, bouncing on her toes in anticipation.

"Jeremiah Sullivan? No, not now. Didn't I just tell you I needed fuel? Maybe later he can come play here."

"All right," she murmured.

The children scattered while Beth watched for

her husband to make it down to camp with the oxen. They only had maybe an hour before sunset, and she had a lot to do.

"Hello, Mrs. McKinnon."

Beth turned from making her mental lists to see the younger Cole girl standing nearby respectfully waiting for her attention. Beth had moved to help her husband as Robert negotiated the wagons into place before she was distracted.

"Oh, hello, Amy." She looked the girl up and down. Most fourteen-year-olds shied away from wearing all black, but this girl was a queer one. "Are you looking for Claire?"

"Yes, please."

Beth pointed. "She'll be back here any second. If you'd like—"

"Amy!" Claire exclaimed before darting across the last of the space to hug her friend. "Did you—" She glanced over her shoulder, checking how close her mother was before lowering her voice. "Did you get Nora to tell you about him?" she whispered as she pulled Amy away.

Beth smiled to herself. Even out here in the middle of the wilderness, with death around every corner, there was courting going on. She should sit down with Claire later and see if there was any particular boy she had her eye on. But first, to get their camp set up. Robert was unhitching the oxen when she finally made it over to him.

"Elizabeth," Robert said, turning to face her.

She looked at him quizzically.

"Will you come with me, please?"

"I thought I might go get water for the animals."

"That can wait. We must speak first. Please, come with me." He took three steps outside the circle of the wagon, away from the camp.

Beth balked. "No, I couldn't leave the children alone. Not when they're so tired from the day. You know, it was rough on all of us, and now with that stream nearby, I really think it is best if we all stay together."

"No," he said simply. "Not this time."

Beth didn't know quite how to react. It was so seldom that Robert asked her for anything outright that she wasn't even sure she could refuse him.

"Well, um... all right." Beth smoothed down her skirt, flustered. "I can't— I need to get supper ready, now that you're here with the wagons, so—"

"We won't be long." He walked farther, a few yards away, outside the circle of wagons and far enough away that she could not continue the conversation, but he waited for her.

"Goodness," Beth said under her breath. The idea of leaving her children to the dangers of the Oregon Trail made her frantic, but so did fighting with Robert. "Claire, you're in charge. Don't let any of them out of your sight."

"All right, Ma," the girl answered cheerfully, still whispering with her friend.

Looking over her shoulder at her family several times, Beth left the safe interior of the wagon circle and met her husband in the prairie grass a couple dozen yards away. This close to dusk, a small scattering of lightning bugs danced in the tall grass. Fires were starting up around the camp, and women were frying bacon, baking biscuits, brewing coffee, and otherwise nurturing their families.

That was precisely what Beth should be doing at this moment. Whatever Robert wanted to talk to her about had better be important if it was to take her away from taking care of the children.

"Is everything all right?" she asked when she reached him. "What are we doing all the way out here?"

"Elizabeth," he said, taking her hand. The simplicity and strength of his touch surprised her, but she didn't yet respond. "I know you have had a very trying day. Several days. Weeks. If there is anyone on Earth who knows how much you ache for our son, it is me."

She smiled softly. His words were like water on parched earth. This was the comforting and sympathy she'd needed immediately after Alexander's death, and she hadn't realized how much until this moment.

"But even that pain is no reason to behave as you have been," he continued.

Her mouth hung open in shock. She pulled her hand from his own as she took a step back. A million different responses went through her head, but what she really wanted to do was run back to her children to add their father to the list of things she needed to protect them from. If Robert could not support her need to keep them all safe, who would?

She almost didn't hear it when he started

speaking again, but his low tones cut through her distraction.

"Maybe you can talk to the pastor about this," he suggested.

"About what? I don't understand what it is you think I've done that is so terrible. Forgive me," she said, sarcasm in every syllable, "but I was under the impression that you were satisfied with the way I was mothering our children. But of course, if you prefer to do all of this yourself, I'm happy to step aside."

"Elizabeth."

"No, please, explain to me how I could possibly be a better mother than what I am doing. I keep every single one of those children clothed and fed every day. I ask so little of them, and make sure I am constantly between them and danger. I would do more if I could, of course, but I am only one person."

"I know."

"No, Robert, I don't think you do know. I think you probably still blame me—"

"No—"

"Then what is the problem? What precisely is it you think I need to talk to the pastor about?" She threw up her hands in frustration, aware that her voice could be carrying all the way back to camp. But Beth already blamed herself enough for Alexander's death. Knowing that Robert's blame was still smoldering was too much.

"Elizabeth," he began calmly. "You are a

wonderful mother, and I do not blame you for anything. But—"

She opened her mouth to protest, but relented at the pleading look on his face.

"But," he continued, "your constant protectiveness of the children may be doing more harm than good."

"What do you mean?"

"There are things they need to be able to do on their own. Not just skills they need to develop, but they need to be able to trust themselves to do it. We won't always be around to look out for them."

"They're not ready to be on their own, Robert. Just look at what happened this morning, letting Boyd lead that wagon. Poor Mr. Gilroy was held up for hours fixing the broken wheel."

"The wheel only got broken after you took charge of the wagon," he said, with more steel in his voice than before. "Yes, of course, it might have also happened had we let Boyd do it himself. But at least that way, he could have also learned what not to do the next time. As it is, he merely got frustrated and learned that if he complains enough, you will step in and take care of him."

"Well, of course I'm going to take care of him. He's my son!"

"He's twelve. He'll be thirteen soon, and a man much sooner than we want to realize. These are all things he needs to learn himself."

"He will."

"How?"

"When we get to Oregon." Truthfully, Beth

hadn't put any thought into what all Boyd or the other children needed as they grew to adulthood. First, she had to make sure they even lived to adulthood. Tomorrow was never guaranteed.

"Elizabeth, please. Just give them a little bit of space. Let the boys collect water for you, or let Claire go make friends with other girls her own age. We can't protect them from everything."

"But we can try," she retorted. "You will never convince me that it is not a mother's job to take care of her children. As you were unwilling to take us back to Lancaster, I am merely doing my best with what I have."

She offered her husband one last look, angry and hurt, before turning her back and striding back through the grass to the wagons. She still had supper to make, of course. She still had to feed these children, no matter what objections Robert had.

CHAPTER SEVENTEEN

Beth woke early the following morning, well before dawn and before anyone else in her family was stirring. Little Tara was curled into her side under the quilt, and Beth moved carefully to keep from waking her. She felt as though she had tossed and turned all night. Her muscles ached a bit, even, so little rest had she enjoyed.

The previous evening, after their fight, she had done all she could to avoid Robert. Even now, waking with the sounds of snoring children all around her, she was grateful that he had a bedroll to sleep in under the wagon instead of inside with them. She couldn't bring herself to be civil to him just yet—she was far too insulted by his insinuations. It wasn't until she'd had to refill Ross's cup of drinking water three times during the night that she realized that her husband might have a point.

Back in Lancaster, the children had been responsible for numerous chores all over the farm. Every day they had something they needed to take care of. Somehow though, here, on the plains of North America, when there was just as much to do, Beth had taken on all of it in her quest to help keep them safe. She had said yes to their needs so many times she may have forgotten that she could say no. After all, Ross was plenty old enough to fetch his own water to drink—it was only in a bucket just outside the wagon, after all. That was not something she needed to do for him.

It was with this turmoil in her heart that Beth had gone to bed not long after supper, early for her, but at the same time as the children. She lay in her cot, with Tara kicking her accidentally in her sleep, and thought over whether or not Robert's concern was valid. Now, in the dim light of dawn, Beth still didn't have an answer. She loved her family, she loved her husband, and she had always known him to be kind and wise.

If she couldn't take his advice, whose could she?

With that resolve—or at least, attempt—Beth rose for the day. She combed out and pinned up her hair, and quietly pulled a clean apron from the crate that had been stashed under her cot. Today would be another laundry day, but maybe this time she could enlist the boys' help to fetch water or the girls to help scrub. If she made it a deliberate goal, perhaps she could let go of a bit of her constant control.

With the full day ahead of her here in camp, Beth had plenty to fill her time. She was hoping to do all the family's laundry and bake extra biscuits if possible. Maybe she would even find a chance to visit Mrs. Fields or Mrs. Hudson. All of that activity would keep her away from Robert and give her more of a chance to think over his concerns.

Beth wasn't the only one with such ambitions; every other member of the wagon company had the same idea. That day that the Sullivan-Mills wagon company spent in camp would be full of visiting and visitors, Martin Jamison's fiddle, neighbors reacquainting themselves, and every person finding a quiet moment of break where they could. The Mills family had butchered one of their cows early that morning, and the scent from the roasting meat floated over all the wagons as they all made breakfast. Pastor Montgomery had planned a church service later that night, while Miss Leah Atkins would be holding small classes throughout the day.

Though her list of things to do was unending, what Beth really wanted was to avoid all of it. There were so many factors and risks and opportunities for her children to get hurt. And yet Beth kept going back to her frustration the night before at having to get out of bed to get Ross more water. The more she thought about Robert's criticism, the more she thought she should at least give it a chance. Maybe he did know something about their children.

"Did you get enough to eat?" she asked Ross as he licked the bacon grease off his fingers.

The children had all slept late, but finally, the scent of frying bacon had roused them from the wagon. Breakfast that morning with the McKinnons had been quieter than usual. It was almost as though the children were afraid of making her angry or drawing more of her attention. Maybe they had heard her raised voice the night before.

"Yes, Mama," Ross said.

Bringing his empty plate over to where his older sister had already started washing the dishes, Ross seemed as though he wanted to say more but was reluctant. He looked off into the center of the wagon circle, toward where Beth imagined he must have friends or some other interest that would keep him from the home fire that day.

Beth then looked at Lizzie, who was drawing dejectedly in the dirt with a small stick where she crouched down. The little girl had been such a bright light when they lived in Pennsylvania, but it seemed to have been quenched. And Beth suspected that wasn't completely to do with the death of Alexander.

Beth tried to remember the last time she had seen her children playing carefree with others, and she couldn't. When any of the other children from neighboring wagons came to the McKinnons' camp-site, she forced them to stay as close as possible, under her watchful eye. But even that hadn't happened for more than a week.

Loath though she was to take the risk and relent to Robert's prodding, Beth realized it might be best.

But only under very specific circumstances.

"I have some news for you all today," she said to her children, scattered around their campsite. Robert had already eaten and gone to help Sean Gilroy. He had wanted to pay the man back for being so helpful in repairing their wheel. As such, Beth had full say over what the children would do that day, and she was resolved to at least try. "I've decided that today might be a good day for you to attend class with Miss Atkins."

"Can I go play with Norman Kirk instead?" Boyd asked hurriedly. "He was going to go down to the water to look for frogs."

"No. Absolutely not." Beth's impatience flared. "I said class with Miss Atkins, and that's what I meant. When you're not with her, I need you here with me."

Boyd's shoulders sank, dejected, but he nodded.

"When?" Claire asked, scrubbing the dishes even faster.

"I checked with her early this morning before you all were up. Lizzie will be in her morning class and the other three of you in the afternoon. I'll walk you over myself and come get you again at the end."

"Ma, it's just over there—" Boyd began.

"Over there, through the wide-open space that is full of cattle and horses and other creatures that could crush you without a second thought? Absolutely not, Boyd. Of course, you don't have to go. You can always stay here with me."

"No. Thank you. I want to go."

"Do you think Marigold will be there?" Lizzie asked excitedly.

"Maybe." Beth smiled at her little girl. "That would be nice, wouldn't it? I just need you to wash your face and hands first, and then we'll walk over in about thirty minutes."

The girl was ready well before the appointed time. She chattered animatedly about all she was hoping to see and do. The more possibilities she mentioned, the more Beth questioned if this was the safest place for her children.

But then she imagined Robert's face if she had to tell them she kept all of the family near her the whole day, and she forced herself to not rescind her promise. When it was time for them to seek out Miss Atkins's class, Beth steeled herself.

Beth thought it was rather generous of her to let the three older children stay at camp without her while she walked Lizzie over to the clearing where Miss Atkins was holding class. She carried Tara with her, though, unwilling to let the toddler out of her sight, even for the short time she would be gone.

The lesson was to be held in a quiet corner of the campsite, under a copse of trees that both provided shade and kept the noise of the children far away from the rest of the camp. Though Beth wouldn't be able to see it from her own campsite, it would be easy to catch a glimpse of the little group anytime she walked to the water.

Lizzie barely glanced at her mother once they drew close enough. Her friends Marigold Abbott and Jeremiah Sullivan were already there, sitting in the grass around where Miss Atkins had established her own seat. The woman patiently answered all of Beth's questions, reassured her as best she could, and finally, gently insisted that she needed to get the class starting.

Beth made her way back to her own campsite with her heart pounding.

Later, when she walked the older children over to their class in the afternoon, the tension had lessened somewhat. It might take many more times for this to be easy, but at least Beth had done it. She even found herself forgetting for minutes at a time that her children were far away from her as she went about her chores that day.

The older children returned to the McKinnons' campsite late that afternoon. Beth had long since finished the laundry she needed to do and couldn't manufacture any more reasons to gather water, so she had not seen the class in more than an hour. When Claire, Boyd, and Ross came striding back to camp earlier than she had expected, relief overwhelmed her.

"How was your time?" she asked, trying to calm her heart.

Ross held up his palm, which even from this distance she could see was scratched up and bleeding.

Beth gasped.

"I'm okay, Mama. Really, it's nothing."

"It's not nothing." She hurried to his side to take a closer look. "Did Miss Atkins at least clean it for you?"

"Claire made me rinse it in the stream."

"Well, it looks like that wasn't enough," Beth said. "Come here. Sit. Tell me what happened."

After having the children away from her all afternoon, it did Beth a world of good to fuss over her son, clean and dress his wound, superficial though it may be, and reassure herself that he was being taken care of now. She pushed from her mind the panic at his being injured at all, reminding herself that it was already done. All she could do was treat it. Between the two of them, Boyd and Ross did not stop talking. Apparently, Miss Atkins had used the afternoon to talk about the life cycle of frogs.

"She said we should start seeing tadpoles soon, and that's how I scraped up my hand."

"Looking for tadpoles?" Beth asked with a frown.

"Yeah. I was leaning on a rock to look into the little pool and slipped in."

Beth gasped.

"I'm all right, Mama. Really. I just got my arm wet. But it dried, see?" Ross waved his hand. "You didn't even notice."

He seemed so proud of himself that Beth felt somewhat bad for scolding him.

Her throat tightened, and she felt tears threaten. The fact that Alexander had died while playing in the shallows of a river filled the air, unsaid between them. Beth focused her attention on the wound to keep herself from crying at the memory.

This was what Robert had wanted her to deal with. This was precisely the thing that she had been afraid would happen. And she had been right.

"Well," she said, willing her voice to calm. "I'm glad you're not hurt too badly. But I think I'll have to have a more urgent word with Miss Atkins before I let you go to any more of her classes."

"But—"

"No," she said sharply. "If anything were to happen to you, Ross, I would never forgive myself. Please do not contradict me. It will be fine. You'll see."

Beth told herself she didn't see the morose expressions of the children around her.

When the company left the following morning, Beth once again instructed her children to stay close and ride in the wagon if needed, though they complained about the jarring.

"Well, then, walk in the sun," she suggested in response. "As long as you stay within my sight I'm satisfied."

She pushed their hurt and confused expressions out of her mind, as she walked alongside her husband through the tall grass along the Oregon Trail.

CHAPTER EIGHTEEN

Beth was grateful for several days of uneventful travel. After crossing the Platte, the stony field, the broken wheel, the argument with Robert, and so much more of the day-to-day stress, merely having to cook for her family and walk westward seemed almost like a chance to rest. It was true that the heat seemed unbearable at times, but there was something cleansing about it, the starkness providing a clean slate. Beth relished these days. Under such conditions, the Sullivan-Mills wagon company was able to press forward more than a dozen miles each day, getting them ever closer to their goal of being over the Cascade Mountains before the first snowfall.

After several days of this rhythm, it was an unnerving surprise when morning came and went without any indication that the caravan would be leaving camp. Claire had finished washing the dishes after breakfast and had already put them away, which was usually the very last thing they had time to do before wheels started to roll. This morning, however, she wandered back over to the smoldering coals of the campsite, looking a bit lost.

"Why are we still here?" she asked her father, who, like her seemed unsure what to do with himself. The animals had been hitched up, but now they stood merely pawing the dirt with nowhere to go.

He shook his head, peering toward the wagons that usually led the caravan out of camp.

"I can go see, Ma," Boyd suggested. "I could run and go ask someone, maybe. Maybe the Sullivans can tell me."

"Thank you, but no," she said. "We're just fine here. No one will leave without us, and if we need to know why there is a delay, someone will let us know. You'll be fine here."

Boyd sat down again with a frustrated sigh.

Her children's frustrations and complaints wore on Beth. When they'd lived in Pennsylvania, they had usually been so well behaved, following her instructions whenever she gave them. Somehow, out here on the Oregon Trail, they seemed to have acquired a taste of rebelliousness. No matter how many times she explained why she needed them to stay close, they always seemed to resent it. The freedom of their friends like the Kirks and Coles didn't help.

A short moment later, they heard a commotion in the Gladwells' camp nearby, and Beth stood to look.

"We're moving, I think. Boyd, Ross, both of you go help your father with the teams. Claire, go ahead and take Tara and Lizzie into the wagon. We should be on the trail again soon."

Though the delay in leaving worried Beth somewhat, she had plenty of other things on her mind. Throughout the day, she checked on each of her children in turn. Ever since the day in camp when they had been allowed to attend Miss Atkins's classes, all four of the oldest children had been incessantly asking to return. Beth wasn't fooled. She knew perfectly well it was the socializing and the getting away from chores that had them so eager to practice their math and reading.

That day passed like any other, though there seemed to be an unspoken pall of worry over the members of the company. When they stopped for a midday meal, far fewer visits and playfulness were to be heard. Beth wondered about it—she assumed there must be a reason they'd been delayed in leaving, but she could only guess what it might be. No one was telling them.

That evening, the wagons pulled into a tight circle, as usual, guarding against any attackers from the plains and settling in for the night. Though it went against her every instinct, Beth had continued to try to do as Robert had requested. She forced herself to be more lenient about the children's comings and goings when she could. As such, Ross seemed positively bursting with joy to be entrusted with the task of bringing them water from the spring, even if he could only carry one bucket at a time.

Boyd was helping his father with the animals. Tara sat in the dirt nearly under the wagon, making variously sized piles of small stones, knocking them down and then piling them up again. Claire was brushing through Lizzie's long black hair, getting ready to plait it in fresh braids.

As Beth pulled together the food and pans she needed to make the McKinnons' supper, a tall figure approached their camp, hat in hand.

"Yes?" Beth called out, drawing the man closer. "Is everything all right?"

When he walked closer to the light, Beth saw that it was Daniel Mills, the son of the wagon company leader and one of the young men who stepped in to help whichever family needed it most. Though she had not yet spoken to him, she understood that her husband respected the Mills family, and she wondered what could have brought this man to their campsite.

"Mr. Mills?" she asked.

"Yes, ma'am. I'm sorry to bother you all," he said, glancing around at the family. "I'm afraid I have some bad news."

Beth froze, petrified at what it could be and already thinking over what she needed to do to protect her family. She swallowed hard. "What is it?"

As Daniel Mills stepped slightly closer, Beth felt her husband's presence approach from behind.

"We've had another death, ma'am. Young Jeremiah Sullivan."

"No," she whispered. She seemed rooted to the ground; in her utter terror, Beth was frozen in place.

"I'm afraid he came down with what the doc diagnosed as measles, and he passed this afternoon."

"This afternoon!" Beth exclaimed. "You mean to tell me we have measles in camp! Why didn't anyone warn us? How long had he been sick?"

"We're very sorry for the Sullivans," Robert added. "Please tell them if there's anything they need..."

"I will, sir. Thank you." Daniel cleared his throat and addressed Beth. "As I understand it, Jeremiah didn't show any symptoms until this morning, and it was decided to allow the Sullivans to continue on with us. If you'll excuse me, ma'am, I need to be getting to the next family." He nodded good-bye and left before he could be asked any more questions.

"Measles!" Beth felt a wave of panic wash over her. "Lizzie, was Jeremiah Sullivan in your class the other day? When was the last time you saw him?"

Lizzie's eyes widened in fear—though whether it was the thought of measles or her mother's panic, Beth didn't know. The little girl nodded cautiously.

"Ma, what happened to Jeremiah?"

In two long strides, Beth was across the campsite at her daughter's side. Ignoring the girl's question, Beth placed a hand to the girl's forehead, frantically looking her over for any sign of illness.

"How do you feel? Are you tired? Hot at all? Lizzie, tell me you didn't talk to Jeremiah that day."

Lizzie's eyes welled up with tears. "I did, though. I sat right by him. Am I going to die too, Ma?"

Too late, Beth realized her panic was spilling over to scare her daughter. She caught herself before another desperate fear escaped her lips. "Oh, no, Lizzie, no, I'm sure you will be just fine."

She hoped she was telling the truth. In her youth, she had seen the way measles could destroy a whole family. One of her cousins had come down with it, and within two weeks, her uncle, aunt, and every other member of that family had fallen ill. By the end of a month, two of Beth's cousins had passed, and her uncle was never the same. She had only been seven years old, but she remembered it so vividly.

And now to think her own child could have been exposed to the dreaded disease.

But she would be safe if Beth herself had anything to do with it.

"Lizzie, I want you to go to bed right now and rest. I wish I had known... Well, it's too late now. The best thing you can do is stay put. Sleep if you can. Let me know the moment you feel the tiniest bit sick, all right? Promise me."

Lizzie nodded, tears spilling down her cheeks now.

"Okay now. Go on into the wagon. I'll bring you supper when it's done. I won't let anything happen to you."

Once the little girl had gone, Beth turned to see the fear and concern on the faces of the rest of the family.

"Ma?" Claire asked tentatively.

But in the state she was in, it was all Beth could

do to finish preparing supper. She shook her head at her daughter. Her hands trembled, and her mind whirred as she considered everything it meant for them to have measles in the camp. If her family spoke to her that night, she heard not a word of it. At one point, Robert put a firm hand on her arm and whispered to her.

"Calm yourself. Calm the children," he instructed her. But he might as well have asked her to fly as to calm herself.

Measles!

Beth sat up late into the night, staring into the smolders of her campfire and worrying over all the other illnesses and injuries her family might suffer. There was no escaping the dangers of the Oregon Trail. Even on days like today, after being lulled into a false sense of safety, death seemed to be creeping up on them.

The following morning, after breakfast, the Sullivans buried Jeremiah. Robert stood at the edge of their campsite and looked questioningly at his wife. She knew what he was asking, but she had already thought about it and decided she couldn't possibly attend the funeral of another child. Even if they still had their precious Alexander, she wasn't sure she could do it. What kind of world were they living in when men and women had to suffer such losses so frequently?

She shook her head at him wordlessly and returned to staring into the fire.

CHAPTER NINETEEN

Though Beth watched Lizzie carefully over the next few days—indeed, did not let her out of her sight—the little girl did not develop any symptoms of what could be suspected to be measles. Lizzie asked her mother seemingly every hour whether or not she would be okay, and the child's fear only spurred Beth on. She lost count of the number of times she had prayed during those first forty-eight hours after they learned of Jeremiah's death. Vacillating between anger and fear, Beth didn't dare to hope they would be so lucky as to not catch measles. She didn't even have room in her heart to feel sorrow for the Sullivan family, so consumed was she watching her daughter for signs of illness.

Eventually, Beth tried to accept that Lizzie was not getting sick. Enough time had passed that maybe her prayers or insistence on the girl resting had worked. Such realization was not enough for her to let up on any of the restrictions she had placed on the other children, however. There were far too many other dangers lurking along every mile of the Oregon Trail. All the evidence she needed for her vigilance was the fact that Lizzie was exposed to measles. If she had stayed close to home, that never would have happened.

Though, when Beth tried to explain that to her husband, he refused to discuss it. Robert had always been rather quiet, but in the days since Beth had avoided the little boy's funeral, he had less and less to say to her.

As the wagon company continued westward, Beth spent most of her time walking in the grass parallel to the wagons, near enough to Boyd to be on hand should he need her help, but far enough that she wasn't expected to talk to her husband. Communication between Robert and her had been strained. Though she wished she could make allowances and please him, she absolutely could not if it meant putting her children in harm's way. As such, Beth spent more time with the children and less time by her husband's side.

This stretch of the Oregon Trail seemed to go on forever, grassy plains extending in every direction. Eventually, she knew, they would come to the granite landmarks that thrust into the sky. Ross had read them the passage from the guidebook just a couple days ago, though Beth couldn't quite imagine what such monuments would look like. Never before had she seen anything like what the guidebook described. There were still miles and miles of grassland to cross before that point, though.

Every day, they woke before dawn, ate a quick meal, and were soon on the road moving west. Every night, she had sweat through her dress, walked a dozen miles in the sun, and still had to fetch water and prepare supper for her family before falling into bed. It was unending, and it was exhausting. Without even the comfort of her own bed, such backbreaking work did nothing to lessen her fury toward Robert.

In the afternoons, as Beth walked step by step through the tall prairie grass, she had time to look around and marvel at where she had found herself. It was so different from where she had imagined she would be at this point in her life.

All through the years she was growing up in Lancaster, she loved that community and that land with all her heart. The only thing she had ever wanted was a home and a family of her own in the same part of the country where her parents and her grandparents had all raised their own families. She had dreamed of that very thing since she was small. The farmlands of Lancaster, Pennsylvania, was the most perfect place to live in her eyes.

Now, however, that she had seen so much more of not only the country but of the continent as a whole, Beth had to acknowledge that there was a strange beauty in much more of God's creation. So much of the landscape consisted of the natural world that she had never imagined. Over the months they had been traveling westward, she had afforded herself so little time to actually look around and appreciate the terrain they were crossing through.

But every so often, she felt herself relaxing enough to take a breath, have a moment, and witness their surroundings.

The prairie grass was patchy and bare closest to the trail. There, thousands of animals had passed and made their meals. There, hundreds of pairs of feet had walked, keeping the dirt exposed. Farther away from the trail, she found herself occasionally knee-deep in a sea of green and yellow grass, peppered here and there with the bright rainbow of wildflowers. Later in the year, this may be all dry or eaten, but crossing through this open territory in late spring almost helped Beth forget what she had left behind in Pennsylvania.

All around her, the prairie stretched as flat as a flapjack. The blue sky above seemed to continue forever, almost bearing down on her in its cloudless state. The brightness encompassed her. Beth felt as though she were part of the very scenery she had been inspecting, floating along, consumed by the nature and beauty that surrounded her.

High above, a large bird circled the caravan once before continuing its way north. Its wide, black wingspan cut through the gentle blue sky, drawing her attention.

She wondered what the bird saw from there, or what it was looking for. The fraught nature of life out here on the prairie surrounded her constantly. The bird above was looking for safety and sustenance just as much as Beth herself was. But humans were supposed to be different, Beth thought. She was supposed to make friendships and have room for something in her brain other than danger.

If she had learned anything while traveling across the continent this far, it was how close they were to the animals that lived alongside them.

"Beth!"

She turned to see Emma Fields picking her way through the tall grass toward her. Waiting for the older woman to catch up, Beth looked again to the sky, but the bird had flown past the horizon and was out of sight.

"I heard you all had a bit of a scare," the older woman said, once she was closer.

"What did you hear?"

"Robert called on us to make sure we knew that Marigold had been sitting with Jeremiah the day before he took sick. And that Lizzie had been there with them."

"Robert told you that?" Her Robert, who was usually so circumspect? Beth could barely wrap her mind around it.

"And he mentioned how much you were praying and worrying over the poor child. We were mighty grateful no one else came down with measles, I don't mind telling you. I'm not sure how this wagon company was spared that."

"That was my thought—I still worry that measles is lying dormant somewhere and that Lizzie will start to show symptoms again any minute. I'm all but making myself sick thinking about it."

Emma peered at Beth. "Are you sick?"

Making fists to try to keep her hands from shaking,

Beth tried to make her tone light. She didn't need any more people telling her she was making too big of a deal over this. "Oh, no, but when I thought my child might be taken ill, I just thought... That is, I couldn't..."

She trailed off, uncertain how to explain herself.

"Oh, darlin'," Emma said with a reassuring pat. "I understand. But don't you forget that your little ones need you to be as good as you can be. Making yourself sick with worry doesn't help anyone."

With a sigh, Beth remembered how scared Lizzie had been that first night, panicked by Beth's own panic. "I'm trying," she murmured.

"I don't doubt it. And I'm not one to tell you how to raise your children, so if you need to tell an old woman to keep quiet, do so."

Beth smiled at that. "I'm trying," she repeated. "I don't know how you can be so unbothered."

With a laugh, Emma turned to look back at her wagon and her daughter's wagon behind that. "Practice. Trust. Age." She winked at Beth. "You'll get the hang of it. Just keep doing your best, and it'll come."

Before Beth could respond, they were interrupted by a joyful cry.

"Mama!"

The two women looked to see both Ross and Lizzie hurrying through the grass toward them.

"They seem perfectly healthy," Emma remarked.

"Is everything all right?" Beth asked. "Do you need me?"

"Mama, look!" Lizzie exclaimed.

The children reached them and excitedly

gestured ahead toward the west. Lizzie pointed toward the horizon, and Beth squinted her eyes against the setting sun.

"What is it? What do you see?"

"There, look, there, you see? It's a... It's something. There's a thing there."

Beth smiled. The monotony and ever-sameness of the landscape seemed to have made any variant an occasion worth celebrating.

She shook her head. "No, I'm sorry, I don't see it. But I'll keep looking. Maybe we can get closer."

"Well, I best be seeing to my own little ones," Emma said with a smile. "I imagine Marigold will be just as excited as these two are." She placed a hand on the tops of the children's heads. "You two be good for your mama, now." Offering Beth a broad smile as she walked away, she added, "And you be good to yourself, Beth. Like I said, making yourself sick with worry is only going to make everyone worry more."

Beth didn't respond, as Ross had called for her attention again, but she knew her friend was likely right. She just had to keep trying.

Later that night, as they were making camp, Ross returned from fetching water to inform his family that the tiny dark spot on the horizon was, in fact, Courthouse Rock, the very granite landmark that he had read to them about just a few days earlier.

"We're almost there!" he exclaimed. "We're almost to the part of the trail where all these giants are going to surround us. Remember, Lizzie? I told you?"

As Ross and Lizzie reveled in their excitement, Beth climbed into the supply wagon to pull out what she intended to make for dinner that night. She scooped her tin cup into the bag of flour and was dismayed to find it only half full when she withdrew it. That bag should have been able to last them another week or so, at least. Was she using more than she had rationed out? Or was there some other explanation? Maybe the company was taking longer to travel than she had accounted for.

There was still flour, of course. The McKinnons still had a lot of food left for their trip, but now she began to worry over whether or not that food would last them the whole way. Robert had assured her it was enough, and even if it hadn't been, that they would stop at several forts between Missouri and Oregon, and they could buy supplies there.

Beth told herself all would be just fine as she opened the new bag of flour for their supper, but she had to admit that it worried her. Just when she had promised herself she would try to quit worrying so much.

CHAPTER TWENTY

One afternoon, as the wagon company passed through more flat plains, the Gladwells' wagon ahead of Robert slowed briefly. From where Beth was walking with Lizzie, she noticed the hold-up immediately. The entire stretch of wagons had ceased. Before she could wonder why, Daniel Mills was riding his horse down the length of the caravan, calling to the men.

"Buffalo!" he shouted. "Make camp, grab your guns, and meet on the north side in ten minutes."

He was gone again before what he had said even registered with Beth.

Buffalo!

Robert didn't say a word, but he sprang into action. Hurriedly, the wagons were pulled into a circle, each man parking his own wagon by the next as quickly as he could. Robert found his gun, swung onto his horse and set off with the rest of the men, leaving all the oxen for Boyd to take care of.

"Wait, can I go?" Boyd called after his father. But Robert was long gone.

"I'll help you," Beth told her son, placing a hand on his shoulder. Beth watched her husband ride off without even a word to her.

"But I want to hunt, too."

"Maybe you can go next time. But first, we have to see to the oxen. They don't know about buffalo and are wondering why we're leaving them all hitched up like this. Come on. We'll see to the camp, and then maybe have a quiet afternoon. We'll probably be here the rest of the day."

"With no chores?"

Beth laughed. "Let's take care of the chores we already have, and then we'll see. We want to be ready if your father comes home with lots of meat, don't we?"

Seeing to the animals without the help of his father didn't take as long as Boyd had expected, and he was back to teasing his siblings in no time. Beth considered spending her afternoon doing laundry or getting ahead on some baking, but in the end decided what she most needed to do was give her children some real, focused, family time.

"What would you all like to do today?" she asked her little crew.

They all looked at her with expressions of surprise intermingled with the beginnings of hope.

"Anything?" Ross asked.

"Well, probably not anything, but tell me your ideas. We'll talk them all over together." Unspoken was her expectation that however they spent the afternoon would be as safe as possible, in their own camp if possible.

Accordingly, a short time later, Beth was leading her family in a game of charades. Boyd was reluctant at first—he had wanted to leave the safe circle of wagons—but soon, his inclination to perform and make his family laugh had won out. As Beth watched her son trying to act out "General Jackson," she wished Robert was there. He should see how happy and safe and smart and capable their little family was.

Though, she admitted to herself with a smile, they were not skilled at charades. The game had almost wound down when Boyd stood suddenly and looked toward the south.

"Do you hear that?"

He shushed the others, and Beth strained her ears to hear what her son was talking about.

"Is that thunder?" she asked, almost to herself.

No one answered, each person listening with their breath held; it was as though all the McKinnons sensed this was something they should not ignore.

"I don't think it's thunder," Claire said warily.

Beth's next thought was maybe it was the hooves of the buffalo herd that the men were hunting. Maybe they had inadvertently driven them toward camp. But before she could open her mouth to suggest it, a second noise joined the heavy thumping and erased all doubt.

A piercing yell, indecipherable words, but the glee and aggression in the man's tone were clear.

"Is that—" Claire whispered.

"Indians!" Beth said in a panic. "God protect us. They must have seen the men leaving and—"

She cut herself off as another volley of war whoops cut through the air.

Indians were attacking! Indians were coming, and Robert had left her alone with the children. Indians were coming to attack her children, and Robert had left her without a weapon. Beth felt rooted to the ground, watching helplessly as all of her worst fears seemed to come true all at once. The Indians would kill them, or worse. The children would be kidnapped. She would be injured. Their food would be stolen, and they would be left to starve in the middle of the prairie.

Oh, how could Robert have left them?

After what could have been thirty seconds or thirty days, Beth felt herself being pulled out of her terrified descent by her son.

"Mama, come on," Ross pleaded with her. "We're going to hide."

Beth looked around her campsite, feeling utterly unmoored. Claire had already scooped up Tara and was handing the toddler into Boyd's waiting arms in the sleeping wagon.

"Hide?"

"Come *on*," Ross insisted. He was now resorting to pushing her from behind. That effort served to unbalance Beth and force her to move her feet to keep from falling. "Maybe if we're very quiet, they won't find us."

"Right. Yes." She was still too stunned to know what she was saying.

Lizzie reached the sleeping wagon ahead of them, climbing in behind Claire. Prince had taken shelter under the wagon and had started barking at the intruders, though none were near yet.

As Ross led Beth to the wagon, she looked over her shoulder to see that there was now a breach in the south side of the circle of wagons. In their haste to hunt, the men had neglected to chain the wheels together as they usually did, and the natives had easily exploited that weakness. Two of the wagons had been pulled apart, and the warriors poured through the gap, some riding, some running, all scattering throughout the emigrants' camp.

What they were after, Beth could only guess.

"Mama," Ross said, more sharply this time. "We have to hide!"

Still dull in her haze of fear, Beth felt her son's hands on her back, pushing her toward the wagon where the rest of her children were already hiding in the dark. Following his insistence was the only thing she could do at that moment. All other thoughts of running or fighting had left her mind completely. Numbly, she climbed up into the wagon, where little hands pulled her quickly in, deeper, crouching between the cots. Beth closed her eyes, willing herself to disappear as the sounds of attacking Indians grew louder.

Tara began to whimper, and Claire whispered softly to her.

"You're okay, little girl. You're okay. We're okay.

　　　　

But it's time to be quiet, remember? We need to be quiet quiet quiet."

Tara nuzzled her face into her older sister's neck.

"Ow, Mama!" Ross said in a whisper.

Beth looked down and realized she had been clutching his hands so tightly his fingertips were turning white. She let go and backed up another foot into the depths of the wagon.

Judging by the sounds of chaos in the camp all around them, it seemed as though the Indians had fully infiltrated the circle of wagons. A scattering of rifles firing told them that at least not all the men had left with the hunt, though it was clear that far too few remained. Prince continued to bark from the safety of under the wagon. Beyond that, Beth heard crying children, women screaming, and the cruel laughter of the attackers.

She closed her eyes, trying to shut it all out.

Lizzie began to cry softly.

"Lizzie," Claire said gently. "Hush, please."

But Claire was already occupied with comforting Tara. There was nothing she could do beyond reminding her sister that quiet was needed. Even though she trembled almost uncontrollably, Beth forced herself out of her fear to take care of her daughter. As she should have been from the beginning.

"It's all right. We're okay. Everything will be fine," Beth whispered into her ear while at the same time trying to muffle the sounds of her daughter's crying.

Without warning, the canvas flap flew open, and

a long, dark face peered into the gap at them. Beth's breath caught in her lungs and all thought of violence dissipated. The warrior met her eyes briefly before he scanned the interior of their sleeping wagon.

In the interminable moment in which the attacker seemed to assess what they had, Beth's mind was bombarded by images of death, destruction, loss. Of the broken bodies of each of her children. Of herself stripped and desolate. Of the wagon overturned and empty. Every possible disaster ran through her mind in that flash.

While Beth imagined chaos, however, her son made a decision. Boyd stepped into the aisle between the cots, blocking the Indian's view of what was inside. He was still shorter than Beth, but he squared his shoulders, standing straight and brave like a man twice his age might.

"Go away," he said, though his voice shook.

Claire and Ross, in the same moment, also stood in the aisle behind their brother.

Beth felt lightheaded, as all strength left her body. From where she was huddled near the back of the wagon, she couldn't even see the Indian any longer and had no way to guess what he might do next.

There was a short beat of silence, then she heard the attacker scoff before closing the flap of canvas and abandoning them with no further molestation.

Beth's hands started shaking.

"Is he gone?" Ross asked in a strangled high-pitch voice.

"Hush," Claire whispered.

"Okay," Beth said, trying to steady herself. "Back away from the opening. Now, Boyd. All of you. Sit down."

With hands still shaking, Beth picked her way over the children to where the canvas hung down, blocking their view of the campsite. She pulled them all back, though not daring to look out of the wagon herself.

"Please," she said. "Sit. Please."

Finally, they obeyed, and Beth let out a long breath of relief. They sat in silence, punctuated by Tara's whimpering. Soon, the sound of Indian war-whoops diminished into the distance, and Beth collapsed onto the cot.

CHAPTER TWENTY-ONE

Beth had been shaken to her core. Only a mere handful of hours earlier, her life and the lives of her children had been virtually under the knife.

Even now, she still felt vulnerable. The native attackers had dispersed. The camp's chaos was slowly being brought under control. The hysteria of the day was starting to pass, remaining animals counted, and injuries treated. But Beth herself could not think about anything but the peril her family had been in just a few hours prior.

The danger of the Indian attack alone was enough to turn her world upside down. To add to that, the knowledge of how her children had handled such a nightmare was making her question everything she had once believed. She had frozen; her children had been at risk, and Beth McKinnon had been unable to put together a coherent thought. She had been utterly useless in the face of actual danger. How could she have let this happen? It wasn't until the men returned from the hunt, Robert rushing concernedly to her side, that Beth began to put words to how she felt.

"Elizabeth," her husband said, crouching next to her.

She was resting on a bag of rice that had been pulled out of the wagon but left behind for whatever reason. Perhaps the warrior stealing it hadn't accounted for the weight or had seen something else more tempting. Beth herself hadn't had the energy to lift it back into the wagon, so in the meantime, she had been using it as a low seat outside the wagon. Robert had dismounted their horse and tossed the reins to Ross, but now all of the children were gathered around, marveling at the rich slabs of meat he had brought back. That would keep them fed for a while.

"I'm all right," she assured him shakily. "I'm all right. I can't rightly believe it, but... We're all fine, Robert, I think. But..."

She tried to communicate the ocean of emotions she was feeling, but nothing that came to mind did it justice.

"No one got hurt?"

"No. Well, none of us. Others, probably. I know that Mrs. Martell was practically racing from one side of the camp to the other in the aftermath. No one died, as far as I know. I can't imagine what else happened. So many vulnerable people..."

"I'm so sorry, Elizabeth," he said in a low voice. "I shouldn't have gone. We shouldn't have left you all alone."

It was that apologetic comment that pulled her out of her stupor. Eyes bright, she turned to him. "Yes, of course you should have. It was only right that you take the opportunity. Buffalo meat! Think of it. How were you to know there were warriors out there just waiting for their chance?"

She trailed off, thinking about the possibility of those warriors just watching from far away, ready to jump on the opportunity as soon as enough men were gone. Why, for all she knew they had even done their part to herd the big animals across the emigrants' path to bait the men. Could they even do that?

"I wish things had gone differently," Robert said, "but I'm glad you're safe."

He placed his hand on her knee, and she covered it with her own.

"I don't know what I would do if anything had happened to any of you," he continued. "Thank you for all you do for our family."

Robert leaned his forehead against hers, bringing them close together. Closing her eyes, Beth took a long slow breath, breathing in the scent of her husband, the coppery blood from the buffalo side, the grass plain beyond the circle of wagons. She was safe, she reminded herself. He was here; the rest of the men were back, and if the attackers returned, she wouldn't be left on her own.

Her mind flashed back to the first instance she had seen the Indians attacking their camp.

"I need to tell you something, though," she said softly.

He straightened again but remained crouched at her side with a concerned expression.

"I didn't..." Her disappointment in herself overcame her, but she forced herself to start again. "I didn't actually do anything. It was the children. I just, Robert, I froze. It was petrifying. I was so scared. I couldn't even tell them to hide. I was absolutely useless. Ross pushed me toward the wagon, in fact, and Claire looked after her sisters. They even —" Here, her voice broke. "The children even stood up to the Indian that came to our wagon. While I did nothing. I'm so sorry. I failed as a mother."

She looked down at her lap. Robert was silent, and she couldn't bear to look at him and see her own disappointment reflected in his face. When she thought about how many terrible things could have happened because she wasn't quick enough to react, it was enough to cause Beth McKinnon to break down completely.

"Look at me, please," Robert said softly.

Beth took a deep breath and raised her eyes to him.

"You did not fail, Elizabeth." His eyes bore into her as though willing her to accept what he was saying. "What you've done is teach these children how to react in such a dangerous situation. Their actions are a testament to your role in their lives as a mother, more than anything else."

"But I froze. I didn't do a single thing to—"

"And yet everyone is just fine. This is just what I was hoping for when I asked you a week ago. They're all growing up. Claire will have suitors soon, and Boyd will need to start thinking about his own future. The fact that such cool heads prevailed, and they knew enough even without your detailed guidance to keep them all from harm just proves what we've been talking about."

"What *you've* been talking about," Beth corrected with a smile. "I don't mind admitting that I was wrong, Robert, but... I don't know that I will agree that I didn't fail."

He smiled at her and chuckled. "I should have expected you would be hard on yourself. But all I care about is that none of you are hurt. Losing Alexander was enough for one family."

She sighed and made a promise to herself that she would at least think about what he was saying. There would not be a day that passed that she wouldn't wish she had acted more assertively. But maybe he was right that this whole event showed what the children were capable of outside of her direction.

Besides, there were other pressing things to tell him.

"We're fine," she reiterated, "but our food... Robert, they all but cleaned us out. There must have been two or more men, maybe. Or a horse with saddlebags, judging by how much of our supplies have been stolen. We were safe in the sleeping wagon, but that left the supply wagon completely unguarded."

He patted the bag of rice underneath her. "They left this, though?"

"Yes, thank goodness, but oh Robert! They took

so much more. The only reason we still have this sack is probably that they must have been weighed down with everything else they took from us. What will we do? There's still so long until we get to Oregon."

"There are forts between here and there. We should be able to purchase more supplies. And there's the buffalo meat I brought home today. And of course, there may be opportunity for more hunting as we go."

Beth shook her head in despair. The whole thing made her tired, but she had so much more to deal with before she could rest.

"Have you talked to anyone else?" he asked, gesturing to the Gladwell family nearby. "See who else lost food or other things?"

"I haven't felt up to it. No, I haven't."

"Have you done a full inventory to determine what has been stolen? Maybe it's not as bad as you think."

"No, I haven't."

"All right."

They were silent together, each thinking about what the other had said and what challenges were still ahead of them.

"Well," he began slowly, "I think we've probably been quite lucky. No one got hurt. Nothing irre-placeable got damaged."

Beth nodded.

"And, I know I can count on you to help the family through the worst of what is to come."

Beth nodded again but couldn't bring herself to

speak. How different she and Robert were now out here in the wilderness versus in Lancaster when he would barely say a word. This was the first time she began to think that maybe this adventure westward could hold some good for them.

"Why don't we start by treating all this buffalo meat? At the very least, we can eat well tonight."

He stood and offered her his hand. Beth pulled herself to her feet, took a deep breath, and turned to face the next challenge head-on.

The following morning, the Sullivan-Mills wagon company could not leave camp fast enough. Three times the number of guards had been replaced overnight. Though so many men had gone without sleep, everyone felt it was better to leave this place —and the risk of another attack—behind.

CHAPTER TWENTY-TWO

After leaving behind the site of their Indian attack, the Sullivan-Mills wagon company, as a whole, seemed to be anxious to get to the next big stop on their journey. They'd had a very eventful, very draining day. The boon of the buffalo meat helped each member of camp, and everything else could be gratefully forgotten. Fort Laramie was a few days' journey ahead of them. There the emigrants could rest for half a day and hopefully replace at least some of the items that had been stolen from them.

Beth had tried to shake off the fear and doubt that had plagued her the entire journey. She was grateful for the chance to look forward and plan how she needed to best spend the resources they had left —both the time they would be at the fort and the little money they had left to buy supplies. Without that planning to focus her energy on, she was afraid she would spend too much time ruminating over that harrowing moment when she knew her family was under attack and did not a thing. She'd always had a tendency to ruminate; she knew this about herself, and it was something Robert's steady presence often pulled her out of. Ever since Alexander's death, Beth felt as though she had more or less been in a constant state of agitation, constantly churning through her pain. She, frankly, had not allowed herself to rest one moment since she found out they had to leave Pennsylvania.

Beth's nerves were wrought.

But now, she had a chance to reset.

It was true that the risk of another Indian attack would never abate. It was also true that the family's depleted stores worried her, to say nothing of every other danger that stalked the emigrants on their journey. But after her reaction to the warrior in her camp, Beth was realizing that worrying didn't help. Robert would be so pleased if she could let go of at least some of her worry.

She imagined she would fail repeatedly. But for her family's sake, at the very least, she wanted to try.

Accordingly, the very first morning after leaving the site of the Indian attack behind, Beth had worked up the nerve to give the children a tiny bit more freedom. It required a courage and vulnerability that she usually avoided. But she would try.

The wagon company had rolled out of camp as early as possible and had every indication of making quite a bit of distance that day. With the longer days of summer, they had many hours of travel ahead of them.

Walking next to the sleeping wagon, Beth heard

her daughters playing together within. She was near enough to hear the three girls while still walking along the trail in sight of her sons. That very first step of making any big change was always the hardest, no matter how much she told herself it was necessary. There was always a moment when she had to forget any potential consequences and just do it.

As she wavered in her resolution to speak to her children, Beth was reminded of one magical afternoon of her youth when she had been about Claire's age. She had been invited to have tea and cake for her friend Theodora Ward's birthday, and somehow events had become wilder than Mrs. Ward had suspected. Theodora's cousin Daisy was visiting from Philadelphia and had begun spouting off all the amazing and glamorous things she did in the big city, including, apparently, swimming in the Schuylkill River.

Even at that age, Beth doubted that the girl was actually permitted to swim in such a busy thoroughfare. Still, she couldn't allow this stranger to show off so. They had just as many adventures in Lancaster as in the city, after all. When Theodora had rashly claimed that they went swimming in Long's pond all the time, Beth backed her up, despite the fact that she had never been in the water beyond wading up to her ankles on a hot day.

Of course, with a half dozen fifteen-year-old girls, one thing led to another, and soon Theodora and her cousin were leading the others to the pond for a swim. Beth had no idea how she could possibly get out of it without exposing her lie—not to mention Theodora's. Instead, she found herself stripped to her bloomers and undershirt, standing with bare toes in the water, willing herself to find the courage to go in. The other girls were already splashing and laughing in the chest-high pond while Beth stood wavering on the shore.

Finally, Beth realized that she just had to do it. She just had to go. She had to stop thinking about it so much and simply take the step. It wasn't necessarily courage, to Beth, so much as it was refusing to let her fear stop her. She had closed her eyes, held her breath, and forced herself to run the twenty yards through the water to her friends. By the time she stopped to think about what she was doing, it was already done.

It was with this same mental state that Beth knew she would need to let go of the tight grasp she had been exacting over her children heretofore. There would never be a time when she was truly ready to let them spread their wings and go out safely into the world, but that didn't matter. She would need to do it anyway. It was not that she needed to be particularly brave about it; she just needed to stop letting being afraid stop her.

Lizzie's giggle floated out of the wagon, drawing Beth's attention. Those sweet daughters of hers were always staying put just as she told them to, always taking care of each other, always foregoing their own desires for whatever their mother required of them. Beth felt a pang of guilt. Those girls had the rest of their lives to acquiesce to what other people needed. Now, in their girlhood, she could at least try to give them some freedom, some of that same taste of wildness she'd had in her youth.

"Claire?" she called, hurrying to the back of the wagon. "Lizzie? Girls?"

Their laughter stopped, and Lizzie poked her head out through the gap in the canvas.

"Is everything okay, Mama?"

"It is, thank you."

Beth carefully stepped up into the wagon—not an easy feat when it was still moving, and she wore a long skirt. Once she had settled onto the foot of her daughter's cot, next to Lizzie, Beth gave her daughters a careful look. Tara and Claire sat on the cot opposite, both with their feet tucked up underneath them. Across the narrow aisle, Lizzie sat leaning forward, so she could see what Claire had in her hands.

"And what is the story with Mr. and Mrs. Petunia today?" Beth asked when she saw Claire was holding the two corn husk dolls she'd had since she was a child. As long as these—now delicate and precious—dolls had been in their home, Claire had given them such personality, though most of those stories she pulled from the Bible or books she was reading.

"Today," Claire said with authority and pomp, "Mrs. Petunia is going to be fitted for a new ballgown."

"Oh, really?" Beth said with a laugh. "That does sound like a nice day. Is that something you girls would like to do sometime?"

She caught Lizzie and Claire exchanging a smirk.

"Well, you know of course, dear mother," Claire

said, "how very many balls we have in the upcoming season."

"Very funny, I know. Maybe if enough other families move to Oregon, we will have a ball or two in, say, thirty years or so."

Claire laughed a little sadly.

"In the meantime," Beth added, hastening to cheer her daughters, "you could always pretend. In fact, why don't you two take the rest of the day to go play? I'll manage Tara. You don't have to be cooped up in the wagon all day."

"Really?" Claire said. "If... If we could. If you don't mind, if you think you could do without me."

Here it was, Beth thought. This was the moment when she would have to force herself to take the plunge into the scary unknown. She must do it before she thought too much about it.

"I don't mind. Why don't you go see what your friends are doing? The Cole girls, or Marigold or maybe Abby Mills?" she suggested, speaking quickly. "I can keep an eye on Tara, and you can have a bit of a day off. If you like. Of course, if you'd rather—"

"That sounds wonderful," Claire said, immediately dropping the dolls and jumping to her feet. In the cramped space, Beth had to lean back, lest she be elbowed inadvertently. Tara grasped at the dolls on the cot next to her, and Beth hurried to scoop them up and out of her destructive little hands.

"Be back by supper."

"Yes, Ma!"

Claire was already halfway out of the moving

wagon, as though she feared her mother would change her mind if she stayed too long.

"Be careful," Beth called after them, trying to keep the fear out of her tone.

Left alone with her youngest, Beth tried to focus on little Tara. The girl had already suffered so much grief and trauma in her short life.

"Why don't we get out a bit today?" Beth suggested. "Do you want to get out of the wagon?"

"YES!" Tara shouted jubilantly.

Beth laughed as she stood. "All right then. Mama's got you."

She climbed carefully out of the moving vehicle and then lifted Tara out after her. Carrying the child clear of the moving wheels, Beth took them both out to the wide grass field that the trail cut through. Her arms would likely get tired carrying the toddler for very long, but the chance to take this first big step in letting go of her need to keep a constant grip on them, and stress over her children's safety was worth it.

"Look," Beth said, pointing to the long caravan of animals, wagons and travelers heading west.

"Goat!" Tara said. "Mama, I want to see the goat."

At least two of the families were herding goats west. More had their own small herds of cattle, though many of the animals had been stolen by the Indians. Prince was darting through the grass around Beth's feet as she walked, and she was grateful for his noise and action. Any snake or other creature would be far away, and she wouldn't have to worry about where she stepped.

"I see the goats," Beth murmured. "What else do you see?"

They spent the afternoon talking about all the new and exciting sights that Tara was finally getting time with, finally outside the wagon for more than just mealtime. The other girls came back before supper, just as they had been instructed, and Beth went to bed that night proud of her choices.

CHAPTER TWENTY-THREE

"Is that it, Ma?" Boyd asked, pointing to what seemed to be a structure of some kind low on the horizon.

Beth shaded her eyes with her hand. It was late afternoon, and the bright sun overhead played tricks on her vision. She had spent the morning walking with her oldest son as he led the team of oxen. With every step, she tried to distract herself from what the other McKinnon children were doing when not under her direct supervision. It had been a difficult several days of trying to give them all more freedom.

"I think so. I think your father said we should get to Fort Laramie in the early afternoon tomorrow. Seems like we should be able to make that distance in that time, doesn't it?"

"Yeah, it does." Boyd nodded seriously. "As long as we leave early enough tomorrow morning."

Beth had noticed how much more mature the boy had become in the short time since they left

Independence. With the added responsibility placed on his young shoulders, he had begun to take himself more seriously. She smiled to herself, thinking about how she should tell her husband he had been right. Give credit where credit was due, after all.

The following morning, the fort loomed even larger on the horizon, and Beth was almost surprised when it took them a full six hours to reach it.

As the wagon company drew closer to the fort, Beth found herself worrying more and more about whether or not they would be able to purchase the supplies her family needed. They had lost so much to the Indian attack, and she had five growing children. Fort Laramie had originally been a trading post out here on the frontier before being sold to the U.S. Army last year. Beth reminded herself of this as the caravan pulled into a circle to make camp outside the fort walls; whoever was in charge here should at least have resources and the foundation to keep plenty of supplies on hand. The only question would be if all of the other wagon trains this summer had stripped them bare.

Being within sight of the first real structure they had seen since leaving Independence sent a pleasant jolt through Beth. From where they made camp, she could see two guard towers, one at each corner of the wall closest to the wagons. She walked briskly toward it. It was almost as though she had forgotten what it was like to have a roof and four walls. The moment her eyes fell on Fort Laramie, she wanted to already be in Oregon more than ever. The safety and security that such a defense provided were what her heart longed for.

After seeing to the animals and securing the wagons, Robert disappeared into their sleeping wagon briefly to collect the cash the McKinnons still had for their journey.

"Do you want me to come with you?" Beth asked as her husband tucked the money into the inside pocket of his coat.

"No, I can manage. You just worry about things here."

"Do you need me to make you a list? Of course, get more bacon if you can. We can always use more meat. The children will eat it."

"Bacon, yes."

"And rice, beans, flour, cornmeal. Goodness, I feel like we're running low on all of that. Jerky, too. Maybe even dried apples. I think we have a lot of those still, but more could be useful."

"Elizabeth, I'll get everything I can. I promise."

"And don't forget—salt! I had almost forgotten, but between the Indians and what we needed for the buffalo, we're almost out. We'll need a lot if you do more hunting to keep the meat longer."

"I know," Robert said. "Boyd? Come with me, son. I might need another pair of arms."

"Can I go, too?" Ross asked.

Robert assented immediately, and soon the three were striding across the terrain toward the open gates of the fort. As Beth watched them go, she couldn't help but feel a pang of grief, missing her fourth little man. If Alexander had been here, he too would have wanted to accompany his father, to help, to be included. Though she often tried to set aside such thoughts, Beth couldn't help but remember the tiny grave they had left behind along the banks of the Kansas River. Her little boy would forever be part of the wilderness in the middle of the continent.

These thoughts were interrupted by Lizzie pulling on her elbow.

"Yes?"

"Mama, can I go to the water with Martha Sullivan? It's so hot! We can take off our shoes and—"

Beth felt her heart leap up into her throat. "No, no. No," she stammered out before taking a deep breath to calm herself. "No, Lizzie, I think, maybe… Let's stay away from the river, please. You understand, don't you?"

She couldn't bring herself to say Alexander's name out loud. Not yet. Nor could she bear to risk any of her other children near water if she wasn't nearby. Even with Miss Atkins watching, Ross had fallen into the stream trying to catch a tadpole. The thought of small Lizzie anywhere near a current made her weak.

"I'm sorry, dear," she said kindly, but Lizzie had already sulked off to the stretch of prairie on the outside of the wagon circle. Beth almost called to her to come back, but when the little girl sat in the high grass, with Prince settling down next to her, she decided to leave her be. She would be safe enough with the dog and was easily within Beth's sight.

"Ma?" Claire appeared at her other elbow.

Beth suppressed a sigh before giving her oldest daughter her attention. This was her life—everyone wanted something from her.

"Can I go see what Amy is doing? She told me yesterday that she had found a bird's nest at the last creek that she was studying."

"Oh, well... Yes, I suppose you've earned that. Thank you for looking after Tara so much. Go ahead, dear. Just..." Claire had already started to dart away across the campsite. "You come tell me if you go *anywhere* other than her family's campsite, all right?"

"Yes, Ma!" she called back.

Beth glanced back to Lizzie and saw that Martha and Patience Sullivan were sitting with her in the grass.

"Girls, I'm going to collect some water. You stay right there!"

Lizzie waved her acquiescence to her mother and then turned her attention back to her guests.

Beth spent the next thirty minutes going back and forth to the water, collecting enough to wash some of the family's clothing. How her boys managed to get so filthy just walking along the trail, she would never understand. But this had to be done. There wouldn't be any water after this for a few days, and they couldn't go any longer in what they had on.

By the time she had finished gathering as much water as she needed, Beth noticed that the Sullivan girls had left, though Lizzie stayed out in the grass still. She seemed to be making a flower chain from all the wildflowers easily within reach. Beth was grateful her daughter seemed to be getting over her disappointment.

She was partway through heating the water for her clothes when she was interrupted by a visitor.

"Mrs. McKinnon?"

Beth looked up to see Mrs. Sullivan standing at the edge of her campsite, with her daughter Martha just behind her elbow. Martha waved excitedly at Lizzie, and Beth felt a stab of anger. She had been very clear telling the little girl she could not just go play in the water, and now she had... what? Betrayed her mother to Mrs. Sullivan?

"Can I help you?" she answered somewhat coldly. First, the wife of one captain came to try to change her mind after Alexander died, and now the wife of the other came to question her choices?

"I wonder if we might be able to tempt Lizzie to join us at the stream this afternoon? Your oldest daughter—Claire?—is, of course, welcome too. It would be such a nice treat for the girls, don't you think?"

"Well, Claire is already with other friends today," she responded, adding 'safe' and 'away from water' in her own mind.

"I may not stay all afternoon, but my oldest daughter, Hannah, will be with them. Keeping a close eye. In fact, I aim to make sure she has nothing else to hold her attention other than the girls. I assure you it will be very safe for all of them."

"Do they not have more important ways to spend their day? Surely with so many children, you must have an unending number of chores. I know I do." Beth tried to sound light-hearted about her deflection, but inwardly she was panicking.

"Oh, of course I do," Mrs. Sullivan said with a laugh. "But I want my girls to know fun as well. There will always be more chores, but wading in cool water on a hot summer day is a treat."

Beth felt penned in. She wished Robert were here to back her up, but as it was, she found herself with fewer and fewer options. Would she give in to this woman's request and let her precious child out of her sight? Or would she have to turn her down, possibly be rude, and then later judged by whatever other women Mrs. Sullivan chose to tell this story to?

She glanced at Lizzie, who had been listening to the entire conversation avidly, though silently. Once again, Beth's mind returned to that childhood dare of swimming in Long's pond, and she had to admit that it had been a magical day for her. Whatever else she had done that day, she couldn't recall, but the small adventure with her friends had lingered.

She had let Claire run off with her friends. Maybe it wasn't fair to Lizzie to deny her the same privilege.

"Hannah will be there, you say?"

"Yes, and my Hannah is about as responsible a young woman as you could ever meet. I don't know what I would do without her as my right hand many days. Not only that, but I believe our wagon is closest to the water, of everyone in the camp, so I may even be able to hear them playing as I do my laundry."

"Well..." Beth took a deep steeling breath. "All right. If Hannah takes charge of the girls, then I suppose I can see my way to letting Lizzie join them."

Behind her, Lizzie laughed in delight.

"But you are to be home before supper, Miss," Beth reminded her daughter.

"Of course, Mama."

"They'll be in good hands," Mrs. Sullivan assured her one last time before leading all three little girls away.

Beth watched them go with a small pang in her heart. As much as she was trying to do better about giving her children space and freedom, none of that diminished her fear.

CHAPTER TWENTY-FOUR

Throughout the afternoon they were camped at the fort, Beth's hands were busy doing the family's laundry and keeping track of Tara, but her mind was with all her loved ones. Everyone seemed so far away from her. Of course, she couldn't help but worry. She would keep it to herself, she vowed. This would be a test of her resolve.

She busied herself wringing out all the wet clothes.

Robert and the boys returned from Fort Laramie with their arms full. It wasn't as much food as the Indians had stolen from the McKinnons, but it would tide them over a good while. And besides, as Robert later confessed to his wife, he wasn't sure they could spare much more cash, even if supplies to purchase had been unlimited. They would be fine, he assured her.

She had been so caught up with making sure her family reached Oregon at all—and one never would

—that she had completely put from her mind everything they would need to do to make a home once they arrived. Continuing to camp while they built their house would be a trial, but at least she knew there would be an endpoint. Robert would build much of the furniture they needed, and she had stashed in the wagons her linens and other supplies. There was so much to think about, but Beth remained confident that she had planned well and thoroughly. Especially if Robert was judicious about how much to spend on supplies now.

Claire came back to the McKinnons' camp not much later and helped her mother put away all the new purchases and reorganize the supply wagon. She kept having to repeat her questions, however, as Beth was too distracted looking for Lizzie. The afternoon grew later and later, and still, her daughter did not appear. The fact that it was still well before she had asked Lizzie to return was irrelevant—Beth couldn't help but imagine all the things that had gone wrong with her daughter out of her sight.

Once the wagon was sorted and set, Beth still had time before she had to begin supper—before Lizzie needed to be back—and she felt a bit lost.

"Why don't you just go to the water?" Robert suggested kindly. "Claire is perfectly capable of taking care of Tara, and the boys are helping me with the leather. You can go make sure Lizzie is safe and reassure yourself that your choice was a good one."

Beth nodded absentmindedly. She wanted him to be right, but it seemed so hard for her to believe that her daughter would be able to enjoy such an eventful afternoon unscathed. She would just have to go see for herself.

The wagon company had made their camp on the north side of the stream, a tributary of the Platte River. Beth passed a half dozen different families and campsites on her way toward the water. Though she didn't intend to eavesdrop, she couldn't help but pick up phrases and conversations as she went. The mood of the camp after the Indian attack had felt desperate and afraid. But now that they were so near the soldiers at the fort, more of her neighbors seemed relaxed and optimistic. It was enough to make Beth doubt her own fears, and she found herself actually looking forward to seeing Lizzie carefree as she played with her friends.

Passing between the Hatchley and Harper wagons, Beth crossed the open grass toward the tall shrubs that lined the stream. She could hear many voices near the water, though most people were blocked from sight by the tall plants. Listening for the sound of little girls, Beth was able to almost pinpoint where her daughter was and pushed between the undergrowth.

At a glance, she saw that her fears had been realized. Everything that she had warned Mrs. Sullivan about, all of her objections and her certainties were coming to pass. The little girls were playing in water up to their waist, and not a soul was watching them. Hannah Sullivan stood on the shore only half-turned toward them. Instead, the bulk of her attention was being held by a broad young man with honey-brown hair. Patience, the oldest of the girls in the water, stood in the middle of the current and gestured wildly for Lizzie to join her.

In the split second as Beth watched, her daughter stepped fearlessly into the running water. But Lizzie didn't take two steps before losing her balance. She slipped, or tripped, or the current was too strong for her. Whatever the problem, the little girl lost her footing, and she almost went completely under.

Both Beth and Lizzie let out a startled yelp at the same time. The sound was enough to draw Hannah's attention, and in moments the oldest Sullivan was in the water, fetching Lizzie to her feet before Beth even reached them.

"Goodness," Hannah was saying as Beth approached. She had her strong arm around Lizzie's waist, holding her tightly. "Are you all right? It's slippery, isn't it?"

"Lizzie!" Beth screamed, wading into the water to her daughter. When she got close enough, she lifted the little girl bodily out of the water, tearing her from Hannah's grasp and clutching her to her chest.

Hannah said nothing, but her face registered shock.

"Mama put me down," Lizzie whined.

Beth waded back out of the water, not letting go of Lizzie until she could be placed safely on the shore.

"Lizzie, darling, I'm sorry. I'm so sorry. I thought

Miss Sullivan would be watching you better. I never should have put you in such danger!"

"Mrs. McKinnon—" Hannah began.

"Mama, I'm fine," Lizzie protested bewilderedly.

"You're soaked through!" Beth exclaimed. "Let's get you home so you can change and get dry before you get sick. I don't know what I was thinking."

"Mama—" Lizzie whined.

"Come."

Without even a glance at the young woman who had cared for her daughter all afternoon, Beth grabbed her daughter's wet hand.

"Pick up your feet, Lizzie," Beth scolded.

She pulled her along back through the shrubs away from the water, through the circle of wagons, to where their family's campfire still smoldered. Lizzie protested all the way.

"We need to get those wet clothes off of you," Beth insisted. "You're lucky I got there when I did. That Miss Sullivan would have just plopped you on your feet but let you catch your death of cold."

Lizzie had stopped protesting by this time. Beth rushed around to build up the fire, dry off her daughter and find warm clothing for her as quickly as possible.

"Let's get you under a quilt," she said, trying not to panic. Soon, she was able to get Lizzie into the warm interior of the wagon and into dry clothing.

"Elizabeth?" Robert called from outside.

"Stay here, warm up," Beth told her daughter, tucking the quilt up under her chin. "I'll bring you supper when it's ready, but don't you worry about a thing."

"Mama, I'm not cold," said Lizzie plaintively. "I don't want to lay in here."

"We can't be too careful," she insisted before turning her attention to her husband and the rest of the family.

"Is she all right?" Robert asked when Beth appeared from the wagon.

She began her explanation, her voice shaking. Only half the story had spilled out when Robert climbed into the wagon himself to see. After speaking briefly to their daughter, both McKinnons emerged into the sunlight.

Beth didn't dare argue with her husband in front of the girl, but as soon as she had gone off to play with her sisters, she rounded on him.

"Did you hear what I said? She fell in the *water*. She could have drowned just like her brother. Then where would we be?" she demanded in a hiss.

Her anger made her cruel; she knew this about herself and had always tried to control her temper, but when it came to the safety of her children, she couldn't understand his actions.

He glanced at the children, still close enough to overhear. "Come with me," he said firmly as he led his wife outside the circle of wagons.

Beth began to protest—she still had to start supper—but Robert didn't stop until he was far enough away from the camp that no one would hear their discussion.

"We have talked about this," he said in a low voice as she approached him through the tall grass.

"I know," she insisted. "And I am trying. I am. Claire was with friends all day too. I think I deserve some credit for that."

"You do." He bowed his head in acknowledgment. "And I know it must have been hard to let Lizzie go."

"Do you? It seems to me that you have no problem pushing our children into situations they might not be ready for or that might be dangerous for them. Did you even consider any of this when you decided we were to move to Oregon? Robert, I don't know how... I'm trying."

He caught her up in a hug, whispering in her ear as he let her cry against his shoulder. All the pain and stress of the preceding months felt like a weight, pressing her into the dirt. There was a tension that she had not yet released, and every time she and Robert had this discussion, she felt like more expectations were being heaped on her.

"I'm so tired," she said despondently, half-muffled with her face in him.

"I know." He squeezed her more tightly. "I know, my love."

That made Beth cry harder. It was only when she was most broken, most vulnerable, that he used those words with her. This man, her beloved husband who had taken care of her for so long, was simply trying to help her through this as well. He loved her so much. He loved their family. He saw her so clearly.

"I'm trying," she said, finally pulling away to look him in the eye. "I tried to let them go. After Alexander, it seemed near impossible, but I know you're probably right. It's so hard. I think about finding Lizzie floating face down or about Boyd being crushed under the oxen and—"

"Elizabeth," Robert said sharply, cutting her off from any more imaginings. "You can't keep doing this to yourself. You're tired because you're trying too hard to control every detail of their lives. You're hanging on too tightly. Please don't forget that I am also here to help keep them safe. Every other man and woman in this camp wants our children to stay safe. You don't have to keep trying to do this on your own."

The two looked at each other for a long moment as Robert gently rubbed her upper arms, trying to steady her.

"I don't know..." she said.

"Let's just let Lizzie stay up this evening, out of bed. We can make her stay in camp, near the fire, and if she shows any sign of sickness tomorrow, you can tell me 'I told you so.' But let's just try."

"It feels scary," she whispered.

"It is." Robert wrapped an arm around her shoulder and started guiding her back to their camp. "But so is traveling on this trail at all. Having children is scary. Life is scary, Elizabeth. That's why we have each other."

She leaned her head on his shoulder and let him lead her to the wagon where they would give their daughter the good news.

Lizzie didn't show a single indication of getting sick after her close call in the river, and Beth had to admit that—again—Robert had been right. He had been right from the very start when he assured her that traveling to Oregon would be the best thing for their family. He had been right again a couple of weeks ago when he tried to keep her from worrying about them all so much. Beth still struggled with guilt, however. She tried to tell herself that Alexander's death had not been her fault, had not really been anyone's fault. There was a chance she would never forgive herself for that, but she was trying.

After leaving Fort Laramie, the terrain the Sullivan-Mills wagon company crossed was dry and dusty. Not only was there no water for miles—that stream where Lizzie had fallen was the last fresh water for a while—but there were hardly any plants. Mr. Mills had directed the men of the company to gather as much grass as they could manage to help feed their animals along that stretch of trail. Still, many families also fell to supplementing the animals' feed with oats or even the little sugar they had as well.

Beth tried to ration the family's supplies as carefully as she could. Every day was a delicate balancing between making sure every member of her family—human and animal—had enough food and water while still also making sure that enough lasted for the remaining time on the trail. Though Fort Laramie had supplies to be purchased, Beth had no faith that all the other forts along the way would, too.

And so, she spent every day under the hot sun, doing mental calculations about how much the children could eat that night. As the wagon company moved ever westward, Beth carried Tara in her arms as she walked along the trail. Claire, Ross, and Lizzie were rarely seen near the family's wagons throughout the day. Though it frightened her greatly, Beth was becoming accustomed to this new reality.

After all the discussions Beth and Robert had had about her stress in keeping the children safe, she didn't think it prudent to admit that she was worried about the family's food supplies. She was probably just overreacting—at least that's what she told herself. She and Robert had made sure to purchase more than what was recommended before they left Independence, and he had acquired more at the fort. There was the Indian attack, and the risk of more. Beth was constantly on guard for spoilage of any of the remaining food. And there was, of course, the chance that their supplies would be running low before the company reached Oregon, but Beth had promised Robert she would stop worrying so much. Instead, she kept all this to herself and rationed her own meals as much as she could.

In order to get to the next source of water as soon as possible, the Sullivan-Mills caravan was pushed to cover fifteen miles every day. It was a grueling, punishing pace, especially since Beth spent most of it carrying her toddler. Tara could walk a tiny portion of that fifteen miles, but Beth didn't feel up to letting the child free on her own two feet. Giving Claire or Boyd space was one thing. Giving a two-year-old such free rein was quite another, and Beth didn't think Robert would object.

With so much asked of them and with so little sustenance, many of the animals of the company were showing signs of weakening or even starvation. It seemed as though this was a common problem with most wagons that passed by this stretch of the Oregon Trail. As Beth walked alongside her husband or son each day, the bright sun overhead would reflect on something ahead of them that would catch her eye. Mahogany wardrobes, luxurious mirrors, and other heavy pieces of furniture were abandoned by the side of the trail. Objects that the owners had so carefully packed and carted all the way from the east coast could no longer be part of their journey. Pieces that were evidently valuable— either financially or emotionally—had to be left behind. As she passed yet another crate full of well-protected china dishes, Beth was reminded that everyone left something along the Oregon Trail. She had lost her youngest son, but that was by far the only real sacrifice.

And so, she spent her days constantly worrying in her mind over the safety of her children, the speed the caravan traveled westward, the amount of food left in their wagon, what they could dump if the vehicles needed to lose any weight, and innumerable other things. The constant concerns exhausted her, but she kept it all to herself. Robert would not want to hear it and would try to talk her out of it.

Thus, she was otherwise occupied and startled when her husband called out one afternoon.

"Whoa, there!" Robert said urgently, reining in his team with little warning.

The unexpected stop drew Beth's attention immediately. She had again been walking alongside the trail with Tara in her arms, but when something seemed to be wrong with the caravan, she wanted to do what she could do to help.

"Boyd, are you all right?" she called, as the boy also strove to slow his own team and the wagon behind them.

Beth glanced back to see that Curtis Fields had heard the commotion and was slowing his own wagon, but she still couldn't tell why the Gladwells had stopped just ahead of them. From her vantage, Beth could see that Ralph Ulmer—in the wagon ahead of the Gladwells—seemed to be driving his wagon just fine.

Something had made the Gladwells stop.

"Claire, take your sister, please," Beth said. She

handed the toddler over to Claire, who had also been walking through the grass with them.

Thus unencumbered, Beth picked up her skirts to run lightly to her husband's side.

"Are you all right? What happened?"

He shook his head. "Dunno. Do you want to take the reins, and I'll go check?"

"No, I'll go." She wouldn't be able to stand just waiting. Better that she knew as soon as possible what the problem was, so she could plan for it if necessary.

As such, she was the first one on hand and the first one to offer to help.

"What can I do?" she asked breathlessly as she approached.

Mr. and Mrs. Gladwell were huddled together, talking urgently near their team of oxen. They didn't seem to hear Beth approach and were, in fact, startled when she spoke up.

"Is everything all right?"

Linus Gladwell didn't respond before ducking away to go to his team. As Beth watched him leave, she noticed what the problem was. She couldn't possibly help with this.

"Oh no," she said in a low voice.

Like most of the Sullivan-Mills wagon company, the Gladwells drove a wagon to Oregon pulled by a team of four enormous oxen. These animals were all about two thousand pounds each, which meant that they needed to consume a good amount of grass and water each day to maintain their strength. Though the land nearest the trail had been a bit sparse, Beth had thought that the wagon company stopped in more fertile stretches for long enough for the animals to all get their fill.

That apparently was not the case.

One of the Gladwells' four oxen lay in the dirt, pulling down the heads and necks of the other animals that shared their yoke.

"Did it just...?"

"Madison just stopped walking," Sarah Gladwell said in a despaired whisper, "and before Linus could coax her again, she dropped. I wouldn't be surprised if she hurt an ankle or something under her."

"Can we get her up again? Do you have any oats to give her or...? I don't know what to do."

Beth felt that familiar freezing of fear. Every helpful action or suggestion she may have come up with yesterday had completely left her brain. She didn't know how to help, and she didn't truly know how to see this from happening to her own animals.

Another woman arrived at that moment and bombarded the Gladwells with her own questions. More and more neighbors came to offer their help or expertise, and Beth found herself being nudged further outside the circle. She couldn't even be offended by that, given that she had been so unhelpful. All she could do was watch as others sprang into action.

Eventually, she turned away. All her worrying was doing nothing to help the situation.

With slow steps, she returned to where Robert still stood with his stalled team and explained the situation.

"Go let Boyd know," he suggested. "And the Fieldses. That's something you can do to help."

She nodded numbly and made her way down the wagon train.

Beth tried to reassure herself that her own family wasn't about to lose an animal, that her husband and son must be taking better care of their teams than the Gladwells were. Furthermore, even in the completely unlikely scenario that they did lose an animal, the McKinnons drove two wagons. They could consolidate or move weight around if they needed to. They would be fine.

She told herself that over and over—the McKinnons would be fine. It was not easy for her to believe it, but maybe the repetition would help. They had already been asked to give up so much; how could they stand to give up more?

They would be fine.

She almost believed it.

Before long, the wagons got moving again, with the depleted body of the Gladwells' ox pulled to the side of the trail. She averted her eyes and walked in a wide arc through the grass around it.

Beth tried to put the whole affair out of her mind, even as she all but hovered over her own animals. She wouldn't lose another member of this family even if she had to give up her own food to feed the oxen. The following day, she spent some of the afternoon riding inside the McKinnons' supply wagon, going over—again—all that they still had and making lists of what she still hoped to get.

That night, she was surprised to hear that the day outside had been eventful.

"What were those wagons going by today, Pa?" Ross asked. "They were going the wrong way."

"I think those folks are heading back east."

Beth looked at him sharply. Turnarounds? She had missed them somehow in the commotion, and after all her insistence that they go back themselves. Now that they had come so far, Beth couldn't imagine returning to Pennsylvania. They had a ways to go, still, but every mile west they traveled was that much closer to their new home and their new life.

CHAPTER TWENTY-SIX

Beth kept her fears to herself. They threatened to overwhelm her at times, but she didn't want to worry anyone else. She already knew how her husband would react to her concerns, and she could always tell herself everything would be fine. Everything would be fine if they just stayed the course. They were nearly halfway to Oregon already. They couldn't be like the turnarounds. She knew that now. They had to keep looking forward, keep looking to the next landmark.

Courthouse Rock had marked the beginning of several weeks' worth of monumental landmarks indicating their way west to Oregon. The days of monotonous repetition of sky and plains were behind them. There were days of travel between the large granite sites, but they dominated the horizon and the emigrants' view throughout those days.

Just as Fort Laramie had drawn Boyd's attention days before they reached it, Independence Rock appeared on the horizon and anchored them to their destination. It was lower to the ground than Beth had expected, and yet at the same time, it compelled her. It was neither pointed nor steep, and that made it feel somehow more accessible than the other immense boulders they had passed along the way. She spent several days relishing the possibility of relaxing in its shadow for an afternoon.

When the day finally arrived, Beth actually walked on ahead of her family's wagons, with Tara in her arms, to take in the campsite and the imposing Independence Rock before she was called to make her camp.

"See, baby?" she cooed in her daughter's ear. "Isn't it big?"

With eyes wide and unblinking, Tara nodded. "It's a mountain?"

"Not exactly." Beth fumbled with how to describe the phenomenon to her small daughter. "We'll be in the mountains soon enough. This is just a... a big rock."

All around her, the Sullivan-Mills wagon company was arranging itself in a tight circle, chaining the wheels together securely as they made camp for the rest of the day. The sun was still high overhead, and Beth scanned the wagons for her own. With a broad smile, she strode across the packed earth to where Robert and Boyd were getting the animals settled.

"Mama!" Ross came running up to her when she approached, almost knocking over his brother in his haste. "Can we go up there? Can we? We can climb it, see?"

"Sit here, darling," Beth said to Tara as she got her settled. "Mama will be right back." She turned to Ross. "Now then, what is it you want to do?"

He grabbed her hand and pulled her a couple steps toward the enormous rock that dominated their camp. With his arm extended as far as he could manage, Ross indicated the very top, and Beth followed his finger, squinting into the bright sky to see silhouettes of people along the ridge of the rock. There were at least a dozen up there already, far more than she would have expected. Maybe it wasn't as dangerous as it looked.

"I don't know..."

"Oh yeah!" Boyd said enthusiastically once he noticed what his brother was doing. "We could get to the top and maybe see all the way to Oregon."

Robert chuckled, overhearing this. Beth caught his eye, and they exchanged a smile. He shrugged, and Beth seemed to be able to read his thoughts. She hesitated, then nodded slightly.

"I'll take you, boys," Robert said to their sons. "Let's get these animals taken care of, and then we'll go see how high we can climb."

"Really?" Ross said excitedly, looking between his parents.

"Do you want me to change my mind?" Beth asked.

"No, no. No. Thank you!" he called over his shoulder as he ran to find the water bucket.

Beth watched her husband as he, in turn,

watched the joyful reactions of their children. She had missed this easy camaraderie that they had shared back in Pennsylvania. So much of their lives had changed in the intervening months. She hadn't realized what was missing, but this silent conversation brought back such a feeling of security for her.

She could trust those boys with their father. The rest of the afternoon, she could feel confident knowing they were being looked after while still having a fun adventure.

Beth had her quiet afternoon in the shade. It might not have been as relaxing as she had hoped, but she was working toward that. Knowing that the boys were with Robert went a long way toward calming her anxious heart.

After supper, all of the McKinnons left Prince to guard their campsite and followed the small crowd leaving the circle of wagons. They headed to the clearing near the rock, where Pastor Montgomery gathered his itinerant congregation for an evening service. The poor man was trying so hard to give the emigrants some semblance of home and security, but with all the other stress, he wasn't able to hold services consistently.

This night, at Independence Rock, there was still plenty of light until sunset, but camping on the east side of the granite mound meant that they were able to settle in the shade, sitting on smaller stones or on quilts laid out in the grass out of the hot sun.

Lizzie helped her spread out the family's largest quilt as the boys joked and played with the Kirk boys.

"Come on now, beloveds," Beth said gently. "Sit down, please."

She took Tara from Claire's arms and settled with the child in the middle of the quilt, with Lizzie on her other side. Robert stood behind them, toward the back of a crowd, but Boyd and Ross were now playing tag with Norman Kirk, running around the grown-ups as they all waited for the pastor to begin.

Beth hadn't realized how much she had missed the peace and community of a worship service until her family settled in the midst of several dozen of their friends and neighbors that evening. Back in Lancaster, she had felt just as at home with the Lynches or other families as she did with her own. There was a special sort of intimacy in worshipping together, and Beth realized that all of her fretting about the day-to-day dangers had disconnected her from that companionship.

She would have to try harder.

But somehow now, such an effort seemed possible, welcome, even. Beth felt as though she had worn herself out in worrying, and sitting here, surrounded by other hopefuls on their way to Oregon, she felt as though she wasn't truly alone anymore.

"Mama?" Claire tugged gently on her sleeve. "Amy Cole is waving to me. Can I go sit with them?"

Beth looked to where her daughter was pointing —the two Cole girls sat in the grass just a few feet from their parents, clearly safe in the middle of the crowd. Her immediate reaction was that it would be lovely for her daughter. In fact, Beth surprised herself by being completely at ease with the idea of Claire with her friends for the evening.

"Of course, my love. You go have fun. I just want you home before dark, please."

Claire's expression quickly morphed from questioning to shock, so fast Beth was worried.

"What? What's wrong?"

Claire grinned, happier than Beth had seen her in months. "You just said 'my love.'"

Frowning, Beth tried to recall what she had just said. "I did?"

"You haven't said anything like that since Alexander died," Claire added softly. "Remember, Ma? You used to always call us all kinds of silly things like beloved and angel face and all of that. I didn't realize how much I missed it."

With a small laugh, Beth hugged her daughter close. "I guess you're right, genius daughter of mine. I'll have to pay better attention now."

"I love you, Mama," Claire said before striding off across the clearing to her friends.

Beth watched Claire go with the Cole girls to sit with them in the grass with a few other older children. She hadn't realized it until Claire pointed it out, but it was true—she hadn't used any of the common endearments that had so peppered her vocabulary. Her mind had been too busy concerned with the literal life-and-death matters facing her family for Beth to be able to relax enough to even think such words. Though she hadn't realized it, something must have changed in her; she must be feeling safer and more able to let her children live their own lives.

Claire had noticed. Poor Claire, thought Beth. Her girlhood was being marred by her mother's clutching need of her. She would have to see what she could do to give her daughter more space.

One of the young men sat down in the grass near to Claire, whether deliberately or not, Beth didn't know. There was a pang of nostalgia—her girl was growing up. She would never again be her little girl. Soon she'd be meeting a young man, collecting her own trousseau like Poppy Lynch, and leaving the family.

But she was Beth's to cherish until then.

"Thank you all for coming tonight." Pastor Montgomery projected out over the crowd as he took his place at the front. "I hope this evening serves as a balm to your souls. But first, let's pray."

Beth closed her eyes and bowed her head, clutching her daughters' hands in her own with gratitude swelling her heart.

The wagon company pushed hard for several days after leaving Independence Rock. They had many miles to cover, and time seemed to be growing short. The next big campsite they would stay at was Pacific Springs, and the promise of that fresh water and sweet grass for the animals kept them going through exhaustion and physical pain. There was no opportunity to dawdle. They needed to get there as soon as possible; too many other families were at risk of losing their draft animals for there to be any delay.

Leaving Independence Rock the following morning felt almost like a fresh start. Beth smiled to herself to think that Claire had noticed a change in her, a change that she didn't see coming.

It was curious to feel such a change in herself. Though Beth could proudly say that she had been trying to reach this state—more trust, more ease— she never truly believed it was available to her. But now, she was feeling more secure in trusting her children and herself and was ready to give them all more chances to be on their own. They deserved the opportunity to grow up in their own way. She couldn't help but think about how Alexander would have loved climbing up to the top of the stone like his brothers or how he would have had Prince following at his heels every step of the journey to Oregon. Each thought of her son brought her pain, but it was slowly being tempered by bittersweet gratitude for the time she had with him.

About mid-morning, she left Tara with Claire in the wagon and walked to her husband and the oxen of the family's lead wagon. When she reached him, Robert was whistling softly, one of the hymns that Pastor Montgomery had led everyone in singing the night before.

"Good morning," he said cheerfully when he saw her. "I want to tell you that I think the boys will be talking about their climb up Independence Rock for years."

"Oh?"

"I'm proud of you for setting aside your fear to let them do that."

She blushed and looked away. "I'm not sure that's really anything that deserves pride. It's not like I let them go off by themselves after all."

"True. But I know it wasn't easy for you."

"Thank you," she murmured.

They walked in silence for another few minutes. So much had changed since they had left Pennsylvania—from losing Alexander to Robert becoming more communicative—that she had to make a concerted effort to remember their life there. Somehow, it now felt as though they had always been meant to come west. The idea that she could have lived her whole life in that one town seemed far away from her now.

"Do you remember," Beth began, "last Christmas at your brother's house? How he kept mentioning stories of friends who had gone west?"

Robert was silent so long that Beth wondered if maybe he hadn't heard her. "I had forgotten," he said finally. "He must have known then that he wanted us off the farm."

"I'm sorry," she said, stricken by his tone. Through all the pain of the circumstances surrounding their leaving Pennsylvania, Beth hadn't let herself think about it all from her husband's point of view. "I know you were close. It must have been so hard to hear him asking you to leave."

"Asking *us* to leave," Robert corrected her quietly.

Beth didn't know precisely how to word her next question. They walked in quiet contemplation for a few moments.

"Did it seem like he was asking you to choose?"

"Choose? Between you and him?" Robert looked ahead, again quiet for a long time before finally responding. "Yes. I think that's exactly it. He's always been the older brother and had some measure of control over me."

"I can't believe he would do that to you, though."

"Well... Stuart even putting me in that position made the decision easier."

"I'm sorry," she said again.

Robert remained as stoic as ever, barely even squeezing back when Beth slipped her hand into his. They walked in silence for a while before he spoke again.

"It seems so strange to think we'll never see them again."

Beth gasped slightly. "I hadn't even thought of that. You're right. Somehow saying good-bye to everyone in the town felt more final than saying good-bye to family." She peered at him carefully. "Are you all right?"

He nodded, finally holding her hand tightly in his. "I still believe what I told you all those months ago. This is the best thing for our family."

She tried to smile at him.

"Though, of course, I wish we hadn't lost our son," he added softly.

Three quick tears spilled down Beth's cheeks before she wiped them away. She would never be done mourning her son, but at least she could try to be done punishing Robert for it.

"I know," she whispered. "Me too."

Reaching Pacific Springs felt like the end of a race, and yet they still couldn't rest. There was still so far to go. The wagon company remained at that camp long enough to eat, sleep and again fill every single container they carried with water. Though she had read through the Oregon Trail guidebook Robert bought in Independence, Beth hadn't realized how much of this continent stretched without fresh water available. She marveled at the animals and Indians who made this seemingly inhospitable land their home. All she could do was keep heading west to the relative haven of the Oregon Territory.

That first night after leaving Pacific Springs, Beth was putting together supper for her family when she heard a gasp come from the camp next to them.

"What happened?" Ross asked his mother, but she could only shake her head.

"I'm not sure, love, but I'm sure everything is fine."

When Sarah Gladwell approached their camp a few minutes later, Beth had already wiped her hands on her apron, readying to see what she could do to help. The other woman looked as though she hadn't slept in days. Something was causing her even more stress than the normal wear of life on the trail.

"How are you?" Beth asked her guest. "Is there something wrong?"

Mrs. Gladwell nodded, grimacing. "I hate to even ask; I'm so ashamed. And please don't feel as though you have to say yes. But... well, Sally knocked over a pail of water, and a couple of our smaller bowls and we're just..." She looked down at her hands, clutched in front of her so tightly her knuckles seemed to be turning white. "Any help you can provide, we would be so grateful."

"You want me to give you my family's water?" Beth asked this slowly, incredulously, just to be certain she understood the woman correctly. It was such an extreme request.

"Please," she whispered. "Anything."

Beth considered. Any drop she gave the Gladwells was one fewer than she had for her own family. She could be somewhat confident that she had enough water for the McKinnons, but not at all confident that she had enough to give away.

And yet, she could not help but think about how many people had helped her when she had been struggling under a much heavier burden. Looking at Mrs. Gladwell's pleading eyes reminded her of the pastor's expression when he came to care for the children after Alexander's passing and of Emma Fields checking in on her.

How could Beth turn her back on her neighbor when everyone else had been so kind to her?

"I can't spare a lot," she warned. "But maybe this will be enough to keep you all till tomorrow. After that—"

"Thank you," she said breathlessly.

When Beth handed over the bowl of water she thought she could spare, Mrs. Gladwell's desperate grab reassured her she was making the right choice. As the woman headed back to her own wagon, Beth mentally adjusted how much water each person could have now. She would manage it somehow. If there was one thing she was learning, it was that her family could weather anything that came at them.

. . .

The wagon company pushed farther west, at as fast a pace as Mr. Mills and Mr. Sullivan could manage. Judging by the recommended route to the west coast, they were several days behind schedule. They should have reached Independence Rock by July fourth, but the several days late represented dozens of miles. Those days could be the difference between life and death if they didn't get over the Blue Mountains before the snow fell or if they ran out of food and water before finding new supplies.

The only way to make up the distance was by sacrificing more and more. Pushing harder and harder. Each family, each animal, was stretched to its absolute limit. To Beth, it seemed like they were constantly moving—many days, they didn't even stop for a midday break, and she was forced to dole out cold biscuits and jerky to her children as they walked. Though she tried to stay positive, she always felt in need of a little more rest, a little more food, a little more quiet.

But there was no stopping. Not yet.

CHAPTER TWENTY-EIGHT

The Sullivan-Mills wagon company spent day after day heading west. The monotony of the flat plains was behind them, but every day was a new environment to conquer. As they crossed into the high desert, they left the low prairie behind, and the elevation began to climb almost imperceptibly. Though the distance traversed seemed interminable, small changes were noticeable as they progressed. One morning when Beth woke up, she realized she was curled into as small of a ball as she could manage under the thin quilt on her cot. The cold of the foothills seemed to have snuck up on her. She hesitated to get out of bed at all, and in fact, only did so once she had reminded herself where the family's cold weather attire was stored.

By the time the rest of the McKinnons had risen for the day, Beth had unpacked all of their heavy winter coats, shawls, and extra blankets to sleep under at night. Walking under the sun during the day wasn't so bad, but the high desert cold cut through the wagon canvas and all their layers. As she'd had to cut back their meals little by little, each person in the family seemed more susceptible to the cold at night.

But they would be all right, she reminded herself. Between herself and Robert, they would get all the McKinnon family that remained safely to Oregon.

Any doubt or question or panic, Beth shoved resolutely from her mind. Instead, she busied herself with asking Ross about his time herding cattle with Ethan Goldman or Claire about the bird's nest Amy Cole had been carting westward. Beth herself made time to visit Emma Fields and Margaret Hudson as the Oregon Trail climbed into the foothills, higher in elevation with every rotation of the wheel. This was what life could be like, she told herself. A semblance of normality if one didn't constantly worry about the unknown future.

And with every day farther west, Beth felt more and more comfortable letting her children be on their own. She held back her harping and controlling, and they found joy in her changing. The old camaraderie the family used to share began to creep back. The McKinnon children had always been friends and, given the chance, were becoming so again. One evening, after supper, Beth could not catch her breath from laughing so. Boyd's clowning had focused on his mother for teasing, and his imitation of her was too spot-on to be ignored.

"Oh, angel face, butterfly, lovey, star breath,"

Boyd crooned in a falsetto while miming himself holding up long skirts.

"I have never once called you star breath," Beth protested with a laugh.

That only made the rest of the family laugh harder, and Beth was too happy to be embarrassed.

Before Boyd could sail into her again, there was a polite throat-clearing from behind him.

Everyone looked to see Emma Fields approached the McKinnons' camp. Beth stood to meet her friend but was arrested by the other woman's grave expression. There was a somberness in her manner that Beth had not seen before. Every time Emma had come calling, it had been far more light-hearted. Whatever was making the older woman wring her hands as she did was already worrying Beth.

"Is everything all right?" Beth asked, trying to keep the fear from her tone. She was well aware of the children behind her and the need to keep them calm as well.

"Oh, child, I just needed to... That is, I have some bad news. I wanted to make sure you knew."

As Emma stepped closer, Beth's heart jumped to her throat. Her mind ran through every possibility she could think of, and she mentally reminded herself that all of her still-living children were there with her, none more than ten feet away. Her family was safe. They were all right.

"What is it?"

"Over the last day or so, there's a number of folks have come down with what the doctor is calling Mountain Fever," she said in a low voice.

"What is that? What does that mean?" Her heart raced as she glanced over her shoulder at the children. How could she protect her family from this?

"It's a fever," Emma said gently. "General malaise, exhaustion. I believe a couple of the sick ones are showing signs of hallucinations."

"Everyone is exhausted," Beth snapped. "That doesn't help. What am I looking for?"

"A fever, mostly. Just keep an eye on the little ones," Emma suggested. "Maybe keep them in bed longer if you can. That's what I aim to do."

Beth turned her back on her guest to see all of the children watching her intently.

"As far as I know, the sickness is already in the Hudson camp, the Sullivans, and others."

A groan of defeat escaped Beth's lips, and she turned back to Emma.

"How are we to bear this?" she asked in a whisper.

"The same way we have borne everything else, my dear. Because that is what we must do," Emma said quietly. "I'll go. But go see the doctor if you need to, he said. He'll likely have his hands full, but between him and Mrs. Martell, everyone should be seen to."

"The doctor. Yes. Thank you," Beth said absently.

She couldn't—she *wouldn't*—lose any more of her children.

"Did you hear any of that?" she asked them once Emma had left. "I think it's time for bed, now."

Beth braced herself for protests and complaints,

but they all seemed to sense the seriousness of the situation. Even Robert backed her up, standing and lifting Tara with him.

"You don't have to sleep right away," he said. "But rest in bed, like your mother says."

Claire searched her mother's face questioningly, but Beth couldn't bring herself to explain. When she finally looked at her oldest daughter, her heart broke at the disappointment on her face. After slowly gaining some independence, Claire was now being caged again. Beth looked away.

It was for their own good. She just kept reminding herself that this was all to keep them safe.

The next day flew by in a blur. Beth could not have said how she spent it; it seemed as though every moment she expected to hear Ross tell her he was tired or hear Lizzie complain about being hot. Keeping them all cooped up in the sleeping wagon while Beth drove the team seemed to the children to be a punishment. She apologized and explained but did not relent.

By the end of the day, she was so tired from dealing with all of it that for a moment, Beth feared that she herself had come down with the fever. The muscles in her arms ached with the effort as she unhitched the team of oxen. Robert helped her briefly but then made his excuses to go check on the rest of the company. It had been a tense, uncertain day.

He wasn't gone long enough for her to worry, but the moment Beth saw her husband's expression, panic gripped her. Whatever news he brought from the other men was nothing good, and she was well able to imagine all sorts of different disastrous scenarios.

"What is it?" Beth demanded. "I know there's something, Robert McKinnon. Don't you keep it from me."

"William Sullivan is dead," he said dully. "The fever took him. Maybe a couple of the others too, soon."

"No. Oh, Robert, it can't be!"

"The funeral will be in the morning," he added quietly. "Early. Then we will need to leave again. The sooner we get out of the mountains, the sooner we should all be safe."

Beth slumped against the wagon seat. Another death. Another loss. Another funeral and gravesite left behind as they continue to push their way west.

CHAPTER TWENTY-NINE

William Sullivan's death marked one of the lowest moments for the wagon company since they had left Independence, more even than the Indians' attack, more than any of the other deaths had. He had touched so many lives. The man had been a caretaker of all the other families, and his loss was felt throughout the entire community.

Explaining to her young daughter that her friends' father had just died brought back a rush of memories from just after Alexander's death. Beth knew she should reach out to the widow but could never find the courage and calm to do so. Instead, she was consumed with watching her own children, checking on their well-being, and promising them that she and Robert were not going to die too. It was a fraught several days for all the McKinnons.

Pastor Montgomery held Sullivan's funeral the following morning, but immediately after that, Mills insisted that the company move west again. There was no time for rest, no time for grieving. Every single person in the caravan knew that what William Sullivan wanted most was for his family and the rest of the company to arrive in Oregon safely. The only choice was to continue westward.

With one of the wagon company captains gone, that first evening after a day of hard travel, Captain Mills called a meeting with all the men, one representative from each family, to help make the next decision. They had to choose between two different routes to follow, each with a drawback and a benefit. Beth spent the whole time her husband was gone coming up with a plan for either option. She would be prepared, whatever the men decided. When Robert returned from the meeting, he looked grim. Beth resisted asking him about it in front of the children, but as soon as they had a moment alone, she pressed her husband for details.

"Well, Mills took a vote. You can't ask better than that. So, we all could choose whether to cut across the desert, shaving seven days off the trip, or go the longer route near water and a fort."

"And?"

"I voted with the majority—we'll be taking the trail with grass and water for the animals."

Beth felt a pulse of panic course through her, despite all her supposed planning. "You're not worried about taking longer to get to Oregon? I thought we were already behind more days than we should be."

"The general thought was the water and grass will be better for all, especially the animals, and will be worth the extra time. Plus, we'll have a chance to buy more supplies at Fort Bridger. If we took the cut-off, we would be going around the fort, and we would have to do another full week with no fresh water. I think most of the men are seeing the strain in their teams already, and they didn't want to risk it."

"I just... You know, Robert. I worry about running out of food or getting stuck in the mountains with the snow, or tiring out our team with extra miles or—"

"I know, Elizabeth," he said softly, stepping closer to her. "But there's a risk either way. Going the slightly longer way is what everyone agreed to."

Beth fell silent. She would have to be content with the group's decision. It was not as though she would talk Robert into taking the cutoff by themselves. Everything would be fine, she told herself. It would have to be. She would make it be fine. Just fine.

In order to make up the time in taking the longer route, Mr. Mills spread the word that they would be leaving camp at first light every morning. They would stay on the trail as long as they could manage, before stopping only long enough to get a bit of rest and a bite to eat. Day after day passed in which Beth ate as little as possible so as to save the dwindling supplies they had for the children. Everything would work out once they got to the fort, she told herself.

And Robert had been right that the longer route afforded them far more sustenance than crossing a sparse desert would have. During the week that they took along the longer path, he even had an opportunity to hunt briefly. Beth stepped in to lead his team and wagon, and Robert brought home two game hens. Beth used them to make a hearty soup that would stretch for two meals for each of the McKinnons. It wasn't ideal, but it was bearable.

After several days of constant worry in spite of the more lush surroundings, Beth let out a relieved sigh. The wagon company had crested a low hill, and Fort Bridger was finally visible. It wasn't much to look at—a strong, sturdy wall on four sides to protect against attack—but it represented all the hope she had held for the last couple of weeks. Not only would they be able to supplement their food stores, hopefully, but they would also be camping here for half a day and offering the first real break since the company had decided to take this route.

As Mills led the caravan into a circle to camp for the rest of the day, she didn't even wait for the full company to be settled before she headed off to the fort on her own. Let Robert handle the animals and the wagons; Beth was perfectly capable of purchasing the flour and salt they needed.

Beth's eagerness meant that she was alone when she entered the fort ahead of the rest of the company. There was one guard at the gate, holding his rifle lazily and watching the arrival of the emigrants, but otherwise, not much else to see. Where the other soldiers were, she had no idea. She put such things from her mind and focused on finding the trading center.

Within the four walls of the fort were a cluster of stark buildings, all constructed for strength rather than beauty. The low wooden building in the center had its door standing wide open, almost welcoming, and Beth made her way there.

When she stepped inside, she was initially relieved to find that she had guessed correctly, and this was in fact the supply store. She immediately took in the tall shelving units and the counter in the back where a man stood hunched over a layout of cards spread across the counter. In the next moment, however, she realized that the shelves were virtually bare.

"But..." Beth began, taking several more steps into the room.

The shelves had been pushed to the walls, leaving only open space in the center. The man at the counter looked up and offered her an apologetic expression.

"Afternoon, ma'am," he said, standing up straight.

"Where— Maybe I'm in the wrong place. We're crossing over to Oregon and had hoped to purchase supplies here." Beth couldn't keep the desperation from her voice. If there was nothing here, she didn't know what she would do.

"Yes, ma'am. Well, I'm sorry about that, but we don't have anything—"

"What do you mean you don't have *any*thing?"

"The last company that came through here a few days ago picked us clean. We're hoping to get another shipment before the end of summer, but the goods that were supposed to get here a few weeks ago overturned in the Kansas River."

"You have nothing?" she asked again, hoping that if she could just word it in the right way, he might give her a different answer. "No cornmeal? No ammunition? No calico? Nothing?"

He shook his head. "I really am sorry, ma'am."

Beth spun abruptly on her heel and left, her mind a cloud of exasperation, wondering how on earth she would be able to get past this. She headed back toward her wagon in a daze, hardly recognizing where she was stepping. There was too much to think about for her to pay close attention.

As she exited the walls of the fort, she noticed a group of men and women heading toward her. Dimly, through her frustration, Beth realized these must be emigrants from her own wagon company, but she didn't stop.

"There's nothing," she called as the group approached. Beth was too distracted to even note the individual faces coming toward her. All she wanted was to get back to her own camp and come up with a plan.

"Say that again," one of the men insisted.

"Nothing here," Beth reiterated. "The shelves are stripped bare. They don't even have any ammunition we could use to find our own food. How am I going to feed my babies?"

But by then she had already stridden past the group; no one could answer her question.

"There's nothing," she said again, once she was within shouting distance of her own camp. She didn't care who overheard her. They all needed to know. How could the company survive more time without enough food? She didn't see how they would manage.

All of her children were nearby as she hurried back, and Beth took in their stricken expressions. She should have stayed quiet to not panic them, but it was too late now.

Beth felt a warm presence by her side.

"Let's think about this calmly," Robert said, placing a hand on either of her upper arms.

There was just something about that man's touch that calmed Beth when nothing else could. She took a deep breath, and once her heart stopped racing, she explained what she had found—or, rather, not found—at the fort and what that meant for them.

"And so, whatever food we have left in the supply wagon has to last us for who knows how long!" she finished desperately. "I've already been rationing for myself, but I don't want to— I can't take anything from the mouths of our children. What are we going to do?"

"Elizabeth," he began kindly. "Let's take this step by step. We have food for today, right? And for tomorrow."

She nodded and tried to calm her breath.

"Do we have food for the day after that?"

"Yes." He was right, of course. She knew that. She did this to herself all the time. He was right. Goodness, when would she learn? But still, the fear of her children starving gripped her.

"So, none of our family will starve for at least a

few days," he summarized with a smile. "And we'll reach the Bear River Valley after not long. Do you remember reading about that in the guidebook?"

She shook her head. It sounded vaguely familiar to her, but his voice and explanation were so calming that she didn't dare interrupt.

"It's a beautiful, lush place," he said. "The trail follows a river, and from my understanding, the whole area should be full of game and fish. Probably also some wild onions or other plants we can use to supplement what we have."

"Do we have enough ammunition, though? And hooks for the rods?"

He nodded slowly, deliberately, still trying to keep her calm. "We have everything we need. I promise."

She rubbed her eyes hard, trying to slow her racing heart.

"All right?" he asked, peering into her face. "We're all right, Elizabeth. I promise. You trust me to take care of us, don't you?"

"I do," she said. "Yes. I do."

He was right. Of course he was right. Her husband had always taken good care of the family and had always been a voice of calm, even-keeled reason. Beth felt safe.

CHAPTER THIRTY

After leaving Fort Bridger, with all of the mothers grumbling over the lack of supplies, the trail headed almost due north. With this slight detour, the company could more safely cross the mountains and go around the Great Salt Lake. Ahead of them was both the promise of the lush Bear River Valley with its game and vegetation and then Fort Hall just beyond that. Both offered the chance to shoot, catch or buy more food. Beth found herself constantly consumed by plans and contingencies for what food they had left, though Robert's reassurances had calmed her far more than at any other step along the trail.

There were still several days of travel before they reached the Bear River, though, and Beth spent most of it reminding herself that everything would be fine and that her husband was helping care for the children too. She would be fine. Everything would be okay. It was a near-constant refrain in her mind. Beth may need to remind herself of this several dozen times each day, but that was what was needed in order for her to keep herself and her children calm.

Pulling together supper for all seven McKinnons was still a trial for her, given the uncertainty ahead of them. Though she told Robert she wasn't worried, the truth was that Beth felt herself seize up every time she visited their supply wagon.

They would be fine. She knew, though she had to remind herself. Absolutely fine.

As another long day on the trail came to a close, the wagons had been pulled into a circle for the evening. Beth climbed out of their supply wagon with arms full of what she hoped would be enough food to satisfy all. She would make some semblance of a soup. It might be a bit watery, but at least it would stretch. It seemed as though Boyd was eating more and more every day. He must have grown two or three inches since they had left Pennsylvania earlier that year. There would be plenty in Oregon, Beth reminded herself. She just needed to keep them all fed until then.

Within twenty minutes, she had the pot simmering over the fire. There was only so much time before the sun would be set for the night, and Beth felt rushed. It wasn't until the soup was just about heated through that she looked around for the children.

"Tara, baby, what are you up to?" Beth asked.

The older children had scattered to see friends and do chores, but the baby of the family sat alone in the shade of the wagon. She lay sprawled lazily, resting her face on Prince's belly. "Nothing."

"Well, come out from under there, please. It's almost time to eat."

Tara shook her head stubbornly but grinned as though this was all a game her mother was playing.

"Tara," Beth said more sternly. "Come on now, darling. You know better. Don't make me ask again. You can play with Prince again later."

She turned back to the pan, fully expecting her daughter to toddle over any moment. Though arguably the youngest McKinnon had been a bit coddled, Tara had always been obedient and easygoing. It was a surprise to Beth, therefore, when she looked over her shoulder to see that the little girl was still sitting in the dirt under the wagon.

"Tara, my love. I said come here."

To her credit, the child was no longer under the wagon. She had at least crawled those couple feet since Beth had looked away. But she seemed disinclined to move any farther.

"Tara."

"I'm ready, Mama," she said cheerfully and lifted her arms to be picked up.

"I'm sorry, honey, my hands are full." Beth looked back at her pot of soup. The fire was uneven this evening, and she was afraid of burning the bit of rice at the bottom. There was none to spare. "I can't pick you up. I need you to come to me, please."

"Supper ready, Ma?" Boyd asked as he and Ross strode up to the campsite.

The child was becoming more and more the mature young man that Robert had foreseen.

"Just a couple minutes. Tell me about your day, boys."

Ross launched into a tale of some card game the Davis boys were teaching him while Boyd interrupted periodically with both corrections and teasing. Claire and Lizzie appeared soon after, and Beth tried not to let them all distract her.

Within moments the McKinnons' campsite was a bit chaotic. The boys eagerly hovered, hoping to get the first bowl and the girls teased each other about something or other. Beth didn't catch it as she kept calling for Robert, who had his hands full fixing the handle of one of their buckets. The thought of how much food each person got and how much she could spare from their stores distracted Beth until she realized that Claire was holding Tara right by her side, both waiting for their food.

"All right, girls. Here you are. Claire, put her down so you can carry both bowls."

Beth dished the soup into two small servings and turned back to hand them to the oldest daughter. Tara sat in the dirt at her feet, looking up and watching. Frowning, Beth handed the bowls to Claire and then squatted to be closer to the littlest girl.

"Tara, why are you in the dirt, my girl? Stand up. Claire has your supper if you just go with her."

Tara raised her arms again to be picked up.

"All right, then. I'll help you this last time, but that's it."

Beth pulled her daughter to a standing position but didn't lift her off her feet. Strangely, the girl's knees seemed to buckle under her. Soon Tara sat in the dirt at Beth's feet again.

"Tara, baby, are you all right?"

Beth tried again to pull her daughter to her feet, but Tara's limbs did not seem to want to cooperate. The little girl didn't seem to notice that anything was amiss, however, and Beth tried valiantly to stay calm and not frighten the child.

"I'm hungry, Mama," Tara said simply.

"I know, baby. I know. Let's..." Beth cleared her throat and tried to steady her words. "Can you go with your sister, please? Claire has your supper."

For her part, the oldest McKinnon stood waiting, plates in hand, with a concerned expression.

"Can you stand up, please, beloved?" Beth asked, with her last shred of calm.

In response, Tara lifted her arms again to be picked up. Her mother tried one final time to help the little girl to her feet, but it was as though her muscles had completely wasted away. The almost-three-year-old who had been walking confidently for nearly two years could no longer hold herself up.

"What's wrong with her?" Beth demanded. "What's wrong with my baby?"

Claire looked at her blankly. "I— Ma, I don't know, we've just been—"

"Tara, honey," Beth began, brushing her oldest daughter aside. She caught up Tara in her arms, trying not to shake the little girl in her panic and frustration. "Tara, what's wrong? Are you sick? Are you feeling okay?"

Tara seemed remarkably fine, grinned at her mother, and nodded. "I'm hungry, though."

"Did she eat today?" Beth demanded of Claire. "How much has she eaten? Maybe she's hungry. Maybe— Oh, goodness, maybe she caught something. Could Mountain Fever do this?"

"What's wrong?" Robert appeared at her side, holding Beth's arm and steadying her. "Whatever it is, we'll figure it out."

He spoke slowly and deliberately, as though willing his wife's heart rate to slow. She explained as best she could, but her worry and speculation overpowered any attempts at rational thought.

"She can't— She's not walking. She's not even standing! Her legs seem to be broken, or she's too weak to hold herself up or, I don't know, Robert. I don't know how this happened. What do we do?"

"Why don't we call the doctor?" he suggested. "That seems like the most logical step—we ask for help. You put her to bed and get her to eat something, and I'll go find Dr. Martell. How does that sound?"

Beth felt tears spilling down her cheeks. The thought of another one of her precious children being lost to her or being in any way harmed by this trip west to Oregon overwhelmed her to the point of rendering her speechless. Just as with the Indian attack, and when Lizzie had been subsumed by the creek, Beth was useless in a true moment of crisis.

Freezing up and letting her panic overtake her was in no way helping her family.

Thank goodness for Robert. And Claire.

Thank goodness for all of them.

Beth nodded at her husband's suggestion. "You're right. Yes, I'll do that. Tara, baby, are you ready?"

The little girl lifted her arms again. "I'm hungry, Mama."

"I know, my love, I know," she whispered into the little girl's hair as she carried her to their sleeping wagon. Claire followed closely behind. "Let's get you settled, and then you can eat your supper."

After getting her to eat—there seemed to be no problem with her appetite—Beth tucked Tara into bed. She sat for a long time by her side, waiting for the toddler to fall asleep. Whatever had happened to her youngest daughter, she would never forgive herself for not noticing sooner. First, Alexander had been lost forever, and now, her baby may never walk again.

This journey had taken so much more than she had been willing to give. Nothing would ever be the same.

CHAPTER THIRTY-ONE

Less than an hour after Tara had finally fallen asleep, Beth was still sitting by her side. Occasionally she would feel the little girl's head for a fever or brush hair away from her face, but none of that distracted her from her worry.

She heard a soft whisper through the opening of the canvas covering the wagon.

"Elizabeth?"

Beth stood and moved to the end of the wagon, where she could whisper to her husband.

"Is the doctor with you?"

"Yes, ma'am," another voice said. "I'm here."

"Oh, thank goodness. Please come in. Please, doctor. I don't know what's wrong with her."

She backed up to give the doctor more room and felt a wave of dread at whatever news he was about to give her.

"Did my husband explain to you the problem?" she asked. Robert waited outside the wagon but under the canvas flap so he could hear everything. "I don't know when this started, but she doesn't seem to be in any pain. She just... I don't know what happened."

Beth felt as though she was rambling while the doctor knelt down at Tara's side.

"Your husband explained the issue. Do you want to wake her up for me?" he asked gently.

"Are you sure that's a good idea?" Beth demanded. "If she's sick, then she needs all the rest she can get."

"Of course, you're right, Mrs. McKinnon." The doctor glanced at Robert.

"Elizabeth, let's let the doctor look at her."

She was too overcome with her own shame and exhaustion to argue anymore, so she did as the men asked. Kneeling down at the head of the cot, Beth gently brushed the little girl's honey-brown locks off her face.

"Tara..."

She stirred without waking. Beth gently placed a hand on the girl's arm.

"Tara, darling, wake up, please."

Blinking rapidly, the little girl smiled into her mother's face and then yawned. "Is it morning?"

"No, belovedest, not yet. But there's someone who wants to talk to you." She glanced at the doctor before moving out of his way.

"Tara, I'm Doctor Martell."

Her eyes widened. "Am I sick?"

"I don't know yet. That's why I'm here. Can you do something for me? Can you tell me if this hurts?"

The doctor proceeded to conduct a range of tests on the two-year-old, from checking the reflexes of her legs to asking her to count as high as she could. To Beth's eyes, there seemed to be no rhyme or reason to what he was doing. Checking the child's temperature seemed to be a reasonable precaution, but then he followed it up by asking her what she had done the previous day while the wagons were rolling.

All Beth wanted were answers, and so far, this man didn't seem capable of providing any of what she needed. She took a couple of deep breaths, resisting the impulse to dissolve into anxious tears. Whatever happened, whatever the problem, her baby needed her to be strong.

Finally, the doctor seemed to have all the information he needed.

"Why don't you lay back down, dear, and finish your nap. I'm going to talk to your mama and papa, and everything will be fine."

The three adults climbed back out of the wagon, and Beth noticed that Tara remained sitting up and watching them alertly. Dr. Martell led the two parents several feet away from the wagon, and the other children, before turning to give them his full attention.

"Well?" Beth demanded. "What is it? How can we make this better?"

"Tell me, Mrs. McKinnon, during the day, when your husband is driving your wagon, what are you typically doing?"

She blinked at him, confused. "What does that have to do with anything?" she snapped.

"Elizabeth," Robert said softly.

She took a deep breath. "Usually, I walk next to the wagons. Sometimes with my husband, sometimes with my son."

"What about your daughters?"

"What about my daughters?"

"Do you ever walk with them?"

"Occasionally." She looked off across the high desert, trying to remember. "Not often. Usually, Claire takes charge of the two little ones, and they ride in the wagon. She's wonderful with the girls," Beth added, fearing the doctor would somehow blame Claire for what was wrong with the baby. "I'm sure Claire didn't do anything to her."

"No, I'm sure you're right," he said. "All right, just another couple of questions."

"Why all these questions?" Beth asked, exasperated.

"I'm just trying to rule some things out," he responded pleasantly.

His smile infuriated Beth; the doctor didn't seem to be taking this seriously at all. Maybe she would have been better off not even bothering with him but instead nursing her daughter on her own.

"What about when we stop in camp?" he continued. "What do you do with that time?"

"Are you serious?"

"Elizabeth—"

"I don't understand what any of this has to do with Tara. But besides that, doctor, I would think that what I do when we're in camp should be obvious. I assume it's the same that your own wife does, right? Cooking, cleaning, repairing everything, and then more cooking, cleaning, gathering water constantly, more cooking and more cleaning over and over again."

"And what do your daughters do while you're taking care of all of that?"

"Well, Claire is usually in charge of the two younger ones. I need someone to make sure they stay out of trouble, and of course, since Tara is too young to be left on her own, someone needs to watch her. They usually ride in the sleeping wagon and tell stories or play games. I think Claire was helping Lizzie with her reading, but how can that... Wait. Do you think the other girls could come down with the same thing that is ailing Tara? Oh, my heavens."

Beth suppressed a sob, holding her hand to her bosom and trying to calm herself. All this time, and all this care, and now everything was falling apart.

"I apologize, Mrs. McKinnon; I didn't intend to worry you so much. I'm simply trying to understand what little Tara's day-to-day activities are like."

"And that will help you diagnose her?" Robert asked.

The doctor chuckled lightly. "I think so, yes. If I may be honest, I suspect, Mrs. McKinnon, Mr. McKinnon, that what we have here is merely a case of little Tara being *too* well cared for."

The words didn't make any sense to Beth. "What?"

"She's the youngest child, is she not? And she's not old enough to be given any chores or responsibility on her own, of course."

"Doctor, she's two years old," Beth said, interrupting.

"Just so. And that's just what I mean. At two years old, she's still learning and still figuring out how things work, is she not?"

"I suppose so."

"And while there are, of course, plenty of things you still need to do for her, she is old enough for *some* things."

"I'm sorry," Beth said. "I don't mean to be rude, but I simply don't know what you're trying to say."

"Mrs. McKinnon," he said with a gentle smile, "it is my belief that the little girl has simply been coddled a bit too much. Everyone around her loves her and does everything for her. She has learned that all she has to do is stay put and she'll still get everything she could need."

Beth barked out a laugh, part in relief, part in disbelief. A million thoughts rushed through her head, but she voiced only the most important.

"Are you serious? What are you saying? My baby is all right?"

"Yes, little Tara seems perfectly healthy. She's obviously well-loved, but I think what we need to do now is not protect her quite so much."

"Oh, well, I don't know," Beth stammered, immediately backtracking.

"Don't misunderstand." The doctor held up a hand to halt her objections. "I just mean let her come claim her own supper, instead of you taking it to her. Or letting her run in the grass for a bit instead of being cooped up inside the wagon."

"But she's so little..."

"Of course, she will have to ride in the wagon sometimes and be carried sometimes. Just not *all* the time. Let her learn again what it means to be free."

"Doc," Robert interjected as Beth turned over that word—free—in her mind. "I just want to be absolutely clear. You're saying that our Tara is not sick."

"Not sick," he repeated. "Just a bit spoiled." He chuckled. "No offense meant."

Beth and Robert stared at each other disbelieving, and the doctor said his goodbyes.

"Could he be wrong?" she asked in a petrified whisper.

"It's possible. But, I think, unlikely."

She just nodded.

"This is something we can fix, Elizabeth. This is a problem with a clear solution. There's nothing to worry about."

"There's always something to worry about," she said, offering him a half smile.

"Tara will be back to her old self in no time," he continued in a whisper.

Beth leaned in to her husband, letting him hold her, letting him support her.

She found herself believing in his optimism easily and then surprised at herself at that ease. This could have been a life-changing crisis, and with her husband's help, she was finally able to take it in stride.

It took some cajoling and encouragement, but that very next morning, Beth convinced Tara to stand on her own. It was like teaching the child to walk all over again, only with months of her already learning that she didn't really have to. Beth could be patient, however. The hardest part would be curtailing her own inclinations to bend over backward to put her little girl at ease.

That afternoon, the company crested the hill just before they plunged into the Bear River Valley. Beth was doing just as the doctor had instructed and was walking in the grass with her youngest daughter. The relief on Claire's face when she learned she didn't have to stay in the wagon with the little girl made Beth feel a touch guilty, but she put that behind her. She was doing better now. They were all doing better.

Tara's little legs only carried her so fast, and Beth had accepted the fact that her family's wagons would get farther and farther ahead while she walked more slowly with the toddler. She kept Prince with them, for safety, as they stepped through the grass that grew above Tara's waist. She seemed to have some trouble not being able to see her own feet, and she walked step by slow step, peering down into the grass, feeling the firm earth under her feet.

CHAPTER THIRTY-TWO

The wagon company's time spent following the trail through the Bear River Valley lifted Beth's spirits immensely. How could it not when she was surrounded by such bounty? For the first time she spent days not worrying about food or the children's safety. It was a truly idyllic location, and now that Beth knew what to look for, Tara's strength and balance improved by leaps and bounds.

"Every day in Oregon will be like this," Robert assured her as he cleaned the half a dozen trout he caught that day.

"It's rather too bad we can't stay here," Beth replied, teasing.

"It might be lonely," he said with a grin, "with everyone else moving on to Oregon."

"Yes, that's true. Claire might never forgive us if we kept her away from her friends. Can you imagine?"

The two laughed companionably. Their marriage

had been so good before the dreaded news of heading west. It could be so again, Beth knew. Even just having the stress of enough food lifted for a few days had done wonders for her.

Little Tara walked unevenly across the dirt toward them. Her balance was improving by the day, and Beth found herself not worrying over the child for hours at a time.

Where the Oregon Trail climbed out of the Bear River Valley, the shift between green, lush landscape and stark high desert was striking. Gone was the chance of game behind every tree or in every stream. Once again, the emigrants had only the water they could carry out of the valley to sustain them. Fortunately, however, they had only two days of scrub brush and sun before reaching the walls of Fort Hall.

After crossing through all of the states in the east and then the open territories of the plains, Beth felt as though they had experienced all that North America had to offer. But here, the land around Fort Hall was different than anything else they had come across. The structure itself was two stories tall, windowless, and built from roughly hewn logs, and the land that stretched around it for yards was no more welcoming. Black lava plains and barren ground stretched for yards around the structure.

But it truly didn't matter what it looked like— Fort Hall had supplies. Spread throughout all the families of the Sullivan-Mills wagon company, there wasn't an over-abundance, but there was enough for now. Robert would be at her side to help her scavenge or acquire more when the time came, but for now she could simply enjoy what they were able to obtain. Her fear and anxiety never truly went away —and likely wouldn't as long as they were living on the trail—but putting her trust in Robert did help.

They camped at Fort Hall for half a day, and for practically the first time since they had left Alexander's grave, Beth had allowed each of her children to spend the day how—and where—they liked. She didn't even see Boyd until supper had already started. The girls had their friends. Ross had a science lesson with Miss Atkins. Even Tara didn't need her mother and spent the afternoon playing with the dog. Prince was so good with the little girl that Beth actually felt she had no supervising to do whatsoever. The freedom almost unnerved her, but she was grateful.

After leaving Fort Hall, the caravan headed farther west to the Snake River. The trail cut along the top of a deep canyon and followed the curve of the river as it headed downstream. The trail was level, though not wide, and situated dozens of feet above the actual running water. As Beth walked alongside the wagons, she could hear the water, though not see it at all.

There had not been accessible fresh water for a couple days, and they still had another couple days of traveling along the Snake River until they reached Shoshone Falls. If only the river weren't so far below them, she thought. She had gone out of her way to obtain promises from Boyd and Ross that they wouldn't try to climb down the steep cliff face. There had been a rumor that a couple of the older boys had attempted the descent, but Beth was not about to confirm for her own boys if such a thing were possible. She found herself more and more comfortable with giving them freedoms in the way they spent their time, but such a risk was out of the question.

Though the sun was still high in the afternoon sky, the Gladwells' wagon ahead of them pulled off the trail toward the rest of the caravan. Everyone seemed to be settling in place for the rest of the day.

"It's early to be making camp, isn't it?"

Robert nodded. "Something must have happened."

Beth watched her husband for a moment longer before laughing out loud.

He looked at her quizzically.

"How is it you never seem the least bit curious?" she asked. "Anything could have happened—good or bad—and you're just calmly making camp, confident that nothing more is needed."

"What more is needed?" He shrugged. "Someone will make sure we know if there's something we need to know."

"But how will you be prepared for whatever that is? What if you're needed to lend your muscle or gun, or what if we're somehow wildly off course?"

"Elizabeth." He took both of her hands in his. "I never worry if I'm prepared for anything because I'm certain you've already worried about all that for me."

Beth flushed, embarrassed, before seeing the

twinkle in his eyes. "Oh!" she said with a relieved laugh. "You're teasing me."

Laughing heartily and pulling her close, her husband agreed. "I'm teasing you."

"Fine then." She pecked him on the cheek and started toward the supply wagon. "I'll do the worrying for both of us."

As worried as she was about making good time to Oregon, having unexpected extra time in camp that evening could be an advantage. As Beth assessed what she needed to do that afternoon and what food she could make for their supper, she thought again about how lucky she was to have found a man like Robert. He had always been a balance to her worst impulses, and together they had made a home full of love and safety.

For more than an hour, they heard nary a word about why the wagon company stopped when Benjamin Findley came by the camp. He was the oldest son of Captain Mills's good friend, and Beth had seen his face here and there assisting with whatever errands Mills needed done. If a messenger was needed, Benjamin was a common choice.

"Mr. McKinnon, the captain asked that I relay some news." He removed his hat and nodded politely at Beth. "There has been... It's been an eventful afternoon." He cleared his throat and then smiled brightly. "It is my understanding that Mrs. Van Anda's child will be joining us before morning."

Beth gasped. "Oh, goodness, that poor woman. The Oregon Trail is no place to have a child. I'm so glad the captain stopped the company for the day for her."

"Yes, ma'am. Also, there was, um, an accident. Mr. John Harper."

"Is he hurt bad?" Robert asked. "Is there something we can do?"

Benjamin shook his head. "He... he died, sir. Fell into the canyon when he went to fill his canteen. A few of the other men are in the process of retrieving his body for his sister, but..." He replaced his hat and stepped back a pace. "I must tell the next family. We'll leave camp again tomorrow morning after the funeral. Good evening."

"Ross!" Beth called before Benjamin had barely retreated. "Boyd! Boys, come here, please."

"Elizabeth," Robert began, "they will be—"

But he was interrupted by the two boys appearing from the direction of the Kirks' wagon.

"Did you call us, Ma?" Boyd said as he sauntered into camp.

His jaunty confidence stabbed Beth in the heart. It took all her willpower not to simply hold him to her and never let him go in that moment.

"Boys," she began. "Do you remember what we talked about with the river, all the way down at the bottom of the gorge?"

"Yes, why? Did someone find a path? I'll go!" Boyd volunteered.

"No!" Beth startled her sons with her vehemence. "Listen carefully to me, boys." She held out her arms, drawing them close to her. "I know that I can be a bit... overcautious, but I beg you to please trust my judgment. A man has..." She took a deep breath. "Mr. Harper fell to his death in trying to get to the water."

Boyd's mouth hung open in surprise.

"So you see," she continued, "it is no place for anyone, man or boy. Promise me you'll stay far away from the edge. Promise me. This isn't like when we crossed the Platte," she insisted. "This isn't like with... with Alexander. There is a very real danger here. Please promise me."

She felt Robert behind her, also staring down at the boys.

"Yes, Ma," Boyd whispered. "We'll stay away."

"We'll stay away," Ross repeated.

And though Beth felt as though she had had this conversation dozens of times with them, somehow this was different. Something in their expressions, or maybe in her own heart, had changed. She trusted them. Yes, her children were still very young and still learning how to move through life, but for the first time since leaving Lancaster, Beth truly felt as though whatever these boys decided she could feel safe with.

When the Sullivan-Mills wagon company left that camp the following day, it was with one fewer man and one additional child than they had had the morning before. Joy and sorrow intermingled as the emigrants continued their trek.

CHAPTER THIRTY-THREE

The wagon company left the grave of John Harper behind in the morning and pushed hard all day to make up the distance they had fallen short of the day previously. None of the emigrants minded the punishing pace, however, knowing what was at the end of that day's travel. Slowly, incrementally, the trail descended to the water. Every step they took brought them closer to the promise of Shoshone Falls.

They arrived in camp after sunset, and the roar of the enormous waterfall lent a current of energy to their work as each person made camp and ate supper in the growing dark. They all seemed to be in a hurry to go to bed—the sooner they slept, the sooner they could wake up to the fresh, swiftly running water and the several hours to take advantage of it.

Beth let the rhythm of the waterfall lull her to sleep.

The next morning, as soon as everyone was through with breakfast, Beth proposed an adventure. Claire and Boyd had already received permission to seek out their friends, but the younger children were hers to care for that day.

"Should we go look at the water?" Beth asked her children.

Lizzie and Ross ran on ahead, yelling 'yes' over their shoulders.

"Be careful," Beth called after them, though she felt confident they would be.

Tara waited with her arms raised to be carried.

"No, sweetheart," Beth said gently. "We're going to walk today. It will be fun." She peered through the brush toward where she knew the water waited. It didn't sound very far away; she was confident Tara could do it.

The little girl protested only briefly before unsteadily climbing to her feet and clutching on to her mother's hand. Step by little step, mother and daughter made their way along the narrow trail to the top of the waterfall.

It took them the better part of an hour, but Beth didn't relent. Though what she wanted most was for her precious child to be taken care of, she remibded herself that this was how that was accomplished, no matter how long it took.

It took them so long, in fact, that Lizzie and Ross met them coming the other way.

"It's pretty, Mama," Lizzie reported. "But we're going back to camp."

"You're not going to wait for us?"

"Do we have to?"

Beth sighed and smiled. "No, that's all right. Go on ahead."

Tara had watched the entire exchange, and when her siblings left again, she collapsed into the dirt.

"Mama, I'm tired," Tara whined.

"I know, darlingest. I know. You can rest if you want to, but Mama is not going to carry you."

"Will Claire?"

"Claire is with her friends today, love. It's just me and you." Beth tried to put more excitement into her tone than she felt. The truth was, forcing her child into anything even remotely uncomfortable felt terrible to her. But she reminded herself of the doctor's words and strengthened her resolve.

"Mama, I'm *tired*," she said again, more loudly this time, as though she hadn't been heard before. Beth almost laughed at the elaborate pout on her face.

"All right, then, let's rest," she said cheerfully. "It's okay to rest. But we'll keep going when you're ready."

The two sat quietly on the edge of the path trodden between the camp and the edge of the water. They were so close, Beth knew. It would have been easier and faster to just carry Tara the remaining steps so they could enjoy the rest of their day. It was tempting enough that Beth had to force herself to remain seated, waiting for the littlest McKinnon to lead the way. There were so many things that would be easier if she just took care of them herself, but the children would never be able to take responsibility for themselves that way.

Finally, after fewer minutes than Beth would have guessed, Tara climbed to her feet again.

"Come on, Mama," she said, offering her hand to her mother. "I'm ready."

Beth smiled with relief and joy, got to her feet, and continued the slow walk to the top of Shoshone Falls, following behind the toddling steps of Tara.

When they finally got back to camp, Beth was surprised to see Robert moving in and out of the supply wagon. Returning to their familiar home, Tara found energy she hadn't had a moment ago; she ran on chubby legs to where her father was working. Beth stood rooted to the ground in shock, however, when she watched him carry out what looked like a crate full of clothes and place it with a pile of other things near the rear wheel of the wagon.

"Where are the children?" she asked. "Is everything all right?"

"Oh, good, you're back," he said when he looked up. "Mills called a meeting this morning."

"Oh no," she murmured. "What happened?"

"Nothing to worry about, Elizabeth. It's just that we've crossed onto Shoshone land, and while they are generous enough to not harass us, they do demand that we compensate them for the time we are here."

"Compensate them how?" Beth had a vision of that earlier Indian attacker ransacking her wagon. "Robert, *where* are the children?"

"Elizabeth." He crossed the ground to where she

still stood, frozen in fear, and placed hands on her shoulders. "The children are safe. Trust me. They're all with their friends, the Coles, the Sullivans, you know. I saw the Indians myself—there are only maybe eight or ten or so who met with Mills and will be back in an hour. Everyone is perfectly safe. I promise you."

She nodded briskly as though trying to reassure herself. "All right. Yes, okay. Tell me about this compensation, though. Why do we have to give up what has been hard-won and sacrificed for?"

"Because the tribe is also making sacrifices. Every day that we are here is a day that they are unable to hunt as they usually do. These men deserve to provide for their families just as we do, and so this is the compromise they have come up with. I am to take what goods we have to spare to the Mills wagon soon, and the Shoshone will come to select what they deem useful."

"Look what I found, Mama!" Tara called out.

When Beth looked, she saw that her daughter had sat in the dirt by the pile of belongings Robert collected. She held up the brass candle snuffer and waved it around excitedly. Beth flinched, worried for a brief moment about the sharp end, the bit of scissors for trimming the wick, so close to her daughter's face. But Tara lowered the tool again, carefully, safely, and Beth let out a slow breath.

She turned to Robert. "The snuffer? That was a gift from your grandmother, darling. We've had it for so many years and brought it so far. What if we need it soon? Is there really nothing else we can offer?"

He smiled kindly but peered into her face. "Elizabeth, you know I have always appreciated how well you prepare for any situation and how well you take care of our children. But can you honestly say there will be a moment when we absolutely need that candle snuffer and can't possibly find any other alternative?"

Beth smiled reluctantly at that. She knew when she was being teased. It had been only a week or so before they left Pennsylvania that the tool was lost and not being used anyway.

"I know it was a gift," he continued, "so if you insist we keep it for sentimental reasons, I won't fight you. But I would like you to consider whether or not this is something absolutely necessary. We can do more good offering it to the Indians."

She didn't respond right away but squatted down next to Tara and held out her hand. "Can Mama see that, please?"

The little girl placed it gently in her palm, and Beth closed her fingers over it. The metal was cold in her hand, and she thought back to the last time she had used the snuffer.

Well, to be more specific, she tried to remember the last time she had used it. In truth, between being misplaced and being put away deep in a drawer, they couldn't have used this gift many times since they had been gifted it. Instead, she had always just held on to it just in case—though in case of what, she couldn't be certain.

If she couldn't trust that she would be able to put out a candle without this specific tool, how on earth would she learn to trust her children's judgment and choice when they are out of her sight?

"You're right," she said finally, getting to her feet again. "I feel like I keep saying that."

Robert laughed and made to climb back into the wagon. "Why don't you help me choose what else to take to Mills? Then I can tell you that you're right."

As Tara played with Prince under the wagon, Beth and Robert spent a quiet twenty minutes going through the rest of their belongings, sorting the food and other supplies they had left, and making difficult decisions.

When Beth picked up the small pair of boots that had once been Alexander's, Robert nodded somberly.

"You're right," he said in a low voice.

That small agreement opened the gates. As much as they both still missed their youngest son, that traumatic pain had dulled into more of a constant ache. It would never heal completely, but giving the boy's clothes and belongings a second life of usefulness, offered to the Shoshone for their own children, went a little way toward creating the next chapter of their lives.

CHAPTER THIRTY-FOUR

After paying the local Indian tribe the toll they had exacted, the wagon company stayed in the camp at Shoshone Falls only until early afternoon. Part of the agreement was that the white people would travel as quickly as they could, that they would leave the Shoshone territory as soon as possible.

The emigrants of the Sullivan-Mills wagon company had one last gorge to traverse before the relative ease of the flat plains above. The trail that had been cut into the side of the canyon was so steep that the men had to make special arrangements and configurations of wagons and animals just to get all of the company to the top again.

With trepidation, Beth eyed the row of heavy wagons being hauled up toward the top of the canyon.

"Boyd, Ross. Come here," Robert called.

Beth opened her mouth to protest—it looked so dangerous. She could too easily imagine a wheel sliding, or an animal losing its footing, and one or other of her sons being crushed in the accident. But then Tara tugged on her skirt, and Beth was pulled out of her imaginings.

When Beth looked down, she saw that not only was her daughter standing on her own—her balance and walking had vastly improved—she was all but bouncing up and down in anticipation. With another glance at her husband and sons, Beth resolved to keep her fears to herself.

Overprotecting her children had not yielded anything good. She would simply have to practice trusting them more.

"Did you need us, Ma?" Boyd prompted. "I need to go help Pa get the animals hitched."

"Yes, of course, it's nothing. Go on ahead, whatever your father needs."

"Me too?" Ross asked, always wanting to follow in his older brother's footsteps.

She hesitated briefly before relenting. "If your father says yes. But if he thinks you would be better off out of the way, you come right back here to me."

Part of her hoped Robert would be as cautious as she wanted to be as she watched her son run after his brother. But she knew that was a futile hope. Her husband had only ever encouraged their children to stretch themselves, and he would find some work he could put Ross to.

The girls surrounded her, hounding her for permission as soon as Ross was gone.

"Mama, Patience is walking up now. Can I go with her?" Lizzie asked. "With her ma. Can I go?"

"I was going to start up too, Ma," Claire added.

"With your sister?"

"With Amy Cole. But I can take Tara if you'd like. And I can walk Lizzie to the Sullivans' wagon for you. It's no problem," she insisted. "But," she glanced over her shoulder to where the Cole girls waited for her, "can I?"

Beth felt torn between being grateful for the girl's help and not wanting all of her children away from her. She knew what was best, though.

"Tara needs to walk at least some of the way."

"Amy and I will look after her," Claire insisted, agreeing to virtually anything as long as it meant she could be a little bit free.

"And you'll make sure that she runs around at least some, won't you?" Beth asked.

"Of course, Ma."

"All right, then. Go ahead."

She watched her daughters go off together with their friends. Claire would be sixteen soon, nearly a grown woman, and was developing all the level-headed kindness she had seen in her father. Beth realized she didn't know what she would have done without her daughter's help all these many miles since Pennsylvania.

Her children were all scattered, spread out, each attending to their own interests and responsibilities with no need of their mother to incessantly remind them to be careful. Which meant that Beth was on her own, at least until the whole caravan made it to the top of the gorge. She was in no rush, and she wandered between the families and the vehicles, watching.

"Oh, bother," she heard a familiar voice exclaim. Beth turned to see Emma Fields shaking her head as she and her husband looked into their wagon.

"Is everything okay?" Beth asked as she crossed to her friend.

The older couple was in the process of chaining their wagon to their son-in-law's, with Bill Abbott handling hitching up both teams together.

"It seems our animals are not up for carting all of this to the top," Emma said, not taking her eyes off the wagon contents. "So we'll have to make some difficult choices."

"I'm sure there's plenty in here we don't need," Curtis grumbled.

"I don't want to be hearing 'I told you so' from you, Curtis Fields," Emma said, teasingly.

"How can you even choose?" Beth asked. "Can I help? I could maybe carry something to the top for you?"

"No, no, don't be silly. Curtis is right, and there is sure to be some things in here that I stashed away when we left West Virginia and haven't thought about since."

Beth was rendered speechless. For a brief moment, she felt defensive, sure that every single thing she had brought with them from Pennsylvania was necessary and regularly utilized—and then she remembered the candle snuffer that they had only just earlier rediscovered that they had.

"Really, if there's something I can do, I'm happy to."

Emma finally looked at her more carefully. "You don't have wagons and little ones of your own to manage?"

Beth spread her hands helplessly. "It seems not. They're all off…" She waved toward where the wagons and small groups of travelers were heading up the trail. "They're making their own way," she finished simply. "If you need me, I'm all yours."

Emma glanced at her husband, who only grumbled and shook his head.

"We're perfectly fine, my dear," she said, turning to Beth and resting a worn hand on her arm. "Really, there's nothing here for you to worry about. In fact, if I could make a suggestion, I think you should take this chance of not having any little ones underfoot to enjoy the freedom. Goodness knows the next time you will only have yourself to worry about, right? You go on ahead. Enjoy the quiet. Trust me."

There was that word again—freedom. Beth had spent so many months worrying about her children's that she had neglected her own.

Emma beamed into Beth's face and then turned away, as though the conversation were closed and however Beth responded was unimportant.

"Oh. Well, yes, all right."

She was a bit startled to be so dismissed, but Beth recognized that the older woman was likely correct. She had raised her own children years ago, after all, and must have many times wished for such moments of quiet as Beth was now afforded.

The Fieldses seemed to have completely forgotten her presence as they discussed what items they might need to leave behind or what could be rescued. Beth backed away slowly, unsure quite what to do with herself.

Soon she found herself completely alone, though in the middle of the crowd. All around her men and women had urgent negotiations. Children laughed, screaming in delight at their games and making Beth's heart pound to see how closely, how carelessly, they got to the big animals that waited patiently.

With a quick glance to the trail that led out of the gorge, Beth noticed that her own family had just begun the ascent. The girls seemed to be farther ahead, but the boys and the wagons were just starting.

And not a single one of the McKinnons needed her.

Beth felt tears spring to her eyes, though she couldn't rightly say why. The moment was emotional in a way she would have never expected. Maybe it was simply that it was a moment that she never would have expected. Being alone, with no one asking a thing of her, was so unlooked for she felt at a loss.

Beth stood—alone in the crowd—for another brief moment, getting her bearings, before finally taking the first steps toward the bottom of the trail. There was no one she had to report to, or look after, or even inform what she was doing. All she had to do was walk up the trail and enjoy her solitude.

When she reached the foot of the trail, there

was a short break in the wagons' ascent when several families with children began their own hike up. Beth followed behind, at the edge of the gathering, and walked alone.

She was alone with her thoughts and her relatively rested body, and she finally had the chance to feel herself alone.

It was...

It was different, and it was slightly unsettling, and it was definitely a sensation that she was not used to. But mostly, it was freeing.

Beth had been a wife and mother for nearly twenty years. Every single day, every single choice, and every single thought revolved around the needs of her family. Even if this was only a short twenty minutes alone without even an animal to think of, to Beth, it seemed like a whole new life.

When she reached the top of the gorge, Beth looked around at the scattered wagons for her own family. As she had taken her time and all but strolled lazily up the trail, the rest of the McKinnons were already waiting for her.

She felt a burst of pride and gratitude at the look on her children's faces when they spotted her, but she made a silent promise to herself that she would embrace the chances she had to be alone and unencumbered as they grew. Such luxury was good for her heart and for her children's independence. For all of their freedom.

CHAPTER THIRTY-FIVE

After leaving Shoshone Falls and climbing up out of the canyon, the Oregon Trail followed the curve of the Snake River farther west until the wagons would need to cross the water to get to Fort Boise a bit north. For the full three days that the Sullivan-Mills wagon company traveled along the river, Beth vacillated between being calm and accepting that her children were old enough to play on their own and being petrified that the water was so close. Learning to be comfortable again was an ongoing process and her poor children had to suffer through every step of it.

Traveling and camping near the river was difficult enough—Beth tried to put all thoughts of actually fording the water from her mind. As she tried to sleep the night before, she tossed and turned so much that Tara whined more and climbed into Lizzie's instead.

But such westward progress was unavoidable. The

night passed swiftly, and soon Beth woke to the day that they would be spending their daylight hours getting the wagons across to the north. They would be fording the water at Three Island Crossing, a narrow stretch of the river that was shallow enough for wagon wheels. Because the area where they could cross was so limited, only a single-file line of wagons could make the fording, and Captain Mills set aside two days for the process. This meant that Beth had plenty of time to wait and to worry as they got closer to the water.

As the wagon caravan slowly inched toward the wide expanse of the Three Island Crossing, flashes of Alexander lying face down in the current flooded Beth's mind. The Snake River here had the potential to be dangerous, but at this time of year, the water was low enough that the wagons could cross the gravel bars that extended the width of the water. In this one place, it was only a foot or two deep where the wagons were going to cross. As long as her children kept their wits about them, everything should be fine.

That's what she kept telling herself, at least.

There was no question that Tara would remain in the wagon, and Lizzie chose to stay with her rather than get wet. But Boyd wanted to lead his own wagon, and Ross could not be talked out of walking alongside his brother, so Beth found herself with her family at risk on all sides. She didn't know quite where to direct her attention, as arrangements were made and the river's currents were closer.

Robert watched her carefully, and Beth did her

best to appear the carefree, cheerful wife he wanted her to be.

Soon it was the McKinnons' turn to cross, and Beth watched her husband lead the team of oxen with their first wagon into the water. He went slowly and carefully through the water. Shallow though it was, it was still strong enough to make him stumble against the current. He would have to be very careful that he wasn't pushed off course, out of the shallow gravel bars.

Claire crept up to her mother's side and squeezed her hand. "Are you okay?"

Beth laughed and shook her head. "I should be asking you that, daughter-mine."

"I know, but... Well, you know. Do you want me to walk with the boys?" she added in a more serious tone.

Beth looked into her daughter's bright, blue eyes and nodded.

Maybe she would never learn to let go of her fear completely, but she could still trust.

Claire nodded back and set off to where Boyd and Ross were about to step into the river.

"All right," Beth said quietly to herself once she was alone again. "All right. We're fine. Everyone is fine. We are safe. The children are safe."

Saying such things out loud helped make them feel more real for Beth, and though every step across the river was scary, she found herself far less frantic than she might have expected.

Lizzie and Tara waved at their mother from the

back of the wagon as it awkwardly rolled off the bank into the water.

"Be careful," she couldn't help but call to the little girls before following herself.

Each of the McKinnon children was growing bigger every day, and the sooner Beth stepped back and allowed them to do so, the better. If there was one thing she had learned on the Oregon Trail thus far, it was that there would always be things about their life that she could not control. Fighting against this truth is what had caused her so much stress and had risked her baby's very strength and independence. Accepting this truth would be the focus of her efforts going forward.

And just like that, all of her family was in the water, leading oxen, riding in a wagon, being part of the whole caravan of travelers heading west toward Oregon. They were all part of the bigger movement and yet all Beth could think about was the next twenty yards or so it took to reach the other bank. She lifted her skirt up out of the water and took her first steps into the river. The gravel bank was narrow but shallow. With every step, Beth felt a little more relieved to find that the crossing wasn't nearly as scary as she had assumed.

Watching her older children lead the wagon ahead of her, she realized that Claire, Boyd, and Ross all seemed happy, contented, even. There was a tense moment as Boyd made sure the team of oxen found their footing, but overall, the trio seemed really to be enjoying themselves that afternoon.

They didn't seem to be afraid at all.

Beth all but laughed in relief.

The last bit of crossing the river went by quickly, as first Robert, then Boyd led their teams up out of the water and brought the heavy wagons behind. With just a few steps, Beth was out of the river, following the wagons toward where they would be making camp while everyone dried off.

Boyd walked on ahead, leading the team of oxen, as the other children followed after him, chattering away.

Robert turned to his wife and offered her a questioning look, inviting her confidences.

Beth beamed at him.

"They're all... safe." She laughed in relief and joy. "I can't... I don't..." She stumbled over what she wanted to say. All of the emotions of the previous months seemed to be whirling about in her mind.

"They're all safe," he repeated.

"I..." She laughed again and threw her arms around her husband's neck. "I'm sorry."

"Elizabeth." He pulled away from her embrace and studied her face.

She felt tears welling up under his concerned gaze. "I'm sorry," she said again. "I've been so worried ever since we left Pennsylvania; I know it must have been trying for you. For all of you. Poor Claire should have a bevy of friends at her age, and Tara shouldn't have ever stopped walking, and the others..." She gestured helplessly. "It breaks my heart to think what I have inflicted on them in the last few months. How frightened they must have been all the time, given my own reactions. I should be making them feel safe, not giving them more things to be frightened of and—"

Her voice cracked, and she couldn't continue. She merely leaned forward, resting her forehead on Robert's chest. He wrapped his arms around her and held her tightly. Though they'd had some difficult conversations since leaving Lancaster, at this moment, he didn't have to say anything. She could feel his support, feel the way he loved her merely through his silence. As difficult as it had all been, Beth could honestly say she had done her best, and Robert would forgive her for all the missteps.

The only thing they could do now was to try again.

She pulled away from his hug with a bright smile. "I wonder if we could coax the children to go visit their friends' families for supper tonight."

Robert laughed, wrapped an arm around Beth's shoulders, and started walking toward their camp-site. "We should definitely try."

CHAPTER THIRTY-SIX

Though it didn't seem like much, the small shift in Beth's outlook—from fearing all she came in contact with to accepting what she could not control—changed everything for the McKinnons. Their mother's altered energy rippled through the children. Giving her children room to grow into the adults they were meant to be was a core responsibility for Beth's role as a mother, and though it was difficult, she was determined. Robert's love and support made an enormous difference, of course. But mostly, Beth simply had to be willing to admit she was wrong and that she might not know everything.

It was an obstacle, but it was far from impossible.

She found herself remembering this over and over again, every day. Slowly the certainty and control with which she had tried to manipulate everything around her faded away. Little by little, her comfort with the unknown grew, and her trust in her children's judgment expanded.

This was why they were going to the Oregon Territory at all—to give their children space and freedom to grow. Losing Alexander in the process was heart-breaking—Beth would never truly get over it—but she vowed to never take this opportunity for a new life in the west for granted.

After leaving the Three Islands Crossing behind, the wagon company spent another couple of days heading northwest toward Fort Boise. There they could rest next to the river, feel safe near the soldiers stationed there, and possibly supplement their supplies. It would be the last such fort they visited before reaching Oregon, so all in the wagon company were pushing hard to get to that camp as soon as possible.

They arrived early in the afternoon. Fort Boise was just a few small buildings behind a stockade wall, but its placement on the Boise River afforded an idyllic location for the Sullivan-Mills wagon company to camp for half a day. Though it was so late in the summer, the stores had not yet been picked clean. The families with the funds could increase their food stores, ammunition, or other necessities they might need in these final weeks.

For they were down to the end of their journey. Beth couldn't say precisely how many miles or how many days were left before they reached the Willamette Valley, but she knew they were in the final stretch. Soon they would be climbing into the Blue Mountains, higher in elevation, away from the grass that had sustained the animals. Soon they would be struggling through the last of their supplies and enduring the drop in temperature as autumn approached.

After Robert returned from the fort with just a box of ammunition and a bag of cornmeal, Beth sighed.

"Well, I suppose it could be worse," she said. "At least there's something here."

"And there looks to be plenty of fish in the river," Robert added, pointing to where several men and boys had already settled in for the afternoon, fishing rods extending over the water.

"I can feel my stomach rumbling already. Do you need help finding our own rods?"

"No, I'm sure the boys know where we put them. In fact..." He looked around for the children. "Why don't we all go?"

"All of us? Go fishing? Even the girls?"

"I think it would be fun," he said with a nod. "Of course, we will need to share the fishing rods, but they can take turns."

For once, Beth didn't even hesitate or consider any other risk.

"Yes," she said promptly. "Let's do that. It sounds like a wonderful day."

Twenty minutes later, Tara clutched Beth's hand as they followed the rest of the McKinnons down the narrow trail from the camp to the water. They weren't the only family who had thought to fish that afternoon, though admittedly, most of the others were men and boys. But Beth felt no embarrassment

at the sight of her daughters sitting on the river-
bank, helping her sons fix bait to the hooks. Such an
outing had been common in their childhood in
Pennsylvania, and there was a taste of nostalgia to
their adventure that afternoon.

The Boise River was a couple hundred feet
across in places, and wound around the fort enough
to offer plenty of space for the several dozen men
and boys who were out to catch themselves some
supper. Beth mentally divided the salt they had
remaining, trying to determine how much fish they
would store for later in the journey and how much
they would need to eat that night.

"Elizabeth," Robert called, jostling her out of her
thoughts.

When she looked up at him in surprise, he
laughed, shaking his head. "Stay here with us, my
love," he said. "Whatever you're worrying over
doesn't need to be attended to now."

The relief and ease she felt then, that her
husband had essentially given her permission to rest,
surprised her, but Beth welcomed it.

"You're right," she responded, crossing the grassy
bank to his side. "Of course."

She sat next to her husband in the grass and
pulled her knees up. Wrapping her arms around
them, Beth rested her face on her knees and settled
in to watch her family. She didn't need to fish; she
didn't even need to insert herself in their conversation. Watching and listening was enough for her.

All her life, she had prayed that her children
would get along. Seeing the tension between Robert

and Stuart had worried Beth the first several years she had known that family, from her courtship into her marriage. The brothers were always at odds. Eventually, she had gotten used to the sharp remarks and veiled criticism, but she never welcomed it. And she never allowed her children to speak to each other that way.

It seemed as though whatever parenting choices she had made worked. From Claire down to Tara, all of the small McKinnons appeared to be friends. Of course, there were quarrels, and even now, she could see Ross's frustration building as Lizzie perpetually hovered too close to him, but it was a sweet, harmonic sibling relationship that promised to grow into true affection as they too grew.

As Beth watched, she smiled to herself, realizing that it was probably better that they all had come fishing, so there were more hands available to actually do the work. Boyd, in particular, seemed far more concerned with getting a laugh from his siblings than noticing when his fishing rod got a nibble. They had all been sitting alongside the river for more than an hour when Boyd tried again.

"If Alexander was here, I bet he would want to throw the fish back," said Boyd with a laugh.

There was a pause as each of the McKinnons, save Tara, grew still at the mention of the missing child. Beth met her husband's eye and could see in his anguished expression the pain and concern he had for her. How would she react to being reminded of her loss?

"Boyd," Claire warned under her breath.

Beth realized that all of them were looking at her, holding their breaths, and bracing against her reaction.

"Like when he insisted on carrying the new kitten back to its mother every time it wandered out of the barn," Beth added with a small smile. "He couldn't understand why an animal would *want* to leave its home."

"Or how he cried when me and Boyd caught frogs last summer," Ross added.

Beth laughed, and at her mirth, the rest of the family joined in. Alexander'd had such a tender heart. That was one of the things all of the McKinnons would miss with him gone from their lives.

Throughout the afternoon, Beth watched as her family laughed and fished and talked excitedly about what they had ahead of them in Oregon. She counted herself lucky to be their mother. Somehow, even little Alexander felt close to her that afternoon. She could easily imagine how he might have grown up to be especially serious like Ross or with a heart for others, like Boyd. Though God, in His wisdom, had not allowed the small boy to travel all the way to Oregon with them, Beth knew that he would always feel close to them. That afternoon fishing with her family, Beth knew that as the years went by, she would continue to feel Alexander. She could imagine his progress, how old he would be when Claire got married, or how he would be as an uncle and adult. Beth finally realized that even in losing a member of her family, they were never truly gone from her.

. . .

After leaving Fort Boise, Captain Mills pushed the wagon company hard, and they traveled several days without stopping for a midday break at all. The next big obstacle would be the Blue Mountains, and with the cold weather coming, the wagon company needed as much time as they could eke out. Beth spent each night in camp cooking long after dark to ensure the family had enough cold biscuits and bacon to eat on their feet the following day.

It turned out that the rushing was fortuitous, in fact, when in the middle of the third day of such a pace, the sky opened up, and a torrential storm soaked any and all person left outside. Beth fetched oilskin wraps for her husband and oldest son, and by the time she had finished and made her way to the wagon where the rest of her children rode, the mud of the trail was so thick that she was almost caught in it.

Once again, the wildness of the Oregon Trail had caught their wagon company by surprise, but this time Beth felt a peace in her soul as she walked through the storm. Her boots and skirt were becoming heavy with mud, but none of this was a problem Beth was unable to handle. The struggle and pain of the journey had molded her into the confident pioneer she never could have been in Pennsylvania.

CHAPTER THIRTY-SEVEN

In early September, Beth McKinnon was walking with her youngest daughter Tara along the Oregon Trail. The rain had stopped the day before, and though the trail and ground underneath their feet were beginning to dry, it was with ruts and potholes that stalled the wagons' progress even more. The uneven ground made riding inside the wagons even more jostling and uncomfortable than before. Tara had whined all morning and wanted to walk outside after so many days of being cooped up against the rain. Now that she was outdoors and set free, she had not yet gotten frustrated, though she had tripped and fallen in the dirt what felt like innumerable times.

"How are you feeling, my love? Do you want me to carry you, so we can catch up with Papa?"

"No!" she exclaimed before running clumsily on ahead.

Even as the distance between them lengthened, Beth could see her daughter breathing hard. The trail was carrying the wagon company into the Blue Mountains, and even the delicate incline was enough to wear on the little girl. The trail would only get more and more difficult the farther west they traveled. But if Tara wanted to stay independent, if she was going to again find her confidence on her feet, Beth wasn't going to stop her. Their beloved dog stayed close by, and Tara was never out of her sight, so Beth could feel confident in letting the child find her freedom if she so chose.

That was precisely what her other children were doing too. She hadn't even seen Claire since the young woman had finished washing the dishes after breakfast. Her friendship with the Cole sisters seemed to have blossomed and deepened even more; they were spending every moment they could together. Ross had his own friends, but just as often as seeing them, he would help his brother with the team of oxen. Though Beth felt a little forlorn that her children were growing up so fast, she couldn't help but be proud of them.

She shivered a little. The later in the year it got, and the higher in the mountains they climbed, the colder the weather grew every day. Even now, it was still the middle of a sunny afternoon, and Beth felt as though she could do with a shawl.

The wagons ahead began to slow, and Beth called after her daughter to slow down. If the caravan was stopping, the men were surely not paying attention to the presence of a little girl who might be underfoot.

"Tara!" Beth called again. "Come back to me, please."

Even from so far away, Beth could see the stubborn expression on her daughter's face. It was plain the little girl was trying to determine if she really needed to listen to her mother or if she could get away with running farther.

"Just for a few minutes," Beth coaxed. "I promise."

Tara's shoulders relaxed, and she trotted back to Beth. "What are they doing, Mama?"

"I'm not sure. We'll have to see when we get going again. Do you want to walk *with* me? If we stay away from the trail, we can walk on ahead."

"Yes!"

Beth smiled. "Do you want to hold my hand, or can I trust you to stay close?"

"I can do it!" she insisted.

Beth chuckled as she held her hands up in surrender. Holding her mother's hand might keep Tara from stumbling—again—into the dirt, but if she didn't want that, Beth wasn't going to force her.

The two walked parallel to the trail, next to the unmoving line of wagons, while Tara peppered her with questions. What was that man doing? Why was that little boy crying? Did she know why they were stopped? Would they be stopped forever? What would they eat for supper? When would they get to Oregon? What kind of bird was that?

Beth laughed as she tried to answer as best she could, but at nearly three years old, Tara would likely never be satisfied with her answers. Each of the McKinnons had been full of questions at this age, Beth remembered, and with the whole new world of the western territories, she could rightly expect Tara to be the most inquisitive of the bunch.

As they drew closer to the front of the wagon train, Beth noticed what was holding everything up.

"See, baby girl?" She pointed. "It looks like the storm knocked few branches across the trail, so Captain Mills had to stop to move them."

Tara nodded seriously, watching where her mother pointed. Daniel Mills had dismounted his horse to help, and the two men were hurrying to move all the big branches off the trail as quickly as they could. Some could be tossed overhand into the trees and brush, but two of the bigger branches needed both sets of strong arms to drag it out of the way.

"Hopefully, there won't be many more obstacles that we have to stop for," she said under her breath.

Not only were the days getting colder, but they were getting shorter. As the summer faded into autumn, the sunset was earlier and earlier, which meant fewer traveling hours each day. When before they had managed to keep westward for twelve hours each day, now they were lucky to get ten hours of travel. Each person was exhausted; every man needed more rest, especially with less food in every meal. This made every day—every mile— a struggle.

And now, stopping for branches just added that much more time to their struggle.

"Here we go, Mama!" Tara yelled as Captain Mills got his wagon team moving again.

As the wagon company climbed farther into the mountains, Beth began to see signs all around her of the need and deprivation that other members of the wagon company were suffering. At least a couple of the older boys had worn completely through their boots and had been seen patching up the soles with the pages of books that had been carted nearly two thousand miles. More and more, the sounds of pitiful, crying children cut the air at supper time. Though Beth tried to remain chipper and distract her own children from the suffering of others, it all seemed futile.

The truth was the Sullivan-Mills wagon company was reaching the end of their journey. They were reaching the end of their stores of energy, the end of their hope and optimism. Most of the families were reaching the end of their supplies if they hadn't already. So many of the guidebooks claimed the trip could be made in four months, but now they had just passed five months on the road.

The breaking point for many of the emigrants was near.

But even as the food stores for the travelers dwindled, so too did the grass, shrubs, and other sustenance for the animals. The higher the trail wound into the mountains, the less foliage and edible plants grew. It worried Beth that she could see the ribs and pelvic bones jutting under the skin of their oxen. But even then, she knew the McKinnons' animals were better off than those of other families. More than one ox collapsed during that final week, never to stand again.

Finally, one afternoon, when the wagon company was traversing along a relatively flat stretch of trail, Captain Mills halted progress and called for the company to make camp for the day. They had pushed themselves as far as they could, and exhausting the animals even more that day wouldn't do any good at all.

Feet dragged as the men pulled the wagons into camp and tended to the animals. They had still a few hours before dusk, and Beth meant to make the most of it. Through some accident or luck, she had no major sewing, cleaning, or any other substantial chore calling for her attention that evening. As soon as the animals had been seen to, she gave her children permission to see their friends or play quietly. She no longer felt anxious when they were out of her sight; this brought a freedom she hadn't really felt in months.

Beth almost didn't know what to do with such freedom.

The longer she thought about it, the more she realized what she was really missing most from their life in Pennsylvania was the companionship and friendship of other women. This was a feeling she had denied herself for all these many months, but as she began to feel more secure in some parts of her life, she found the energy to try to develop other parts of her life.

And of all the new friends she had met thus far on the journey, the older woman in the wagon behind them—Emma Fields—attracted her the most.

With empty hands but a heart full of hope, Beth made her way over to the Fields' camp to see what her friend was doing for the afternoon.

"Did you come to find Lizzie?" Emma asked by way of greeting.

Beth froze, still several paces from their campfire. "What?"

Taking in Beth's terrified and confused expression at a glance, Emma hurried to reassure her. "Oh, darlin', I'm sorry. I assumed you knew. Not long after we all made camp, your little Lizzie came over to see if Marigold wanted to play. They're both under that tree"—she pointed to a tall pine less than ten feet from the Abbotts' wagon—"playing some kind of make believe."

Beth looked to where the older woman pointed. Sure enough, there was her daughter, happy as could be and giving not a thought to her mother standing there.

Only a few weeks ago, such news that her daughter had all but wandered off away from all adults would have sent Beth into a panic, but now...

She took a deep breath and shook off the latent feelings of fear that had bubbled up.

"No, I hadn't realized she came over here," Beth told her friend. "I'm glad to hear it. She loves Marigold. But in fact, I came to see you."

The surprise on Emma's face was almost comical

in its severity. But she rearranged her expression immediately to one of relief.

"Even though I don't have any of that pie to offer you?" she asked with a wink.

Beth laughed. "Next time." She settled herself next to the fire, looking forward to a nice chat.

CHAPTER THIRTY-EIGHT

"Ma," Boyd whined. "Let's just stay here."

Beth had gently shaken the boy awake just before dawn. They would have a small breakfast before trudging through the narrow trail through the mountains for another full day of travel.

"We can just build a cabin or something," he mumbled, with eyes still shut. "Eat those birds I hear trilling already. I don't want to go anywhere today."

"I know, favorite man-child-of-mine," Beth responded indulgently. "Maybe tomorrow. But today, you need to get up."

Boyd groaned but pulled himself to a sitting position as his mother moved to wake up the other children.

The whole family was exhausted. Beth felt as though they had been reaching the end of their journey on the Oregon Trail for months, though, in reality, it had been a mere week or so. They were so close, but each hour felt like days. Soon they would reach the pass that took them to the other side of the mountains. Soon they would start their descent into the Oregon Territory. After spending months and months worrying about the journey, it seemed almost unreal to Beth that it was almost over.

She climbed out of the wagon, confident that the children would be following shortly. One positive aspect of being this high in the mountains was that there were plenty of trees from which to gather firewood. Granted, the closest and driest branches had long since been scooped up, but it only took Beth twenty minutes to find what she needed.

Next, she gathered the food and pans she needed from the supply wagon and began cooking the family's breakfast. While she did, however, her mind was elsewhere, mulling over the spark of an idea that had only just occurred to her.

Without consulting Robert, Beth made her decision. It may have taken her two thousand miles of travel to come to it, but she had finally reached a place where she trusted both her own judgment and that of the rest of her family. She watched fondly as Claire helped Lizzie button into a clean dress before making her way to their supply wagon.

After she had climbed inside and lit the lamp, Beth stood with hands on hips to assess what they still had left and what they could spare. She could only guess how far the wagon company still had to travel—certainly at least ten or more days. But if there were more deaths, injuries, accidents, torrential rain, or any number of other obstacles, they could be delayed. But this was why she had spent the last five months so vigilant and forward-thinking. She had wanted to make absolutely sure when they got to this point in the journey, she could be confident that everything would be fine, that they would all make it safely to Oregon.

And they were so close now.

Close enough that she could let herself relax, a little bit at least. It was an effort for her, it went against so much of her natural inclination, but she knew this was what she had been working toward.

After breakfast, she returned to the family's supply wagon and spent ten minutes inventorying their remaining food. Beth pulled aside most of a bag of rice, some sugar, coffee, two pieces of dried fish, and a handful of other odds and ends. Looking at the small pile in the middle of the wagon floor, it certainly didn't seem like much. It might not truly be enough. But it was what she could spare, and the fact that they had anything to spare was far more than nearly every other family in this wagon company.

In spite of all the setbacks and stress, she was determined to bring some good out of all the anxiety of the previous months. Carrying half of what she had set aside, Beth made her way to the Fields family campsite nearby.

Emma had just finished dishing up a meager breakfast for herself and her husband when Beth approached. Gently setting the bags of food at her feet, Beth called for the other woman's attention.

"Mrs. Fields?"

The older woman looked up at Beth with a smile. "I'm fairly certain I asked you to call me Emma," she teased.

"Emma, yes. I'm sorry." She was distracted by her own purpose in coming there.

She laughed. "There are far worse things for us both to be concerning ourselves with. Can I help you with something? Everything ship-shape with all the McKinnons? I haven't seen Lizzie yet today."

Emma had been bustling around her campsite, putting things away, straightening others, and finally returned to Beth to settle and offer her a seat. There was a low, wide stone pulled near the fire where Beth was directed. But first, she wanted to make clear why she was there at all.

"No, I'm not looking for Lizzie. I just... I wanted to thank you, and I know that, well..." She gestured at the bags of food. "I wanted to help out. If I can. If you want this. If you don't need this, then perhaps your grandchildren do."

Emma glanced down to where Beth had indicated, and her eyes went wide. "Goodness! You brought that for us? Why, I couldn't possibly—"

"Yes, you can. Please, I must insist."

"Beth, I can't—"

"You can," Beth insisted more fiercely. "I've gone over our supplies dozens of times, and we either planned well or have been lucky or..." She shrugged. "Please, just... let me do this for your family. Trust me that my sharing our bounty in no way will put us at risk. You've been so kind to me; I couldn't bear it if we had food just sitting in the wagon that you all needed."

As she finished her speech, she looked down at the bag of coffee rather than meet Emma's eyes. There was a heavy silence, and she could feel the other woman's piercing gaze as though she were weighing every one of Beth's words.

Finally, she looked up at the older woman and saw a smile of pure joy and gratitude on her face.

"And don't forget, you promised the next time you make a pie that you'll save me a piece."

Emma laughed, releasing her tension at being offered such a trove. "Well, goodness, child, I never would have expected such a gift. You're right. I won't fight you on it. I reckon if you say you have some to spare, then you must. It's not like those growing boys of yours would settle for less if they didn't have to." Emma laughed. "Thank you, kindly. I know my family will get good use out of this, and if we find we have too much—"

"Pass it on to someone else," Beth interjected. "Please."

Emma nodded. "Come here."

She gestured to Beth and brought her in for a hug. When she pulled away, the older woman held Beth by the shoulders, peering into her face. Emma looked at her for a long time before letting her go.

"You've got a good heart, Beth McKinnon," she said finally. "You keep it protected through layers and layers of fear, but underneath you're just as generous and gentle as any other woman in this company."

Beth could feel herself blushing but didn't have the words to protest.

Besides, she had to be getting on her way. She still had a bag of cornmeal and a pound of coffee she wanted to take to Mrs. Gladwell.

CHAPTER THIRTY-NINE

As the Sullivan-Mills wagon company climbed higher into the mountains, Beth had her hands full, trying to both keep her family warm enough and keep them fed enough. She had been careful with how much food she had given away, but it was as fine as a razor's edge, ensuring the rest of their food stretched the remainder of the journey. Each morning she woke before the sun to be sure she had at least a small fire going when the rest of the family awoke. The higher they climbed, the harder it was to find enough fuel for a campfire, but Beth always had something.

Now well into September, most families were on the last bits of food they had left. Gratefully, fortunately, somehow, the McKinnons still had enough. She wouldn't come out and admit to herself that it had anything to do with her own skill or planning, but she was certainly pleased with the result. She shuddered to think how her little ones would be suffering if she hadn't started rationing weeks ago or if Robert hadn't been able to fish as much as he did when they crossed through more abundant lands.

There had been stories about the families that had passed through this mountain range a couple of years prior, running out of food long before they made it to Oregon, and Beth had vowed that she would not end up like them. And so, each morning, she scooped out just enough flour for each person to have half a biscuit, just enough coffee to fortify them through the cold. There was no waste on Beth's watch.

In spite of all the hardship the wagon company had been through, in spite of all the sacrifices they had made on their journey west, Beth found herself cautiously optimistic about her family's future. Each of her surviving children had grown so much over the last nine months since they left Pennsylvania. Though she never would have chosen this path for them, it seemed that they were all making the best of it.

She couldn't be certain how many days they had left before the trail crested the mountain and the company began their descent into the Willamette Valley. A rumor had gone around over the last few days that Daniel Mills had ridden on ahead to scout the route so they could prepare as best they could. It seemed as though they should have been in Oregon long ago, but every day was another long slog up the mountain.

Late in September, when Beth found herself even shivering in her shawl in the mornings, the wagon company stopped at midday for a meal. Many of the families didn't have food left for a whole meal, though the McKinnons did. Beth had heated up a pot of beans, hoping to save the last of their flour for supper that evening.

Her children were quiet as they ate, likely too tired to do much more than the bare minimum. Claire accepted the dirty plates from her siblings to wash them when Lizzie suddenly looked up the trail in interest.

"Who is that, Mama?" Lizzie asked.

"Don't point," Beth murmured. "It's not polite."

Inwardly, she marveled that she remembered what proper society thought was polite or not. It had been so long since they had encountered anyone other than the other members of this wagon company or the scruffy trappers and soldiers stationed at the forts.

Nevertheless, she too wondered at what Lizzie was pointing. At least a dozen strangers were spreading throughout the camp. It seemed to be all men, with some older boys. Two or three of them led horses, but the rest all approached on foot, and there didn't seem to be rhyme or reason for how they infiltrated the camp and who they spoke to.

Beth exchanged a glance with her husband. He nodded briefly and stepped forward to meet the closest of the strangers heading toward them. He was a tall, wiry young man with a heavy-looking satchel dangling from his shoulder.

"Can we help you with something, sir?" Robert asked.

"I think maybe I can help you all." He grinned, and Beth felt drawn to him. He seemed so young and so earnest; she couldn't help but trust him. "Are you all hungry?"

From his satchel, he pulled out a sack of oats, coffee and a side of bacon. He held the bags awkwardly in both arms for a moment before stepping forward and thrusting them into Beth's arms. At this exchange, the other children came creeping up to watch and marvel at the stranger in their midst.

"This is... for us?" Beth asked in a daze.

"Yes, ma'am. If you would like, ma'am. One of your men—Mills, I think—came down ahead of y'all to our town to get help. I understand a right many of you folks are running low on basics, and we aim to be good neighbors first and foremost."

"Do you have any jerky?" Boyd asked boldly.

"Boyd," his mother warned.

The man laughed. "It's no trouble at all, ma'am. As it happens, I do have some. Let's see." He rifled in his bag and pulled out a handful, more than enough for all the McKinnon children.

When he handed it over to Boyd, the boy's eyes grew wide.

"Wow, thanks!" he said as he accepted the gift.

"Share that, please," Beth reminded him.

"We can't thank you enough," Robert said, turning his attention back to the man. "What's your name?"

"Hobbs. Teddy Hobbs," He responded simply. "Maybe we'll be neighbors, and you all can make it up to me. Or maybe we won't, and it will just be my good deed for the day. Don't you worry; this is precisely what we all came up the trail to do."

"I don't know if we even need all this," Beth said, still overcome with the generosity of such strangers.

"Well, that's up to you, I'm thinking," Hobbs said. "I'm happy to share it with the next family on down the line, too, of course."

"Thank you," Robert answered for her. "We'll assess what we need and share the extra, but this goes a long way to filling bellies that have not had quite enough for a long time."

"Absolutely, sir. Ma'am." Hobbs tipped his hat to them both. "If you'll excuse me."

He made his way toward the next wagon and was not even out of earshot before Boyd exclaimed.

"Can we make some of that bacon now?"

The morning after the men from the Willamette Valley found their wagons, the Sullivan-Mills company was awake and ready to leave camp earlier than they had in weeks. The boon of the food and the additional hands for labor had given every man, woman, and child a burst of energy that should carry them all the way down the other side of the mountains to their new home.

Even little Tara wanted to run ahead and had to be called back to stay out of the way of the enormous oxen.

Beth felt torn in a million different directions, but in the end, she decided that the only place she wanted to be was by Robert's side. By this time in their journey, her children had proven that they were capable of looking after themselves. They would likely always need their mother, but it needed to be their decision when they did.

Instead, she entrusted Tara into Claire's care, and Beth went ahead to walk alongside Robert as the trail began its final descent.

"I can't believe we made it," Beth said with a sigh of satisfaction. "There were so many times I didn't think we would."

"I never doubted," Robert responded with a smile.

Beth slipped her small hand into his free one and squeezed. "If I admitted you were right, I would never hear the end of it."

He chuckled and squeezed her hand back. They walked together for another couple of hours until the trail curled around the top of a ridge. Beth knew that the view of their future home would be ahead of her any moment. It overwhelmed her to the point that she kept her eyes on her feet until Robert nudged her.

"Look, Elizabeth," Robert murmured. "Look at how far we have come."

At her husband's prompting, Beth looked up and was dazzled by the sight.

As the valley stretched out before them, Beth caught her breath. She had always thought that the land around Lancaster, Pennsylvania, the most beautiful in the world. The years she had spent making her home there had been happy, certainly. But now that she had caught a glimpse of the rest of the continent, Beth knew that her initial outlook had been very narrow.

From where the trail curved down the side of the mountain into the Willamette Valley, Beth could see for miles. The verdant, green rolling hills stretched out toward the west, toward what Beth knew would be the Pacific Ocean not far past the horizon. Slightly to the north was a wide stretch of dark green trees, winding along the ridge of the hills and through the valley. From the foothills of the mountain, curving through the countryside to the coast, was a swift-moving creek that, in the distance, came together with another wide river cutting through the valley.

Even from this height, Beth felt as though she could smell all of it—the clear fresh water, the pine, the last gasp of the summer's wildflowers.

And here and there, from the mountains to as far as she could see, were the low roofs and smoking chimneys of the families that emigrated to Oregon ahead of them.

THE END

When Hannah Sullivan's family decides to head west to the Oregon Territory, she's exhilarated. The small town where she grew up was fine when that's all she had to choose from, but as soon as the horizons and opportunities open up, Hannah finds a whole new world, just built for someone as 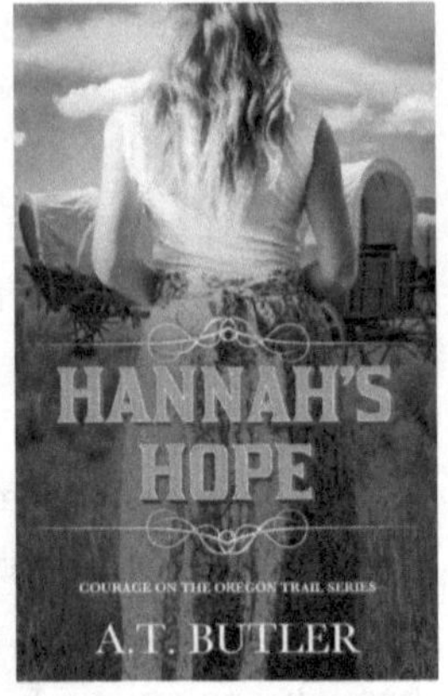 competent, kind and warm as she is.

Sign up for A.T. Butler's mailing list today and receive Hannah's Hope for free! Dive into a story where romance blossoms against all odds, and be the first to hear about new releases, exclusive content, and special offers. Don't miss this chance to fall in love with Hannah and Benjamin's story.

ATButler.com/Hannah

Thank you so much for reading *Unyielding Heart*, the fourth book of the *Courage on the Oregon Trail* series.

Of all eight books in the series (as of this writing), this book was probably the most difficult for me to write.

This is in part because of the story itself—imagining how it must feel to lose a child was heartbreaking.

But it was also quite stressful to be in Beth's head for so long. Yes, by the end, she learned somewhat to relax her worrying and controlling tendencies, but getting to that point was not easy. I know there are some negative reviews on this book about how stressful it was to read; I suppose that just makes the book that much closer to reality.

We all have someone in our life who is a bit of a worry-wart. Some are more controlling than others. And all of them would likely be much happier if they were not consumed by dread all the time. I have a tendency to be risk-averse, and learning to be okay with uncertainty is a regular goal of mine.

I love all of my characters, and as we reach the end of *Unyielding Heart*, I just really hope Beth can *enjoy* her settling in the Oregon Territory, can let her children grow up with the freedom and opportunities that she truly wants for them deep down.

At the time of this writing, I do not currently have plans to give Beth another point-of-view book in the Oregon At Last series, but there's always a chance that could change.

One other small note about this book: I wrote it when I still lived in Texas, not knowing that I would ever live in Pennsylvania, let alone central PA near Lancaster. When I was re-reading this, I was very tempted to add in far more description about how gorgeous it is here. I feel very lucky to have the opportunity to see so much of this country.

Thank you so much for being on this journey with me. The excitement and the hardship and the heart that our pioneers go through every day. We'll be with the Sullivan-Mills wagon company for a long time still.

A.T. Butler

December 2024

The next book in COURAGE ON THE OREGON TRAIL series is available now.

Grab _Wild Promise_ here!
(on Kindle and Kindle Unlimited)

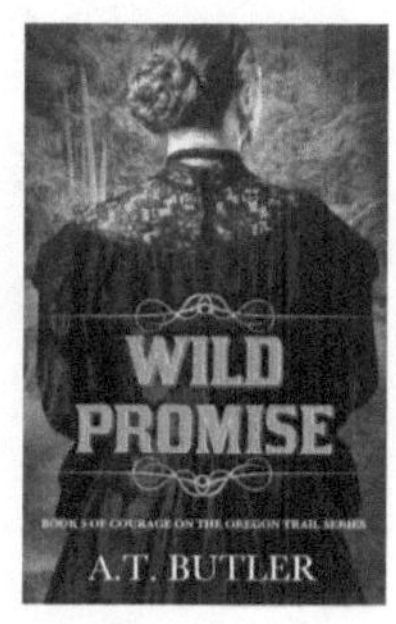

Rebecca Tenney had everything she wanted: a cozy home, generous family, and a marriage to the man of her dreams. She had vowed to follow Andrew Tenney anywhere, so when he began making plans for them to settle in the Oregon Territory, Rebecca was happy to do her part.

When Andrew dies unexpectedly, Rebecca makes the heartfelt promise to him to continue his dream, and to start her new life in Oregon in his memory.

It's only once Rebecca and her family are well on their way to Oregon that she begins to wonder if this is not what she wanted at all. What other opportunities and joys was she leaving behind? What chances of happiness had she let go of? How could Oregon fill the Andrew-sized hole in her heart?

Discovering what she wants, outside her promise to her husband, is all Rebecca can do now.

All the books in the Courage on the Oregon Trail series take place within the same wagon company's trip west and run concurrently. They can be read in any order.

Grab _Wild Promise_ here!
(on Kindle and Kindle Unlimited)

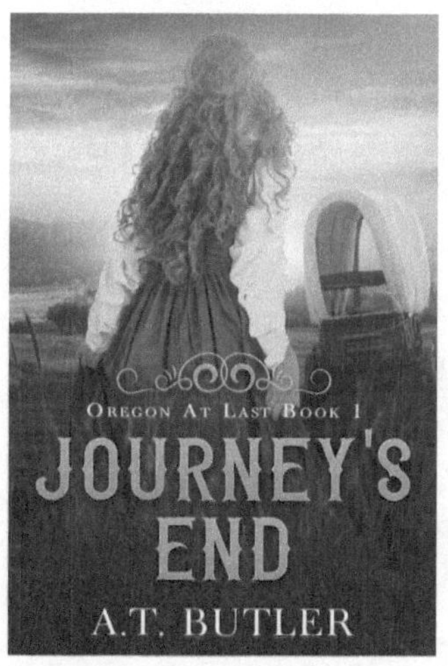

She thought the hardest part was behind her.

The Oregon Territory, October 1850: After nearly a year of living out of a covered wagon, day after day of grueling work and heart-breaking tragedy, Caroline Harper has finally reached the Oregon Territory where her new life will begin.

She thought she had given all she had to give; she thought she had become the strong woman the frontier requires. But every day brings a new challenge for the settlers.

When unexpected obstacles appear that keep her from getting married, from finally finding her security, Caroline learns that becoming the woman she needs to be will be far more difficult than she had realized.

Can Caroline find her new path or will this journey be the end of everything she thought she had achieved?

For all the stories of how these brave pioneers got to Oregon, look for the book series Courage on the Oregon Trail by A.T. Butler.

Oregon At Last Series:
Journey's End (Caroline's story)
Christmas in Oregon (Annie's story)
Snowbound Promises (Nora's story)
The Pastor's Baby (Olivia's story)
Frontier Fortune (Rebecca's story)
Reluctant Spring (Sadie's story)
Summer of Promise (Margaret's story)

ALSO BY A.T. BUTLER

Courage On The Oregon Trail Series:

Westward Courage

Faithful Trail

Frontier Sisters

Unyielding Heart

Wild Promise

Fierce Dreams

Seeking Home

Trouble and Grace

Oregon At Last Series:

Journey's End

Christmas in Oregon

Snowbound Promises

Pastor's Baby

Frontier Fortune

Reluctant Spring

Summer of Promise

Eden Valley Sunrise

Sweet Adventures

Juniper Falls Series:

The Juniper Hotel

Building the Dream

Snowflakes and Sugar Cookies

<u>Marrying a Sweet Sister Series:</u>

The Sweetest Bond

The Sweetest Spark

The Sweetest Shelter

The Sweetest Gamble

<u>Jacob Payne, Bounty Hunter Series:</u>

<u>Trouble By Any Name</u>

<u>Danger in the Canyon</u>

<u>Justice for Jasper</u>

<u>Blood on the Mountain</u>

<u>Outlaw Country</u>

<u>Death By Grit</u>

<u>Desert Rage</u>

<u>Arizona Legend</u>

<u>Fool's Demise</u>

<u>Silent Night</u>

<u>Bountiful Justice Series:</u>

Loyalty's Price

Riding for Justice

Trail of Redemption

Other Western Novels by A.T. Butler:

<u>Hawke's Revenge</u>

Stories from Juniper Falls

ABOUT THE AUTHOR

I grew up in the southwest—California Missions, snakes and constant threat of drought weaving the backdrop of my childhood.

But it wasn't until I moved to Texas a few years ago that the magic and mythology of the American West began to seep into my soul.

I'd love to write about western adventures, strong women and noble men for a long time.

If you enjoyed this book, a review on your favorite retailer would be greatly appreciated.

- A